"Can I interest you in some breakfast, Nurse Bergstrom?"

For an instant passion leaped across the barrier Hailey had created. She wanted to throw herself into Roy's arms, because only there would she find peace. But a little round face swam between them, and the pain cut into her heart. The peace would be short-lived—only the length of time it took for the passion to ebb and resentment to take its place.

"I can't." She looked at him, shook her head and told him the bald truth. "You hurt me, and I'm scared you'll do it again."

"You'd end what there is between us just because you're scared?" There was temper and challenge in his tone. "I thought you were braver than that."

"Well, you thought wrong." She dragged her keys out of her bag and walked around him to open the truck door. "Don't call me, please. Don't wait for me again. It's over."

"Don't do this, Hailey."

She was too tired to argue with him. She started the truck and backed out of the stall. As she drove away she wasn't even crying. Her eyes were dry and burning with an echo of the pain in her heart.

Dear Reader,

Somewhere it says that the way to make God laugh is to tell Him your plans. For me and my original vision of this book, the truth of that saying grew more and more evident as the writing progressed.

The idea for *Vital Signs* was born when my son, Dan Jackart, a Vancouver fireman, told me about a disturbing call that involved an abandoned baby. He explained how deeply the firemen and medical personnel are affected when a baby is endangered, and how everyone wonders how such a tragedy could occur. What kind of mother could do such a terrible thing? In the beginning of this story, I admit that I felt the same way. But as I wrote, I began to see that in the heart of calamity is buried the seed of opportunity, the potential for greater growth and higher love. The story took me by the scruff of the neck and led me along paths that surprised and pleased me and, yes, forced me to change ideas of right and wrong. It became clear that I might as well give up on my agenda and let love follow its own circuitous and surprising path.

This was a book with a mind of its own. I hope it pleases you and touches your heart as it has mine.

Love always,

Bobby

Books by Bobby Hutchinson

HARLEQUIN SUPERROMANCE (EMERGENCY! Titles)

Vital Signs
Bobby Hutchinson

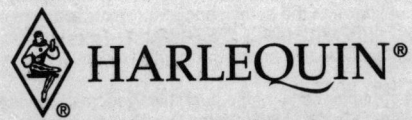

HARLEQUIN®

TORONTO • NEW YORK • LONDON
AMSTERDAM • PARIS • SYDNEY • HAMBURG
STOCKHOLM • ATHENS • TOKYO • MILAN • MADRID
PRAGUE • WARSAW • BUDAPEST • AUCKLAND

ISBN 0-373-71124-7

VITAL SIGNS

This edition published by arrangement with Harlequin Books S.A.

® and TM are trademarks of the publisher. Trademarks indicated with ® are registered in the United States Patent and Trademark Office, the Canadian Trade Marks Office and in other countries.

Visit us at www.eHarlequin.com

Printed in U.S.A.

Heartfelt thanks to social workers Stew Brown and Donna Miller for invaluable assistance and advice on the complex issue of abandonment and parenting.

Vital Signs is dedicated with love and gratitude to my dear and treasured friend Beverly Piebenga, who got me through this one with professional nursing advice, encouragement and, most of all, stir-fries and chocolate. From both my soul and my stomach, thank you, Bev.

PROLOGUE

DAVID RIGGS was two years old when his mother abandoned him one hot Tuesday in July.

Shannon didn't mean to do it. The welfare check had finally come, and she put Davie into the rickety stroller and walked to the corner grocery. The wizened Oriental man smiled at her when she paid her bill.

"No good this heat. S'posed to rain tomorrow. Good thing—too hot for Vancouver, right, missy?"

She agreed with him and bought diapers and soup and some bananas. Davie loved bananas. He chortled when she peeled one and gave it to him. Then they took the bag of dirty clothes to the laundromat, and Shannon took him out of the stroller. Davie discovered a blue plastic laundry basket someone had left behind. He climbed in and pretended it was a boat.

When they got home, Shannon fed him his lunch and he fell asleep on their bed in the bedroom, wearing only a diaper and clutching his favorite stuffed toy.

Shannon was folding clothes on the kitchen table when she heard the knock on her door. Her heart started to hammer when she opened it and saw

Rudy, because she knew he was bringing news about Murphy. He had no other reason to be there.

"Somebody out in the car wants to see you." Rudy's acne-ravaged face twisted into a grin. She knew right away it was Murphy in the car, and her heart nearly jumped out of her chest.

She didn't lock the door, because she'd only be gone a few minutes.

She had to tell Murphy about Davie—had to make him understand why she hadn't had the abortion like she'd agreed before he got sent to jail.

Rudy opened the back door of the car, and she saw Murphy for the first time in almost three years. Her heart hammered and her knees started trembling at the familiar sight of his silky dark curls, his cobalt-blue eyes. Davie looked so much like him, right down to the cleft in his chin.

"Hey, babe, long time no see." Murphy took her hands and pulled her into the car, and she collapsed against his chest, tears pouring down her cheeks. She forgot the times he'd hit her, the times he'd hurt her, the lies he'd told. All she remembered was that he was the first and only man she'd ever loved, and she'd been so lonely so long. When he kissed her, hard and deep, she was instantly wet with wanting him.

And then Rudy started the engine and roared off, and she panicked because her baby was back there alone in the apartment. She screamed at them to let her out, her kid was alone.

"Chill out," Rudy growled, cracking his gum.

"We're only going around the block. I have to make a pickup and I'm late."

Shannon knew he was talking about drugs. Rudy was a dealer. She'd worked for him—that was how she'd met Murphy.

Then Murphy got that scary look on his face and wanted to know what kid she was talking about. So she had to tell him she'd done exactly what he'd said not to do. She'd gone ahead and had the baby, not used the money he'd given her for an abortion.

Murphy got mad, and instead of going around the block, Rudy headed for Stanley Park. She could have jumped out when they stopped at the lights, but she didn't. She went blubbering on about Davie, how sweet he was, how much he looked like Murphy, how proud Murphy would be when he saw him.

But Murphy was pissed off because she hadn't done what he'd told her.

Rudy got the stuff, and she refused when they offered her some.

"Guess you don't love me anymore," Murphy said, and she denied it. He said prove it, and then she let him shoot her up the way he always had before, and after that, nothing was important except the feeling, the feeling she'd fought against and yearned for and dreamed of and managed to avoid since the day she'd found out she was pregnant.

Things were blurry after that. She told herself that Davie would be okay. He always slept a couple of hours, and Tonya was coming today. The door was unlocked. Tonya would be mad at her. Shannon had promised her never again, but she also knew Tonya would take care of Davie.

And for Shannon, time ceased to be.

For Davie, time stretched nearly into eternity, although when he grew older, he had no memory of sliding off the bed, calling for his mother, sobbing until his throat was raw from tears and terrible thirst. He never remembered the endless days or the long nights. He had no recollection of slipping finally into something more than sleep.

For Shannon, it seemed only a few minutes before Rudy pulled up in front of the apartment and she saw the ambulance and the police cars and the firemen, but it must have been longer, maybe lots longer. She couldn't remember. She screamed and tried to get out, but Murphy held her.

"The kid's okay. They're taking care of him. Here, this'll make you feel better."

And after that she didn't try to remember.

CHAPTER ONE

THE EMERGENCY ROOM at St. Joseph's Medical Centre in Vancouver hummed in the midday heat. The sound came from huge air-conditioning units, white noise that the ER staff no longer heard. They heard, instead, the scream of sirens arriving at one of the emergency bays, and the intercom announcement that signaled incoming trauma.

"Trauma alert, emergency department. Paramedics arriving with abandoned baby—male, estimate two years old. Dehydrated, not conscious. ETA four minutes."

"We're set up in room three." Triage nurse Leslie Yates did her best to keep her voice calm and steady, but the one thing that most disturbed her and the rest of the ER staff was a mistreated child.

One of the doctors cursed under his breath, and Leslie knew her own face mirrored the expressions of the rest of the ER staff when the medics arrived with their tiny patient. She found a moment to talk to one of them and he described where and how the child had been found.

"Apartment hotel downtown, a real dump. Must have been ninety degrees in there. The kid was too little to get to a tap. If he hadn't turned on the TV, the neighbor would never have gone to investigate. She got pissed off when the sound went on all night and all morning.''

Leslie notified Social Services just to be sure they knew. It turned out the paramedics had already called, and probably the firemen and police, as well, but it didn't hurt to make sure.

During the next half hour, she dealt with several more incoming crises, but every moment she was aware of the drama going on in trauma room three.

''How's it looking with the boy?'' Leslie asked one of the nurses when she hurried out with blood samples. The young woman shook her head, her expression grim. ''Poor little thing's dehydrated. His vitals are way off the scale.''

Ten minutes later Leslie saw a flurry of frantic activity in and around room three and her stomach tensed. The boy must have arrested. Tension was palpable in the ER as the staff fought to save his life. Leslie did what most of them were doing. She prayed.

By the time her shift ended at three o'clock, the boy had stabilized, much to everyone's relief. He was sent up to pediatric intensive care, and a collective sigh of gratitude could almost be heard throughout the ER. The firemen and the medics who'd attended had called several times to find out how he was doing, and before she went off shift, Leslie made a point of phoning them all to tell them the child was stable.

They all knew the situation might only be temporary, that he could easily go bad again during the night. But at least for now, he was holding his own.

With one last fervent and heartfelt prayer for the little boy's continued well-being, Leslie went home.

ROY ZEDYCK had gotten home late. There'd been an emergency—one of the foster kids he'd recently placed had pulled a fire alarm at his school. Roy had spent the past two hours meeting with the principal, the kid's foster mother and the nine-year-old boy, trying to calm them all down. The boy's explanation for why he'd done such a thing was that life was boring.

This from a kid who'd stolen a car the month before and run it through a neighbor's garden, added bubble bath to a washing machine and dog-napped a mutt outside a grocery store. Roy could only pray that these new foster parents would persevere, that they'd see past the kid's penchant for mischief to the brilliant potential Roy detected. The kid had an IQ right off the scale, but he'd managed to wear out three sets of foster parents in less than a year.

Roy pulled on the trousers to his gray suit—his only good suit. He zipped up the pants, noticing how loose they were around the waist. He'd dropped some weight since he last wore them, and he couldn't afford to lose weight, because he had no intention of buying a new wardrobe.

Must be stress doing it, because it sure as hell wasn't sex. His love life had been at a standstill for weeks, ever since Anna left in search of greener wallets.

It wasn't exercise, either. He hadn't been for a run in ten days, and he'd had to miss the last three pickup rugby games. The court case he'd been involved in had eaten up what little time the job hadn't.

His testimony had resulted in the formation of a commission that would eventually make changes to the system, but Roy couldn't forget that those changes had come about as the result of a child's death. It seemed at times that the world was going to hell, and all social workers could do was spit on the flames. He was weary in a way he hadn't been since he first took the job with the ministry seven years ago this month.

The phone rang, and he shot it a baleful glare. It might be work, and he already had a briefcase filled with files he'd barely looked at. However, he was part of the after-hours unit, and he was on call.

Or it could be his sister, Nicole, who was going with him to the family party at their sister Jennifer's tonight. Or it might be the retirement home where his mother was battling another bout of flu. Whoever it was, he had to answer.

He picked up the receiver and silently cursed. It was his team leader, and that could only mean another emergency.

"Hi, Marty, what's up?"

"That abandoned kid at St. Joe's—did you see the item on him in the newspaper yesterday?"

Roy's heart sank. Abused or abandoned kids were bad; they pulled out emotions already raw from overuse.

"I saw it." There'd been a double murder in North Van, so the article had been buried on a back page of the *Province*.

"I know your caseload is crazy already and Larissa was supposed to be on this one, but she just called me. Her father died, and she's flying back to Calgary tonight."

They'd been shorthanded for the past five years, and with the recent government cutbacks, things had gone from desperate to ridiculous. It took restraint not to remind Marty of that. Roy let him ramble on about their co-workers' latest personal problems.

"Rita's getting married this weekend and Jake's having a hemorrhoid operation. Larissa's done the preliminary work on the case. The kid's name is David Riggs. His mother's known to the ministry— she's on assistance, name's Shannon Riggs. I've got the case file right here. Mother's seventeen, she was on the street at twelve, heavy into drugs, but she straightened out when she got pregnant. One of the downtown volunteers, Tonya Cabral, took her in and helped her get clean. The police and the downtown street workers are watching out for Shannon, but so far no sign. David's two years two months. He was taken to St. Joe's forty-eight hours ago seriously dehydrated. A neighbor found him, called the fire department. Estimates are the boy was alone three days."

Roy shuddered. He'd seen babies like that before. He'd watched one of them die.

"It was touch-and-go as to whether David would pull through, but looks as if he's on the mend now.

He's in St. Joe's—got out of intensive care this morning and was transferred to the pediatric ward. Harry Larue is the attending pediatrician.''

Poor little kid. Intense compassion, deep sadness and bitter anger ate at Roy's gut, the way it always did when an innocent child was the victim of neglect. Along with the other emotions came resignation. This was, after all, social work—the job he'd chosen. It wasn't anyone's fault that he was having second thoughts. It went without saying that he'd do the best he could for David Riggs.

He went through the mental checklist of what needed to be done, then asked Marty where matters stood, how much Larissa had already waded through.

In cases like this, what had to happen immediately was legal removal of the child from the parent, for the boy's protection. Larissa had taken the proper steps; the boy was now a ward of the ministry. Unfortunately that was about all she'd done.

Roy needed to talk to the kid's doctor, the firemen who'd found him, and anyone else who'd been on the scene or knew anything about Shannon and David Riggs. It had to be done immediately, because firefighters and police were busy people, and he wanted to know what their impressions were while they were still fresh in their minds.

It was also important to go see the boy himself, so that he had a feeling for the little person, instead of just a name in a file. It was his policy to do that stat.

''We've managed to keep this out of the headlines

so far, only because of that double murder. Be prepared for reporters, though. They'll be after you because of your involvement in the Sieberg affair.''

Tragedy, Marty, Roy wanted to say. *The Sieberg tragedy, where the authorities sent a little boy back to his birth mother and he died.* But he held his tongue. What did semantics matter when the kid was dead?

''Better refer them to me,'' his team leader said. Marty wasn't a bad guy, but he was a publicity hound who longed to see his name in print. He'd resented the press coverage Roy had gotten during the Sieberg trial. Roy just resented the press coverage.

''Gladly.'' He'd had enough run-ins with the papers to last him a lifetime.

So much for tonight's family dinner. He wasn't going to be able to stay long. He'd just drop off the gift for his sister Dana and then get to work. Nicole could get a ride home with someone else easily enough.

He'd been looking forward to dinner, though. He was famished. Maybe Jennifer would take pity on him and make him up a plate of food to carry with him.

''Okay, Marty, I'll get on this right away.''

''Thanks, Roy.'' Marty added with gallows humor, ''Have a good evening.''

Roy glanced at his watch. Jennifer had said the birthday dinner was at seven-thirty. If he got out of here in five minutes, and *if* Nicole was ready when he got to her place—a big *if,* since his sister wasn't often on time—he could just about manage a quick stop at St. Joe's to see the boy. It was on the way to Jennifer's house, anyway, he rationalized.

Well, almost. Ten minutes out of the way, give or take.

He shrugged into his jacket, ran a brush through his hair—he was two weeks past a date with his barber—and was out the door with a minute to spare.

Things seemed to be going well for a change, because there was a parking spot right in front of Nicole's condo. Roy swung his aging blue Toyota into it and sprinted to the entrance. He punched in her code number and waited impatiently until she buzzed the door open.

Nicole was standing at the door to her condo. She tipped her lovely face up so he could kiss her cheek.

"Hey, handsome, love your suit. Is it new?"

"Vintage. Just had it dry-cleaned. Those guys do wonders." It was an old joke. She'd seen the suit many times before. Nicole was a clothes freak, and she liked to tease him about his total lack of interest in his wardrobe.

"You look as gorgeous as ever," he complimented her. He studied her and hazarded a pretty safe guess. "New dress?"

She nodded. "First time out. I'm testing it on you guys and then I'm going to wear it when that hunk of an airline pilot takes me to dinner on Saturday. Think it's too dressy for a family birthday party?"

"Not at all. It's a good color on you."

Nicole burst into giggles. "Roy, its *black,* you idiot."

"So?" He feigned hurt. "It's still a good color on you. But then, any color would be a good color on you."

It was the truth. His sister was stunning. At five-eleven, she was just three inches shorter than he was, with long, straight, gleaming blond hair. She had the slender figure of a fashion model and a mind like a high-speed computer, and under that golden tan were the muscles of an Amazon. Tonight she was wearing spiky heels, so they were nearly eye to eye.

Nicole was warm and funny and vulnerable. Out of three sisters and two brothers, she was his favorite sibling, a go-for-the-jugular divorce lawyer who dreamed of being a landscape architect. She fantasized about living in a cottage on acres of land where she could grow tomatoes and babies, but for convenience' sake she lived in a condo with a postage stamp for a yard.

Single, as he was. Searching, which he assured himself he wasn't.

She reached up and smoothed his hair back. "You could use a haircut, or are you going for that killer ponytail look? Crooked nose, dimple in your chin—you might just get away with it."

He scowled at her. "It's not a dimple, it's a cleft. And I plan to get a haircut. In fact, I'm thinking of a brush cut."

"I'll get Mom and the sisters to vote tonight on whether or not you should. My money's on the ponytail."

"I won't be around to hear the results. I'm gonna have to cut the evening short, Nicky. I got a call from work just as I was leaving. Can't stay for dinner.''

''Just as well for the rest of us. Jen's making Italian—the cake's gonna be that cream-and-chocolate masterpiece. What's the emergency?''

''An abandoned baby at St. Joe's. I need to meet the little guy and talk to the doctor. You mind if we stop on our way?''

''Not at all. The family knows my car's in for repairs, so it's your head that rolls if we're late.''

''That's what I love about you, Nicky. You're clear that it's every man for himself.''

''It comes from growing up in a house where there was one bathroom and seven bladders.''

''That's something I'm not sorry I missed out on.'' Roy had reunited with his birth family when he was seventeen. His adoptive parents had had two bathrooms and one kid.

He handed her into the car, then took the slight detour that would lead them to St. Joe's.

''Did you hear Dana's pregnant again?''

''Nobody tells me stuff like that. This'll make, what, four for her?''

''Five.'' She shook her head and clucked her tongue. ''Without me to remind you, you'd never remember how many nieces and nephews you've got.''

''It keeps changing all the time.''

''Lucky Dana.'' Nicole's soft brown eyes were wistful. ''What did you get her for her birthday?''

''A Swatch watch. I asked Greg what she might like and that's what he said.''

"I guess she'll need it to time her contractions. I played it safe and got her soap and bubble bath. You can't go wrong with that. She told me the kids used the last of her stash to make potions in the bathtub. They're deep into wizardry. Harry Potter has created a whole new market for bubble bath."

He laughed. "They're good kids. And Dana and Greg are great parents." It was reassuring to know there were people who took care of their kids. He saw so many of the other kind.

"What's with the baby at St. Joe's?"

"Two-year-old David Riggs, found abandoned a few days ago in a downtown apartment."

"I think I saw a small article about him in the paper, but it didn't give his name or anything." Nicole frowned. "How could a mother leave a little kid alone for three days?"

It was more a sad statement than a question. Nicole heard too many horror stories to be surprised by much.

"She's seventeen. She'll probably insist she didn't plan to be away more than a few minutes." He'd heard it so many times before. "David's now in the care of the ministry, so she's gonna have to jump through hoops to get him back."

Unless some idiot judge decides otherwise. Four-year-old Scotty Sieberg had begged to stay with his foster family, and Roy had petitioned the court to leave him there. But Scotty had been handed back to his birth mother. And her boyfriend had shaken the little boy for not picking up his toys, and Scotty had died.

Rage boiled in Roy as he pulled into the lot beside the medical center. He knew he had to shove the Sieberg case into a mental file drawer marked *Don't go there unless you have to.*

"Mind if I come in with you?" Nicole asked.

"Well, I was really planning to leave you out here sweltering in the car," he teased. "But maybe you can come, as long as you cling to me and do that swivel-hip thing you babes do in heels. Nobody here knows that you're my sister, and it'll get me a whole lot of respect from the male members of the staff."

"And here I thought it was the females you wanted to impress. Is there something sensitive and personal you want to tell me, big brother?"

"Only that I need help fighting off the hordes of rabid women after my body."

"In your dreams."

The pediatrics ward was behind a locked door on the fourth floor. Roy presented ID, and the security guard let them in. There was no one at the nurses' station, but they could hear children's excited voices and loud laughter erupting from the playroom at the end of the corridor, so Roy headed that way.

"Sounds like a party," Nicole remarked. "We've come to the right place."

On the floor of the playroom, a group of children sat around a young woman with short, fiery-red curls. Huge, gray rabbit ears were secured to her head by a yellow ribbon. She was wearing a pink T-shirt patterned with garish sunflowers over a pair of green uniform pants, and she was sitting cross-legged, her head bent over a book she was reading aloud.

On the floor beside her, a live rabbit in a wire cage munched on a lettuce leaf, a bored expression on his face. The room was overly warm, and there was a pungent odor of children, antiseptic, urine and rabbit turds.

There was also the ripple of children's laughter, and Roy smiled with pleasure and surprise. A hospital wasn't usually a place where kids enjoyed themselves, and it delighted him to hear them having fun.

The sound of laughter died as one after another of the kids caught sight of Roy and Nicole. The woman stopped reading and turned toward them.

"Hi," she said in a voice that was husky and filled with what musicians called blue notes. "I'm Hailey Bergstrom. What can I do for you?"

She was no beauty. Her nose was long and thin, her mouth too wide in a decidedly square face. Roy noticed those things, but he also noticed that she had unusual eyes, large, tilted, widely spaced. They were a peculiar color, like dark honey.

She made no move to get up. The tag pinned to her chest said she was an RN.

"I'm Roy Zedyck, David Riggs's social worker. This is Nicole Hepburn."

"Hi, Roy. Hello, Nicole." She gave Roy a questioning look. "How can I help you?"

"I wondered if I could see David, and also whether Dr. Larue is around? I'd like to speak to him."

She turned to the kids. "Sorry, you guys, I've gotta go." She rose to her feet, rabbit ears flopping, and the kids sent up a protesting howl. She held out the book to an emaciated girl in a pink tracksuit. The child was bald, and her eyes had immense brown circles under them.

"Brittany, you finish the story, please."

"Noooo, nooooo, we want you, Hailey, *pleeeeeze,*" the kids chorused.

"Brittany can read every bit as well as I can. Stop the noise or Skippy will freak out and have heart palpitations, and we'd have to call Doc Benson."

Her voice dropped to a whisper. "And you know how *grumpy* Doc Benson can be." She pretended to shudder and then stood tall and held her hand to her forehead in a salute. "When duty calls I must obey, or I will live to rue the day."

Roy noted that she was very tall in her flat sandals, probably five-eleven like Nicole.

"C'mon, David's in 4B."

Brittany's clear, high voice followed them down the corridor.

Roy figured that Hailey Bergstrom was oblivious to the fact that she had a huge, furry bunny tail pinned to the seat of her uniform pants. It swished as she walked, emphasizing narrow hips. She was thin rather than slender, with long arms and legs, but there was a vibrancy about her that was almost palpable. She seemed to give off sparks. He wondered idly whether getting too close to her might result in an electric shock.

"David just came up from intensive care this

morning. He's my patient. I thought his case worker's name was Larissa Mott.''

So she'd done her homework, Roy thought. Good for her.

"Larissa's father died, and she's off on bereavement leave. David's got me now.''

She nodded and narrowed her eyes at him. "Any sign of his mother yet?''

Roy shook his head. "Police are watching out for her, but so far no luck. How's he doing?''

"He's a pretty sick little guy. His electrolytes are all out of whack and he won't drink yet. We've got him on IV. There's been a lot of phone calls about him. People saw the article in the *Province*.''

"I'm sure Larissa already covered this, but I'll be leaving written orders of my own that David not be released to anyone, and if anyone tries, I'm to be notified immediately.''

Hailey nodded and opened the door to a two-bed ward. One of the cribs was empty, but in the other a tiny figure wearing a blue pajama top and a diaper lay sprawled on his back, deeply asleep, his curls dark against the white pillow. A stuffed dog, filthy and much the worse for wear, was clutched to his face, and an IV tube was attached to his foot with strips of tape. There were deep, dark circles under his eyes.

Roy looked down at the sleeping child and his heart contracted. Children were fragile and precious, their lives dependent on the adults whose job it was to care for them. This one had been betrayed, and it tore at his gut. It always did. The discouraging thing was that it happened all too often in big cities like this one.

"Were there other visible signs of abuse?" Roy knew he'd get the report, but he wanted to know now.

Hailey held up a cautioning hand, frowned and shook her head at him. "We can discuss that outside the room."

"He's so sweet, so very small." Nicole's voice was husky, and when he looked at her, Roy saw tears shimmering in her eyes. Her gaze was on the baby. "He can't even tell anybody what hurts. That must be awful."

"You're gonna talk a blue streak when you wake up, though, aren't you, David?" Hailey leaned over the crib and in a crooning voice added, "You're such a beautiful, smart boy. We're gonna be great friends, aren't we, little one?" Her hand lightly touched the boy's curls, one finger stroking his cheek. She checked the IV drip and carefully covered his legs with a blanket.

The boy turned his head restlessly to the other side and slept on, and Hailey led the way into the hall, her rabbit ears flopping around her neck.

"No matter how little they are, no matter how deeply asleep or unconscious, they hear us talking, and even the smallest ones pick up on what we're saying," she said to Roy in a ferocious tone. "He was seriously dehydrated when he came in, he arrested down in the ER, he's gaining a little ground, but he's still really sick." Her tone turned sarcastic. "And in answer to your question, other than being alone for three days without anything to eat or drink, he doesn't seem to have been abused. He's well nourished, no bruising or old scars, no broken bones. Real fortunate little guy, wouldn't you say?''

Roy felt like an idiot. ''I'm sorry, Hailey, that was stupid of me. I should have known better than to talk in front of him.'' He was embarrassed, but he also couldn't believe he was being lectured by a woman wearing rabbit ears and a tail.

''Does he have anything of his own, any toys or clothes?'' Nicole asked. She was still looking through the glass door at the small figure in the crib.

''The stuffed dog he's clutching is all that came in with him. It's his security blanket. It needs a wash, but there's no way I'm taking it from him right now.''

''Maybe I can bring him some things?''

Hailey smiled at Nicole. ''That's sweet of you, but don't go overboard. Stuff gets shared in here, and it also gets lost. But it is nice for the kids to have something that belongs just to them.''

''I need to use a phone.'' Roy had to contact the police and the firemen who'd found David.

''There's one at the nurses' station.''

''Thanks. I'll use it on our way out.''

''How on earth do you stand it?'' Nicole was looking at Hailey, and there was awe and admiration in her voice. ''I'd want to kidnap a baby like that and spoil the living daylights out of him.''

''All we can do is love 'em and let 'em go,'' Hailey said with a resigned shrug. ''Nursing is care, not cure.'' She turned her attention to Roy. ''And having said that, do you know anything at all about this so-called mother of his?''

Roy shook his head. ''Sorry, that information's confidential.''

''Figures. Protect the criminal at all costs,'' Hailey said scornfully, giving him another of her scathing glances. ''Makes you wonder what was going on in her head, walking out and leaving him like that.''

''He's lucky to have you as his nurse,'' Nicole said. ''They all are. You're obviously just what these kids need.''

''Hey, thanks.'' Hailey's resentment seemed to evaporate. Her grin was spontaneous and wide, her face animated. She had straight, white teeth, and her amber eyes sparkled. ''It's so good to hear that on the day you're wearing a bunny costume at work.'' She glanced at her wristwatch. ''Whoops, speaking of work, I've gotta go. It's time for meds.'' She turned to Roy. ''Dr. Larue is on his dinner break. He'll be here later this evening if you want to speak with him. Or the aide can give you his cell number.'' She waved a hand at Roy and Nicole and hurried off toward the nurses' station, tail swishing with gay abandon.

Nicole watched her go. ''Now there's an unusual woman for you.''

''Vicious is more like it.'' The looks she'd given him were lethal. He wouldn't want her armed with a hypodermic.

''She's not vicious, she's gutsy.'' Nicole looped an arm through Roy's, and they hurried toward the nurses' desk. "Balls enough to tell you off and enough perspective to accept the parameters of her job. It's evident she really likes being a nurse."

"Nurses, lawyers—power. It's all about power with you females."

But he silently agreed with Nicole. Hailey Bergstrom was an example of someone who'd obviously found the perfect job, and it suited her, even the part that included wearing rabbit ears and a tail.

Or cutting him into chunks and spitting out the pieces.

CHAPTER TWO

FROM THE NURSES' STATION Hailey watched them go down the corridor, Zedyck's arm looped around the woman's shoulders.

They could have posed for a magazine ad, she mused. They made a striking couple, both tall, both blessed with an abundance of physical beauty.

Nicole was a stunner, but based on one short meeting, she also seemed to be a truly nice person, lacking the self-centered attitude that sometimes went with such good looks.

Hailey's mind naturally turned to her older sister, Laura. Laura was drop-dead gorgeous, too, but in Hailey's opinion, Laura was about as self-centered as it was possible to get. She'd carved out a perfect life, by her standards, and wasn't the least bit interested in other people's choices. She'd married Frank, a creep with the same sort of good looks she possessed, produced two perfect kids and decorated a house in the suburbs with a lot of help from Martha Stewart's magazines.

Hailey wouldn't know Martha Stewart if the woman had a stroke in her living room, which was probable if she ever laid eyes on it.

How different could two sisters be?

And it was interesting how beautiful women gravitated to men whose looks complemented their own.

Roy Zedyck was as dark as Nicole was fair, and in spite of his mental lapses, he was good to look at, if your taste ran to crooked noses and grass-green eyes and jawlines out of an old western. Good hair, too. She liked it wavy and covering a guy's shirt collar, the way his did.

For the remaining two hours of her shift, Hailey worked steadily, checking on David often, changing babies and feeding them, telling wild stories and singing nonsense songs as she slowly got her older patients into their pajamas. She ensured that everyone's meds were administered and did her best to make the kids laugh whenever she could. Even the sickest of them rewarded her with tiny smiles, and to her those smiles were precious gifts.

Hailey always took her time with the kids, even though she knew her supervisor, Margaret Cross, repeatedly documented her for spending too much time with the patients and not enough getting the paperwork done before the next shift arrived.

Margaret was a nurse of the old school who made a point of coming to work in a white dress uniform, white stockings and her nursing cap, a regalia that had the other nurses calling her TGONP behind her back—the ghost of nurses past.

It was obvious Margaret hated her, and Hailey pretended she didn't give a flying fig. The head nurse couldn't get her fired, no matter how much she disapproved. That was the beauty of knowing you were excellent at your job. Oh, yeah, and a good union helped, too.

The thing was, there was no way you could rush little kids, nor should you. It was hard enough for them, trapped in here, feeling sick, most of them horribly lonely for their parents. They needed to have some control over their environment, Hailey felt, and if it came in the guise of slowing down the system, so be it. Margaret could have been a general in the armed forces, she believed so strongly in discipline and rules.

When at last the reports had been made to the new shift and Hailey was done for the day, she took off the rabbit ears and tail and rescued her pet, Skippy, from the staff lounge, where he'd been banished after Margaret found him in the playroom.

Hailey was carrying his cage on her way to the elevator when she changed her mind, stowed Skippy back in a corner of the staff lounge and detoured to David's room.

There was another child in the room with David now, but he was asleep. David was wide awake, lying silent in his crib, his stuffed dog held close to his body, his eyes big and scared when he looked up at her. Earlier she'd changed and bathed him, and held him for as long as she could possibly manage it. His electrolytes were still way below normal, which meant that he probably wasn't feeling good at all. His sweet little face was somber, and the anxious, frightened look in his blue eyes tugged at her heartstrings.

"Hey, dumpling, you're wide awake." She

grinned at him and held out her arms, but he just looked up at her with a solemn, wary expression.

"Just you wait, Davie. You're gonna break down and smile at me yet," she teased in a whisper, so as not to wake his roommate.

David smelled clean and fresh, and there was a sweet, elusive baby odor to his skin. She leaned down and pressed her nose against his neck and blew a gentle bubble. He lifted a tentative hand and touched her hair, his eyes wide.

"Some mad mess that mop is, huh, Davie? People keep suggesting I get it styled, but I'm a sucker for the natural look. And you little guys like it. You can get your hands in and really yank. Hey, partner, wanna go for a walk?"

She picked him up. His body stiffened with alarm, but he didn't cry. He pointed at his dog, and she tucked it in his arms. Hauling the IV pole, she carried him on her hip down the corridor to an empty room where there was a rocking chair. Hailey sank into it, and after a while she felt David relax against her.

For forty minutes she rocked and sang him snippets from James Taylor and Janis Joplin. He fell asleep, and because his warm, soft little body comforted her, she went on rocking and singing.

At last one of the other nurses stuck her head in and smiled.

"Hailey, you still here? I thought you'd be long gone by now. You've gotta get a life, girl."

"Hi, Karen. I needed a hug, so I kidnapped David."

"He's a real sweetheart. I heard about him from one of the ER docs."

"He's an angel."

Karen came in and studied David, sleeping soundly against Hailey's chest. "You're right, he is an angel. But then, you say that about all of them. No word on his mom yet?"

Hailey shook her head. "His new social worker was by earlier. The other one's dad died, so she's gone to his funeral. This guy's name is Roy Zedyck."

"Oh, yeah, everybody's heard of him. Big tall guy, great buns. Wow, he's a celebrity. He was the one who was in the news a while back, the inquiry into that little boy who got sent back to his birth mother and ended up dead?"

Hailey shuddered. "I don't watch stuff like that, or read about it, either. What we get in here is quite enough for me."

"Everybody says Robertson's testimony was the reason they set up that independent commission, so there'll be someone else for kids to turn to besides the ministry. Hopefully decisions will be made that are truly in the child's best interest, and not just some arbitrary ruling handed down by one judge."

"Sounds like a good idea."

"I can't believe you haven't heard about it—it was all over the news. Becky's gonna be green. She drools when Zedyck's name is mentioned. But then, Becky drools a lot. I swear she's got an extra few ounces of estrogen going for her."

Hailey laughed. "She's got a good eye for male

beefcake, and in this instance she's dead right. You'd have to be neutered not to notice how sexy Zedyck is.''

And he must have more gray matter than she thought, if he'd impressed the court that way.

"Tell Becky to give it up. He's got a knockout for a lady, gorgeous and caring, really friendly, name of Nicole. She was with him. They were all duded up for a party or something.''

"Lucky them." Karen wrinkled her nose. "How come some people get the full-meal deal and the rest of us have to make do with the forty-nine-cent special?'' Hailey knew that Karen was going through a messy and painful divorce.

"It has to do with astrology." Hailey got to her feet, careful not to disturb David. "I better get home. I left my rabbit in the staff lounge. If I don't get him out of there, somebody'll rat to Margaret and I'll be getting a rabbit reprimand on my file.''

Karen giggled. The ongoing conflict between Hailey and Margaret Cross was constant entertainment for the rest of the pediatric nursing staff. And they were right to laugh. If you didn't laugh about Margaret and her tantrums, you'd be tempted to smother her in the linen closet.

"I'll bring the IV," Karen offered. "You just carry him.''

They paraded down the corridor and Hailey settled David into his crib. She bent and pressed a kiss to his cheek.

"Night, little Davie. Sleep well. The angels will watch over you and keep you safe." She told all her

little patients the same thing when she took leave
of them.

When they were out in the hall again, Karen gave
Hailey a warm smile and a hug. "You need a dozen
or so of your own. You'd make the best mom ever."

Hailey's smile felt strained. Kids of her own was
the thing in life she most wanted. "I'll settle for just
one."

"How's the adoption process coming?" Most of
her co-workers were aware that Hailey had recently
applied for single-parent adoption.

"Slow." Hailey grimaced. "They really check
you out on all fronts. I guess it's a good thing, but
it kind of wears you down after a while."

Karen nodded. "I can imagine." She heaved a
sigh. "I'm glad now that Jim and I didn't have any
kids. It would make this whole divorce thing that
much harder, and God knows it's tough enough as
it is. But I'm getting older, and I guess every woman
wants kids sooner or later."

"For me, I hope it's sooner," Hailey said. "I'm
gonna be thirty in another month. That's old compared with when people used to have kids. My mom
had my sister when she was twenty-four and me two
years later."

"People generally had kids earlier then. Now it
takes time to be able to afford them, and with birth
control we have the option of waiting."

"Some of us, I guess. David's mother's only
seventeen. One of the ER nurses heard it from a
cop."

Karen shook her head and clucked her tongue. "Sometimes there's a good argument for abortion."

"Or adoption."

One of the monitors began to beep.

"Gotta go. Take care and enjoy what's left of your evening." Karen waved a quick goodbye as she hurried off.

Hailey made her way out to the car park and climbed into her battered red half-ton. She'd bought it a year ago, a few months after she purchased her house, trading in her cherished old Grand Prix for it when she realized how many deliveries she'd paid for from Home Depot and how many times she'd wished she could get rid of her own building debris.

The good news was that it took her and the half-ton only twenty minutes to get from St. Joe's to her street. The bad news was that the two-story blue-and-white octogenarian she'd bought had turned out to be a money pit. She was slowly and for the most part single-handedly repairing and remodeling, but it was a painfully time-consuming, expensive process. The front lawn was full of moss, the back devoid of grass because of two tall cedars, a stand of overgrown lilacs and an immense fir tree that prevented sunlight from getting through. The trees did give the property privacy, though, and she'd pay more attention to the yard when she got the inside livable.

Her master plan was to finish the basement first and rent it out so she had additional income, and then turn one of the four upstairs bedrooms, the tiny one next to her own, into a nursery.

She parked on the street. None of the houses had garages. Gazing for a moment at her house, she felt the same thrill she always did when she arrived home. This funny old battered senior citizen of a house was really hers. She'd had to scrimp and save and practically offer the bank her soul to get it, but she wouldn't trade it for anything.

Carrying Skippy's cage, she made her way around to the back, where she'd used chicken wire to construct a pen for the rabbit. After she'd turned him loose and made sure he had food and water, she climbed the rickety wooden back stairs—*gotta do something about those stairs*—unlocked the door and went inside.

The phone on the kitchen counter was ringing. A glance at her watch showed that it was ten-forty-five. She picked up the receiver.

"Hailey?" Her mother's voice made her shut her eyes and wish she'd let the machine take the call. "Where've you been? I called twice before. I thought your shift was over at seven."

"Hi, Mom." Hailey wished, not for the first time, that she'd gotten call display. It wasn't that she didn't want to talk to her mother; it was just that she'd rather choose the times it happened, like Christmas and Easter.

"How you doing, Mom?" Hailey ignored the questions, knowing that Jean really didn't expect an answer. "How come you're calling this late?"

"It's Laura. She was over yesterday, and something's not right with her."

Hailey rolled her eyes heavenward. As far as she

knew, her sister's problems were primarily whether or not to fire the gardener, change the living-room sofa, or enroll Hailey's niece and nephew in yet another extracurricular activity. Poor little mites. At seven and nine their lives were already as regimented as Margaret would like the peds ward to be.

"Have you talked to her recently, Hailey?"

"Not for a couple of weeks." That was about par for her and Laura. The last time Hailey had called, it was on impulse one Saturday morning. She'd wanted to take Christopher and Samantha to the Greek food fair. Of course it hadn't been possible; they'd had karate and swimming lessons. Sometimes she suspected Laura of deliberately keeping the kids busy so they wouldn't be overexposed to their whacko aunt. Christopher had once told her that's how his father referred to Hailey. Chris, bless his heart, had wanted to know if "whacko" had something to do with boxing.

"Well, I wish you'd give her a call—see if she'll open up to you. There's something wrong with her and I can't put my finger on it."

Open up? What planet did Jean live on? Laura hadn't opened up to Hailey since she'd gotten her first period at the age of twelve, when Laura had been kind enough to explain sex and the connection to babies. Hailey had already known, but she didn't let on.

Her stomach rumbled, and she remembered she hadn't eaten since lunch, and then it had been a tuna sandwich gulped on the run.

"Look, Mom, can I call you in the morning? I've

just come home and I need to make some dinner. I'm starving.''

''You're always starving. God knows where you put it, although you could stand to gain a few pounds. In the right places, of course. You will give Laura a call, won't you?'' Jean was nothing if not persistent. And *con*sistent. She'd been on about Hailey's weight, or lack of it, for years, as if the proper diet would pump up her boobs to a 36C and shorten her nose.

A wave of irritation washed over Hailey. She could probably tell her mother she was dying, and Jean would wonder what effect it was going to have on Laura. It had always *been* Laura, but then, in all fairness, Laura was the daughter who looked like Jean, whose values coincided with her own. They actually had serious discussions about things like leg waxing and facials and anti-aging cream.

Hailey wondered sometimes if the balance of attention would have been more even if her father had lived, but Ed Bergstrom had thoughtlessly died of a heart attack when she was eleven, leaving her alone with an alien species.

''I'm worried, Hailey. Do you think maybe she's sick or something and just doesn't want to tell us?''

''She's fine, Mom.'' Hailey heaved an exasperated sigh. ''She'd tell you if anything was wrong with her.''

But Hailey wasn't fine. She was starving, and her mother wasn't giving up. God, anything for a little peace and some food.

''Look, Mom, I'll call her. Not tonight, but soon.

And yes, I'll try to get her to talk to me about what's bothering her.''

She hung up and muttered in a sarcastic tone, ''And how are *you,* Hailey? What's going on in *your* life? Any news about that adoption thing yet?''

The truth was, not much new was going on in her life, so maybe it was a good thing Jean didn't care enough to ask.

She didn't really believe that, Hailey admitted as she put water on to boil for pasta and found some fresh garlic and the jar of sun-dried tomatoes in the fridge, but it was some comfort.

It was better not to have Jean prying into her life, she told herself as she pulled wilted spinach out of the vegetable bin and tore it up for salad. What if she got on that kick again about finding Hailey a nice guy and getting her married off? Jean had driven her nuts about it there for a while two or three years ago. She'd tried to line Hailey up with the least likely candidates: loser sons of the people who worked with Jean in the doctor's office; patients, for God's sake; even a dentist Jean had gone to for a root canal. The dentist hadn't been bad in bed, but after a while Hailey got sick of hearing about molars and incisors and bicuspids, especially right after sex.

Thankfully Jean had given up.

Not that Hailey had done any better on her own. Her last date had been…when? She calculated in her head. It would be about six months ago now, and even at the time, she knew Norman Patino wasn't anybody's idea of an eligible bachelor. But he was male and alive and breathing, and he'd shown some interest in her.

But then she'd gotten to know him better. Or worse. It was one thing for a guy to be overweight and balding—that she could overlook. After all, she was no beauty queen herself. But for him to also be arrogant, self-centered and downright cheap was too much even for somebody who was desperate.

And she *had* been desperate when she dated Norman, Hailey thought as she assembled her meal and sat down at the kitchen table to eat it. She'd been going through a spell when she wanted to get married and have a family so badly she was willing to compromise in all sorts of ways. But even she had limits. Norman bored her cross-eyed and expected her to pay for dinner once too often, and she'd finally realized she was worth more than the compromises she'd been making. It had been satisfying to dump him, and both maddening and sad to hear him blame the failure of their relationship totally on her. He'd accused her of being fussy, which would have been funny if it wasn't so damned sad.

The pasta was good, and she ate her way through a heaping bowlful and then a second. After she put the dishes in the sink, she checked her telephone messages. There was only one, and it made her smile with delight. It was from her paternal grandmother, Ingrid Bergstrom.

CHAPTER THREE

INGRID DIDN'T WASTE time saying all the usual things like hello, how are you, even in a phone message. She simply started off where their last conversation had ended.

"So I went to the community center like I said I was going to, to register for that French course, but the lineup was a mile long, and there was another course being offered in belly dancing, so I signed up for that, instead. It's still multicultural, don't you think?" Ingrid giggled, the wicked, wild giggle that Hailey loved.

"Sam loves the idea," Ingrid went on, "so now I'm going to buy myself some silk shawls and those things you use with your fingers—zills, I think they're called. Phone me when you get a chance. Maybe you could come for brunch tomorrow if you're still on that one-to-nine shift. Don't worry if it's late when you call. I've told Sam I'm staying up to read that last murder mystery you loaned me. Man, that woman can write."

Among other things, Hailey had inherited Ingrid's voice. As she listened to her gran's husky tones move from one octave to another, she remembered once in school hearing her own voice on a tape recorder and being astounded and thrilled because it was exactly like Gran's. It was the first time she'd ever liked anything about herself.

Hailey dialed the familiar number and Ingrid answered immediately.

"Hey, Haileybop, tell me what's going on over at St. Joe's. Any new patients?"

Ingrid loved hearing about Hailey's work. For several years now she'd been one of the volunteers who came to the newborn section to rock and cuddle babies.

Hailey gave her a rundown on the kids Ingrid already knew about, and then she told her about David.

"He's such a darling, Gran. Big blue eyes, black curly hair. He has a filthy stuffed dog he hangs on to for dear life."

"I'll add him to my prayers, and when I'm at St. Joe's, I'll come up and visit him if you're on."

"That would be great. How's Sam?" Hailey adored her step grandpa, who openly admitted he had trouble keeping up with his madcap wife. He was sixty-three, Ingrid seventy-two. They'd married five years before, to the utter horror of Sam's grown family, who considered Ingrid totally unsuitable.

"He's sound asleep. He just finished a catalog shoot for one of those hoity-toity men's stores. He says it was exhausting holding his gut in for so long, so finally he's joining my gym. I told him a long time ago he should. Lifting weights counteracts the force of gravity. It's helped keep my boobs firm, what there is of them, and that's a not-so-minor miracle.''

Hailey giggled. Sam and Ingrid were her favorite people. They were also one of the few married couples she knew who were deliriously happy and had fun together every single day. She also strongly suspected they had sex every single day.

''I wanna be you when I grow up, Gran.''

''Just be yourself, darlin'. You're perfect just the way you are.''

It was a litany Ingrid had repeated to Hailey ever since she was a little girl. It had helped deflect Jean's disappointment in a daughter who lacked the physical beauty and graces that Jean believed were essential to a woman's success.

''So how's about brunch tomorrow? Can you make it?''

''I'd love to.''

''Come over when you get up. I want to try this new recipe for soy muffins.''

''You sure you don't want to go out somewhere? My treat.'' Ingrid wasn't the world's best cook. In fact, she just might be the worlds worst. No one had died from her cooking yet, but sometimes Hailey thought it was a strong possibility.

''Nope. There's way too much sugar and fat in restaurant food.''

There was, but it was also edible.

''Okay, Gran, I'll be there about ten-thirty. Can I bring anything?'' She added in a hopeful tone, ''I can stop and get some of those cinnamon rolls from that little bakery on Fourth.''

"Nope, just bring your appetite. I'll make everything. See you in the morning. Sleep well, honey."

"You too, Gran." Hailey hung up. Talking to Ingrid made her feel as though everything was right with the world, and the feeling persisted as she showered in her decrepit bathroom and climbed into bed.

Her last thought was always for the children in her care at work, and she sent up a prayer for each and every one before she slipped into sleep, adding a special PS for David.

THE FOLLOWING MORNING Hailey took one bite of Ingrid's soy muffins and tried her best to swallow, but it was a challenge. It was truly awful. Across the breakfast table she saw Sam smoothly transferring his own mouthful into his napkin. He raised an eyebrow and crossed his eyes when Ingrid wasn't looking, and Hailey had to stifle a giggle.

"Take another muffin and put some jam on it," Ingrid suggested. "Maybe they need a bit of sweetening."

Nothing was going to improve those babies, Hailey thought. "I'll just have more of the fruit salad, thanks, Gran." She loaded her bowl.

"So what's going to happen to this little David, then? Will he go into foster care?" Ingrid took a bite of her own muffin, chewed doggedly for several moments, swallowed with difficulty, then went to the cupboard and found a box of crackers.

"Maybe I should have put the eggs in," she mused. "I figured the muffins would turn out just as good without, but they're a bit on the heavy side.'' She offered the crackers to Sam and Hailey. ''I cut down on the butter, too. That's probably what did it.''

''So what did you leave in, sweetheart?'' Sam kept a straight face, but his brown eyes were dancing. His thick, white hair shone, his strong, craggy features were tanned a golden brown, and if he had a paunch, it certainly wasn't evident beneath his navy tracksuit. It was easy to see why he was so much in demand as a mature male model.

''The soy flour, of course. I told you, they're soy muffins.''

Hailey and Sam burst into laughter. Ingrid was infamous for changing recipes, and her experiments were always disastrous, but she never gave up. The wonderful thing about her was that she could laugh at herself, as she was doing now.

When Hailey looked at her grandmother, she saw her own face as it would be when she was seventy-two, filled with laugh lines and character. Ingrid was a handsome woman, and Hailey had inherited her tall, lanky body, her square face, even her red hair. Ingrid's was nearly all white now, and what was left of the red had turned rusty, but it still stood out around her head in an incongruous halo of springy, incorrigible curls. The only features Hailey had inherited from her mother's side were what she called her canine eyes.

Ingrid's were a deep green, while Hailey had Jean's toffee color.

''So forget the muffins. I'll get it right the next

time. What about this latest patient of yours, that little David you told me about?''

Sam and Ingrid listened closely as Hailey told them everything she knew about him, which wasn't much. "The Department of Social Services and the courts will decide what eventually happens to him,'' she explained. ''He'll probably go into foster care as soon as he's released from St. Joe's, unless some relative comes forward and offers to care for him.''

''And we all know that's not very likely,'' Ingrid said with a sigh. ''There's so many babies around that nobody seems to want I can't see why they're taking so long to find one for you, honey.''

Ingrid and Sam had eagerly offered to baby-sit their great-grandchild when Hailey finally became a mother. Like Hailey, Ingrid had had little opportunity to get to know Laura's kids, and Hailey figured it probably had a lot to do with her mother. Jean was proprietary about Christopher and Samantha, and because she and Ingrid had never gotten along, it was a safe bet Jean would do her best to keep her beloved grandchildren out of the clutches of the person she'd long ago labeled her dipstick of a mother-in-law. It was easy to see why Frank and Jean got along so well, with vocabularies that contained labels like dipstick and whacko.

Although Sam had three grandchildren, there were problems in his family, too. His son and daughter had united in doing everything they could to keep him from marrying Ingrid, and they still hadn't quite forgiven him for not bowing to their wishes.

He'd married his first wife in his early twenties.

She died when he was fifty-five, and six months later he quit his job as an engineer and began a new career as a model, something he'd always wanted to try. When he began dating Ingrid, his children were aghast; she was the total opposite of what their mother had been.

"I could have a child immediately if I agreed to take one with severe mental or physical handicaps," Hailey said. "I've really considered it, but I see kids like that at work and I know how much time, energy and money it takes to deal with their special needs. I've thought it over carefully, and I just don't think I could manage alone."

Ingrid nodded. "I think you're wise to give it a lot of thought. A child isn't something you can return to the store for a refund if it doesn't work out."

Sam reached across and put his hand over Hailey's, his brown eyes brimming with kindness and affection. "When the time is right, exactly the right little girl or boy will be there for you."

"And the right guy, too," Ingrid said in a decisive voice. "Just remember, they take long enough to show up sometimes. After your grandfather died, I never dreamed I'd meet anyone I wanted to live with again. I certainly didn't go out looking, but Sam came along, anyway. You recall, Hailey, I wouldn't even let him get to first base for the longest time."

Sam rolled his eyes and Hailey hooted. She happened to know that Ingrid had gone to bed with Sam on their third date.

"But eventually you caved," Sam said. "Stubborn bloody woman. I knew from the first time I laid eyes on you that we were meant for each other, but would you listen?'' His voice was gruff and tender, and he gave Ingrid a look that made Hailey feel lonely, but also reconfirmed that there were people who truly cared for one another.

As she drove to work that day, Hailey thought about Ingrid and Sam. Was love preordained? Did two people really come together at a certain point in their lives in spite of their own plans, in spite of themselves?

An old, deep longing made her chest ache. She'd pretty much managed to convince herself that the relationships in her life weren't likely to be the male-female variety. It wasn't that she believed any longer that she was ugly, the way she had as a teenager. In her twenties she'd come to terms with the way she looked, and she'd had her share of dates, but she'd also come to understand that her feeling of alienation from men went much deeper than physical appearance.

Maybe it came from growing up in an all-female household, with a mother who put all her emphasis on beauty and wasn't able to conceal her disappointment at having a daughter who didn't look the way she wanted her to look. Or maybe it had to do with losing her father and not trusting any guy to stay around for the long haul.

Hailey had no illusions as to why she'd chosen pediatric nursing as a career. With children, there were no expectations. With them she could let loose the full force of her madcap personality, truly be the person she was usually too self-conscious to reveal around adults. And pediatric nursing, more than any other career choice, offered the opportunity to hold children close, to care for them, to love them, to make them feel better in any and every way she could devise.

She loved her work. There were times when it was painful, when children couldn't get well and her job was simply to help them die. There were times when she was physically sick from the emotional strain of letting go and saying goodbye. But even then, she never thought for one moment of doing anything else.

But—and it was a but that she managed not to think about most of the time—there was still the dream that every woman had. She wanted the kind of love that Ingrid had found with Sam, and because she was young, Hailey wanted even more. She wanted to know how it felt to carry a living being inside her, to give birth to a baby conceived in passion, to watch and listen to that precious soul as it grew. She wanted to share that experience with a man who felt the way she felt, who wanted what she wanted.

During the past year she'd decided it was time to give up that dream. It was time to compromise. There were children who desperately needed a mother, and she could do that. She'd considered going to a donor bank and having a baby, but she'd come to the conclusion that she had the capacity to love any child. It seemed a waste to grow one of her own when there were babies out there ready-made whose parents didn't want them or couldn't care for them.

She made her way up to the ward. Ordinarily she worked a twelve-hour, seven-to-seven shift, but this week she was filling in on her days off so a friend could go to Mexico. The eight-hour shift gave her a little break from routine.

The first thing Hailey did was check the charts to see how her patients had fared since she'd last seen them.

David had cried off and on all night, but today he was drinking a little more of the clear fluids he needed. A quick survey of his room showed Hailey he was sleeping.

Brittany Whitcomb had had chemo that morning, and Hailey went to check on her next. She was curled into a ball on her bed with the sheet and blanket pulled over her head, and Hailey could tell she was crying.

"Hey, sweetie, how goes it? You feeling crappy?"

There was a tiny nod from under the covers.

"Let's try to figure out what would help. There's ginger ale here—want a sip?"

Negative shake.

Hailey checked the chart. "You've had your anti-nausea meds, so can't offer you any more of that junk. How about if I sing to you?"

Negative shake.

"Darn, I keep hoping one of you guys will miss the fact that I can't carry a tune to save my life." Rhythmically and tenderly she rubbed Brittany's small, thin back through the covers. "So how about a story?"

A tiny nod.

"Once upon a time, there was a beautiful princess named Brittany who lived in a faraway land."

Even though Brittany was twelve, the fairy-tale format seemed to comfort her. For the next ten minutes Hailey wove a fanciful story about a princess who had a lot of bad things happen to her. Her mommy and daddy, the king and queen, divorced. Her big sister, the crown princess, married a prince from another country and left home. Princess Brittany was sad and mad, and then, to top it off, she got sick and had to travel to a healing center a long way from her home.

By incorporating the things Brittany had confided to her from time to time into the story, Hailey could suggest ways for Brittany to manage her feelings about being lonely for her family and feeling sick. When the story was done, the young girl had emerged from the protection of her bedcovers, and although she wasn't smiling, she wasn't crying, either.

"Really, Hailey." Margaret Cross's high-pitched voice made both Hailey and Brittany jump. "It would be nice if we all had time to sit around telling stories, but the fact is, we're shorthanded. Could you come along please and help collect the lunch trays?"

"I'll be right there, Margaret."

The head nurse obviously wanted to hurry the process along. She put a hand on her hip and sniffed several times, but Hailey didn't budge. Finally she turned on her heel and left the room, and Hailey pulled a face and moaned, "*Busted.* I'm gonna get three demerits and I'll bet I won't get any ice cream for dinner."

Brittany smiled at last. They talked for a moment about Brittany's birthday, which was coming up soon, and then Hailey had to go. She left the girl a Stephen King novel she'd smuggled in—Margaret didn't consider Stephen King suitable reading for a twelve-year-old—and went off to collect trays.

A half hour later she was showing two little boys in the playroom how to do a headstand when Roy Zedyck's deep voice sent her toppling from her precarious position.

CHAPTER FOUR

"SORRY, HAILEY, didn't mean to startle you. You okay?" Roy knelt beside her and tried to help her up.

"No." She scowled at him and twisted away. "Owww." She'd fallen hard and her elbow hurt. Rubbing it, she sat up. "Couldn't you whistle or something? I was concentrating on balance here."

"I really apologize. Next time I'll give you fair warning. Wish I could do a headstand." He turned to the boys. "Think if I asked her really nice she'd teach me?"

"Nope," Tommy declared, shaking his head. "'Cause I think she needs more practice."

"Yeah," Ian agreed. "She don't know how to do it right."

Roy laughed and Hailey stopped being annoyed. He was easy with kids, and that made up for scaring her.

"You guys have really hurt my feelings. You're way too critical." She was never embarrassed by anything she did that amused the kids, but having Roy see her topple over like a felled tree had made her self-conscious. She brushed herself off and got to her feet.

He was still smiling at her, so she smiled back. Who could resist?

"I thought I'd drop by and see how David's doing."

Hailey was impressed. In her experience, social workers didn't usually pay daily visits to clients.

"He's been asleep since I came on shift, but let's go check again." She turned to the boys. "You guys practice those stretches I showed you. You're not nearly ready for headstands, either. I'll be back to see how you're doing in—" she checked her watch "—fifteen minutes."

She led the way down the hall and Roy walked beside her, easily keeping pace with her long-legged stride.

"Nicole is probably going to drop by this afternoon with some stuff," he said. "She was shopping for David last time I talked to her."

He had a great voice, rumbly and compelling. She sneaked a sideways peek at him. Hell, he had a great everything.

"How long have you been in pediatrics, Hailey?"

"Ever since I graduated. I wouldn't work anywhere else—I love the kids."

"And they love you. Nicole said it was refreshing to meet someone who'd found the exact job she wanted to do."

"What does Nicole do?" It was obvious he was smitten with the woman. He kept bringing her up.

"She's a lawyer, but her big dream is to have her own gardening business."

"Wow." Hailey was astounded. "I never would

have guessed lawyer. She looks like a fashion model. And gardening. She doesn't look like the type of woman…'' She caught herself. ''Would you just listen to me, making idiotic assumptions?''

''Nobody would guess that someone who looks like Nicole would like to be up to her elbows in compost and dirt.''

''She'd sure clean up good,'' Hailey said. ''She seems like quite a woman,'' she added. ''You're a lucky guy.''

Roy looked surprised. ''Hate to burst your romantic bubble, but Nicole's my sister.''

''Your sister?'' She was astonished.

''Yeah, she got all the looks in the family.''

That was debatable. ''Is there just the two of you?''

''Nope. We've got four more siblings—two sisters, two brothers.''

No wonder he was so easy with kids. ''Lucky you, growing up in a big family. I only have one sister, and I always wanted a brother, as well.'' Maybe instead of, but she didn't say that.

''I didn't actually grow up with them,'' he said. ''I was adopted at birth, and I grew up as an only child. I found my birth family when I was in my late teens. Well, in fact, they found me. It's a complicated story. I'll tell you about it when we have more time.''

''I'd really like to hear.'' God, that sounded lame, but she didn't know what else to say. He hadn't needed to tell her such intimate stuff, but he had, anyway. It made her feel privileged. ''You're sure honest about it.'' That was one more huge thing in his favor. The guy must have some severe faults, but they weren't evident right off the bat.

''I have to be honest, because I have a terrible memory.''

In unison, they recited, ''And a liar needs a good memory.''

They both laughed, and Hailey said, ''One of my gran's favorite sayings. Who drummed it into you?''

''My mom. My adoptive mom, that is.''

''It must get complicated, having two mothers.''

''Two fathers, as well. Different as it's possible to be. My adoptive dad was a farmer who also worked as a handyman. My genetic father is a lawyer.''

''Two dads,'' she marveled. ''Some guys have all the luck. The only one I had died when I was a kid.''

He didn't respond because they'd reached David's room, and Hailey could see through the window that he was awake. For the first time he was sitting up, watching the door, his little face somber. She had yet to see a smile, but she was going to work extra hard to win one. As always, his battered toy dog was clutched to his chest.

''Hey, Davie boy, just look at you, wide awake and rarin' to go.'' She went over to him and checked his diaper. It was dry. She'd be a lot happier when it was soaked all the time, which would mean his body's fluid level was stabilizing. Next she checked the IV level, and then reached her arms out to him. ''Wanna come walk about with Hailey? I should go and make sure my yoga students aren't busting their necks.''

David gave her a long, searching look and then nodded, just once. She felt thrilled at his acceptance of her.

''Why, that's a yes. Let's do it. C'mon, sweetie,'' she cooed. ''Ooh, you're such a big boy.'' She lifted him into her arms, careful to take the dog, and kissed his downy cheek. Resting him on her hip, she pointed at Roy. ''This guy's your special friend. His name's Roy. Can you say Roy?''

David gave Roy a suspicious look and shook his head.

Roy reached out and touched the toy dog with a forefinger. ''Who's this fellow, David? Does your friend have a name?''

They waited, and when David didn't respond, Hailey said, ''That's Dog, silly. Anybody can see that's Dog, right, Davie?''

To her surprise, he shook his head. ''Bonzo,'' he said clearly. He had a husky little voice, and his articulation was excellent.

''Oh, your dog's name is Bonzo. That's a good name for a dog.'' Hailey was elated. He was beginning to talk.

''It's time you and Bonzo met some of the other inmates, young man. Can you bring that pole, Roy?''

''Sure thing.'' With Roy making engine noises and steering the IV, they sailed out into the hallway and down to the playroom. There were now several girls there, as well as the boys, all playing with a building set.

"Hey, everybody, this is David," Hailey said. "And the big guy's Roy." She lowered herself to the floor with David on her lap.

"Are you a doctor, Roy?" Four-year-old Elizabeth had cystic fibrosis. She was giving him the once-over. "'Cause I didn't see you before."

"Nope, not a doctor," Roy said with a wide smile. "I'm David's social worker." He sank down on the rug beside the rest of them, agile and easy. He was wearing jeans, and Hailey noted that they fit him the way jeans ought to fit.

"So what's a social worker?" Elizabeth was noted for asking questions.

Roy was quiet for a moment as he thought that one over.

"It's a person whose job is to help people who have troubles."

"What kind of troubles does David have?"

"That's sort of private between him and me," Roy explained. "But I work with other people, too, and some of them might have problems with money, or with their family, or with getting a job. Mostly I help little kids who have no families find people who love them and want to take care of them."

"So how does that make you *feel?*" Elizabeth was frowning, peering at Roy like a miniature psychologist, and it was all Hailey could do to keep from laughing. It was the question she asked most often of all her patients, and Elizabeth was a quick study. Hailey had found that too often with kids, adults didn't ask how things made them feel. When she did, she always found the kids heartbreakingly honest and forthright in their answers, and she waited to hear what Roy would say.

He was obviously taken aback at first. He glanced at Hailey and lifted one eyebrow. She gave him an encouraging wink.

"Well, I guess sometimes it makes me sad," he began in a hesitant voice, and Hailey was impressed. Most guys she'd met didn't do feelings at all when asked that question. They answered from their head, instead of their heart.

"Do you cry?" Elizabeth was persistent. "I cry when the nurses hammer on me to loosen my mucus."

"Yeah, sometimes I cry," Roy admitted. He was redder than usual, and he didn't meet Hailey's eyes, but she was bowled over by his honesty. "And there're other times that make me laugh, so I guess it balances out."

"Hailey *always* makes us laugh," Elizabeth stated.

Then Tommy, who'd been listening, said, "Hailey really, *really* makes us laugh. Sometimes she gets in trouble for it, too." He leaned toward Roy and said in a stage whisper, "Some people don't like hearing little kids laugh when they're in here."

"No kidding?" Roy looked surprised. "Why is that, do you think?"

Hailey really liked the fact that Roy didn't talk down to the kids.

"They figure we get too excited and it wears us out," Elizabeth explained. It was the answer Margaret had given Hailey when she reprimanded her for making the kids what she called "hysterical and unmanageable."

"I don't agree," Roy declared. "Laughing is good. I always feel better when I laugh a lot."

There was a chorus of agreement.

"So what's wrong with him?" Elizabeth was standing beside Hailey, and she reached out and took one of David's hands in hers. She looked at Roy. "Why's he in the hospital? Why's he need you to help him?"

This was tricky ground. Hailey glanced at Roy, wondering how he'd handle it. All the kids were listening, waiting for his reply.

"David's mommy is having some problems and she can't take care of him just now. He got sick, and he needs to get strong again, and this is a good place to get better."

It was the truth, without going into details.

The kids all studied David for a few minutes, and then Elizabeth put her arms around him and gave him a gentle hug. David's expressive blue eyes grew wide, but he didn't pull away.

"It's not too bad here, David," Elizabeth told him, putting her small face close to his, almost nose to nose. "It's not as good as home, but the nurses are nice, 'specially Hailey, and most of the doctors are okay. They don't hurt you unless they really, really have to. Sometimes Ian and Tommy are bad. They run around like crazy, and once they upset the cart and scissors and stuff fell down, and Margaret got *really* mad, and we had to stay in our rooms.

It's hard when you're in bed at night, though. It's lonely then.''

Hailey had a lump in her throat, and when she looked at Roy, she could see that he, too, was touched by what Elizabeth had said.

"If you get too lonely, honey," Hailey reminded her, "you can just push the buzzer. Whoever's on will come in and talk to you at night."

"I know." Elizabeth nodded. "But I only want my mommy then."

"Mama?" The word was barely above a whisper. "Mama?" David's chin trembled and his face puckered. He whimpered, and Hailey could feel the tension in his arms and legs, but he didn't cry out loud, and that was far more disturbing to her than if he'd howled and had a temper fit. He pointed a forefinger toward the door and repeated in a sad, questioning tone, "Mama come?"

"Sorry, Davie, Mama's not here today." Hailey could see her own reaction mirrored in Roy's stricken expression. "How about we go and get you a new bottle of juice, young man? Does everybody want juice?"

There was a chorus of assent, and Hailey made a production of leading a conga line to the snack area. It was a cop-out for David, but Hailey didn't know what else to do. She couldn't exactly tell the poor kid that his mother was missing in action and not expected to show up, could she?

"I've gotta go. I have a meeting in a few minutes." Roy reached out and touched David's cheek with his finger.

"Bye, David." His voice was husky. "See you again soon." He lifted a finger to his forehead in a salute to Hailey, and for one long moment their eyes met and a silent acknowledgment of the hurt little kids were forced to absorb passed between them. "See you, too, Ms. Bergstrom. Soon."

Hailey took David back to his crib and he settled down with a bottle of apple juice and some toys she'd brought from the playroom. Soon he was asleep, and she went back to her duties, but anger at Shannon Riggs simmered in her. How did you walk away one afternoon and forget you had a baby?

She found herself wondering if Shannon had OD'd, and then was shocked at her callousness when she found herself thinking maybe that would be the best thing that could happen for David.

HAILEY WAS JUST coming back from her supper break when an aide appeared, looking for her.

"There's someone here to see you, Hailey. She's in the waiting room down the hall."

It was Nicole. She had a huge shopping bag on the chair beside her, and she got to her feet when she saw Hailey.

"Hope I'm not interrupting something important. I only have a couple minutes. I'm due to meet a client, but I wanted to drop this stuff off."

Nicole looked entirely different than she had the previous evening. She was wearing a dark pin-striped business suit and designer glasses, and her long hair was pulled to the back of her head in a no-

nonsense bun. She was still beautiful, but now she looked like a woman no one would dare mess with.

"I thought about what you said, that the kids share stuff, so I got some things that I thought could be just for David and some that everyone can use." She upended the bag. "He probably doesn't much care what he's wearing, but I couldn't resist these." There were four small tracksuits, soft fleecy cotton, in bright shades of red, blue, yellow and turquoise.

"With his eyes and hair, these colors should be great on him," Hailey said.

There was also a huge stack of books that Hailey could tell at a glance were perfect for David's age, and several ingenious learning games designed to attach to the bars of a crib. There was also a small fleecy white teddy bear.

"I wouldn't dream of trying to substitute the one he's got," Nicole explained. "I know how much it means to him. I just thought maybe he could have two?"

Nicole was looking at Hailey with an uncertain expression.

"Of course he can. Maybe now I can even get Bonzo away from him long enough to wash. Thanks so much for all this, Nicole." Hailey was examining the games. They were both unique and educational and more expensive than the hospital budget would ever allow. "Wow, these are great. Because of the IV, he has to spend a fair amount of time in his crib, and these will challenge him."

As Hailey repacked the bag, she gave Nicole an

update on David, telling her that he was drinking more liquids and that he'd asked for his mother.

"Wouldn't you just like to strangle her?" Nicole's blue eyes flashed fire behind her glasses.

"Absolutely. Around here, there'd be a lineup for the privilege."

Ian and Tommy, laughing uproariously and clearly bent on destruction, went tearing past the door.

"Gotta go, Nicole. Those two are my patients and they're hellcats when they get going. No telling what they'll get up to. I gotta catch them before they pull a fire alarm or plug the toilets again."

"I don't suppose you'd want to have lunch one of these days?" Again Nicole's voice was uncertain.

"Love to. Only trouble is, I'm starting the seven-to-seven shift tomorrow morning—I've been filling in for another nurse on this shorter one. So it would have to be a late dinner, instead of lunch." Hailey figured that would be out of the question; any woman who looked like Nicole had dates every night of the week.

But to her surprise, Nicole gave her a wide smile and an enthusiastic nod. "That would be perfect. I don't eat till late, anyway. And I'm free any evening that's convenient for you." She pulled a business card out of one of her pockets. "Call me—you set the time. I can work my schedule around yours."

Hailey shot off down the corridor in pursuit of her rambunctious charges, wondering why Nicole would want to see her away from work. The two of them were obviously nothing alike, and what they might have in common beyond discussing David, she couldn't imagine. But her curiosity was piqued, and she found herself looking forward to getting to know the other woman better.

She spent the late afternoon hurrying through the necessary duties so she'd have time to read that evening to the kids at the end of her shift. It was a difficult time for some of them, that hour or so before bedtime, and she hated the fact that they often got stuck in front of the TV because the nurses were busy. Many parents spent the end of their workday with their sick kids, but there were a number of kids on the ward whose parents lived far away or had other children at home to care for and so couldn't make it to St. Joe's.

They were the ones Hailey spoiled a little with balloons and stories and, if their diets permitted, special snacks and little treats from the kitchen.

She picked up David and took him with her to the playroom, where she sat in a rocking chair and read the kids a couple of chapters from a Harry Potter book. Of course the story was way beyond David's level, and he kept looking up at her, a puzzled expression on his face. Once, he reached up and took hold of a fistful of hair.

She smiled at him, and there was the tiniest movement of his mouth, not quite a smile, but close. The other kids demanded equal time on her lap, so she strapped David in a wheelchair. He didn't object. He watched the others, but most of all, he watched Hailey.

A full hour after her shift had ended, she carried

him back to his crib and settled him for the night.
She bent and kissed his cheek, and a dangerous
thought flickered through her mind.

It was probably impossible, but if Roy couldn't
find any relatives who wanted him, was there any
chance that she could take this little boy home with
her?

ROY WAS FRUSTRATED. Four days had passed since
he'd first visited David in St. Joe's, and so far, all
his attempts to find Shannon Riggs or anyone who
could tell him where she was had come to nothing.
First he'd checked her personnel file on the computer, getting whatever details were available about
previous investigations. Then he'd located Tonya
Cabral, the volunteer street worker who'd taken
Shannon under her wing and helped her get off
drugs. Tonya was somewhere in her sixties, a tiny,
birdlike woman with deep lines in her face and dark,
sad eyes. She'd put a wrinkled hand over her mouth
and started to cry when he told her that Shannon had
disappeared, leaving David alone.

"I feel so responsible," she sobbed. "I usually go
over and visit her Tuesdays and Thursdays, but I
came down with a bad migraine and was knocked
out for a few days."

Shannon had gone through a drug-rehab program
prior to David's birth, and she seemed to have stayed
clean, because there was no record of a complaint
regarding her care of David. He'd called the social
worker who'd been involved at that time, and she
confirmed that Shannon took good care of her baby.

She was attending parenting classes and working at getting her high-school diploma.

The troubling thing was that Shannon had never revealed who the baby's father was or given any information about her own background, other than saying she'd grown up in Port Hardy, a coastal village on Vancouver Island. Her file listed her mother and father as deceased, with no other close relatives and no siblings, but from experience, Roy knew that teenagers often did that on their forms. If they were from troubled homes, they didn't want their parents involved in their lives. The social worker had talked to street kids who knew Shannon, and they'd said she was often seen with a man named Murphy. None of them knew much about him or where he lived.

The file wasn't much help to Roy in finding Shannon. Tracing relatives would be difficult, if not impossible. He called the RCMP in Port Hardy and asked them to locate any families by the name of Riggs, but he strongly suspected that Shannon wasn't using her real name.

He was also doing his best to locate her. He'd given her description to the people he knew who drove around downtown Vancouver in vans, distributing clean needles and condoms. He knew several of the firefighters who worked the downtown east side, and he'd asked them to be on the lookout for her. He'd checked emergency departments at all the Lower Mainland hospitals besides St. Joe's, and of course the Vancouver police had Shannon's description.

He'd interviewed the firemen who'd been first on

the scene in the apartment, he'd talked to the paramedics and the staff in the ER, and of course he was
keeping close contact with David's doctor, Harry
Larue.

Roy had other cases, far too many of them to be
able to devote a full working day to David's situation. As always, he was forced to do a great deal of
work on his own time. And he was starting to really
begrudge the fact that his private life and his pro-
fession were one and the same.

CHAPTER FIVE

SHANNON RIGGS came out of drugged oblivion and her first thoughts were of Davie, but the thought of him made the pain in her chest too sharp. She shoved the images of her son down into a dark box in her mind and tried to slam the lid.

Shaking and sweating, she struggled to figure out where she was. It was stifling hot. Sunlight penetrated through a rip in the dark-green curtains, and she could hear the sound of traffic outside. A picture of sunflowers was screwed to the wall, and a closed door must lead to a bathroom. A motel room, she decided.

She propped herself up on one elbow and studied the face of the husky man sleeping beside her. He wasn't Murphy, and to the best of her knowledge she'd never seen him before. Her stomach lurched. She felt nauseated.

She slid out of bed. Her legs were rubbery, and she had trouble making it to the bathroom without falling. Her head felt as if it was about to explode, and the drug need went crawling through her veins like a hungry snake, making her itchy and edgy and frantic and sick.

For an instant memories surfaced, police cars, an

ambulance in front of her apartment, urgent voices floating to her in the hot afternoon. A stretcher with a small figure on it—they were taking Davie away, and she had to stop them.

She'd tried to get out of Rudy's car, but he'd grabbed her, pulled her back inside, then driven off as Murphy held her. She'd writhed and screamed and fought to get loose, but Murphy was strong.

"You're high, baby, they'll toss you in the slammer. The kid's okay. They're takin' care of him. Here, have some of this—it'll make you feel better."

And from then until now, she couldn't remember anything.

She retched into the toilet, gasping for breath, disgust and fear and shame gnawing at her soul. Where was her son? Terror and emptiness made it hard to breathe.

The door opened, and the man stood there, squinting down at her.

"You okay, doll? That was some party, huh? I got some stuff left—you want some?"

She shook her head. She managed to get to her feet, turn on the hot water in the shower and step inside. She pulled the curtain and turned the tap until the spray was as hot as it would get. It beat down on her face, and gradually the pain in her chest became unbearable. She opened her mouth and tried to howl, but no sound came out.

She'd deserted her baby son, the one thing in her life that was precious and clean and innocent. She'd betrayed him, and in doing that, she'd become the person she'd been running from for so many years.

She'd become her own mother.

She wanted to die, but she'd tried before and it wasn't easy.

ROY LOCKED the office door behind him, aware that he was the last one in the building, apart from the cleaning staff. It was almost nine o'clock, and he hadn't eaten since noon. He was famished, and he hated eating alone. He also hadn't seen Nicole for a while. On impulse he dialed her cell-phone number, and after a few rings she answered.

"I'm just leaving the office. If you're not busy, I wondered if you wanted to grab a burger. Or at least talk to me while I wolf a couple down?"

Belatedly he became aware of background noise, music and the murmur of conversation. "Damn, I'm sorry. I'll bet you're out somewhere posh with the pilot. He'll never believe I'm your brother, so just make like this is a wrong number, and I'll talk to you another time. Bye."

"No, no, don't hang up. Hold on just a minute." Nicole said something indistinguishable to someone, and then she was back.

"Roy? Hailey and I are at Tomato on Cambie. She just got off shift and we're having a late dinner. Want to join us? Hailey says it's fine with her."

It was a no-brainer. Roy didn't even take the time to register surprise that his sister and Hailey were out together. "I'll be there in fifteen. Order me whatever their dinner special is—I'm famished."

He spotted them the moment he walked into the funky café. Even in this colorful atmosphere,

Hailey's wild red hair stood out like a beacon. She and Nicole were sitting in a booth beside the windows, plates of delicious-looking food in front of them. He made his way over and slid in beside Nicole.

"Ah, fairest damsels in the land, thank you for taking pity on a starving man." There was a basket of bread on the table with only one piece left, and it didn't look as if the women were going to eat it. He slathered butter on and bit into it.

Hailey smiled a shy greeting at him. She had a first-rate smile—he'd noticed that before. It started in her eyes and moved slowly to her mouth. And that damned hair looked as if an electrical current ran through it.

The waitress appeared as if by magic and put a steaming bowl of soup in front of him, along with another basket of warm, fresh bread.

"Whatever this is, it's my favorite." He took a spoonful and groaned with pleasure. "Ignore me, please. Just go on talking about whatever it was you were talking about before I barged in. I've always wanted to know what females talk about when there aren't any men around."

"Men, of course." Nicole leaned her elbows on the table. "But we'll change the subject now. No point in revealing all our secrets. What are you doing working so late, Roy?"

"The dreaded paperwork. I was warned that if I didn't do something about the mountain on my desk, they'd hold back my paycheck. I'm so far behind I need a rearview mirror." He emptied the soup bowl in a few huge gulps and buttered another chunk of bread. "What else did you order for me?"

"We just told them to serve you the largest of the entrées. I think it was roasted ox or something, wasn't it, Hailey?" Nicole knew that he stuck to a basically vegetarian diet.

"Stewed buffalo tongue." Obviously Hailey had caught on, as well. She shot him a mischievous look.

"Tonight I'm hungry enough to eat raw venison." Roy grinned at her. He liked Hailey's husky voice, the way it wandered up and down like a musical instrument she couldn't quite control.

"Nicole was about to tell me how she got interested in landscape architecture," Hailey added, taking a forkful of her dinner. It looked like fresh fish in some sort of wonderful sauce.

"Subtitled dirt to dirt in five generations, much to the horror of my upwardly mobile family." Nicole laughed. "Our distant ancestors had a gardening business in Milan, but then the family moved to Vancouver and our great-grandfather—who was a hunk if those black-and-white photos are to be believed—capitalized on his looks and married up. Great-grandma was no beauty, but she had pots of money. Her father was one of the early lumber barons. They had a slew of kids—must have had a great sexual relationship—and everyone got university educations, invested in real estate, went into law, expanded the family fortune. My grandpa and my father and two of my brothers are lawyers. Roy, of course, is a social worker. Two aunts are doctors, and one cousin went into politics. Me, I'm the black sheep, a throwback to earlier times. I went into law to fulfil family tradition, but I was born with the good earth under my fingernails. My first memory is pulling up my grandmother's daffodils to see how big the bulbs were.''

''So when are you going to follow your heart and start your own gardening business?'' Hailey asked.

Nicole sighed. ''Soon, I hope. Someday soon.'' She turned the conversation back to Hailey. ''How old were you when you knew you wanted to be a nurse?''

''Eleven.''

''And? How come so young?'' Nicole wasn't about to let her off the hook with a one-word answer.

Hailey shrugged. ''My dad had a heart attack that year. He was in hospital a week before he died, and the nurses were so good to my sister and me. I developed a huge crush on them. And once I was in training, I knew right away I wanted to work in pediatrics.'' She flashed her wide smile again. ''I never really wanted to grow up, see, and being around kids all the time is a great way to avoid it.''

''None of your own?'' Roy found he was curious about her, about whether she was married or had a live-in lover.

He was about to butter more bread when the waitress set a plate heaped with vegetables and baked salmon in front of him. He eyed it with unabated hunger.

''Not yet.'' Hailey shook her head. ''I'm single. But I really want a family of my own, so I've applied for single-parent adoption. It's just taking longer than I thought to get the paperwork finished.''

''Wow, that's so brave of you.'' Nicole's voice reflected her admiration. ''I've thought lots of times about doing the same thing, but I've never gone further than daydreaming about it. Tell me how the process works. Are there many restrictions?''

Roy ate and listened, amazed. He knew Nicole loved kids, but he'd never heard her admit that she'd even considered single-parent adoption.

''Not anymore,'' Hailey said. ''Oh, you have to prove there'll be male input into the child's life, some sort of father figure. And of course you have to show that you'll be able to love the child unconditionally and that you're able to put a roof over its head. But that's about all. You can either go for a private adoption or through Social Services. There's a significant difference financially, which was the determining factor for me. Social Services is cheaper. It can cost up to a thousand for a child under the age of three, but if you take a kid over that age, it's free. And if you feel you can manage an emotionally, mentally or physically disabled child, there's not as long a waiting period as there is for a newborn. Privately you'll pay upward of ten thousand for a baby.'' She added in an apologetic tone, ''Here I am going on about it when Roy's an expert. He can probably tell you a lot more about it than I can.''

''Not really.'' He shook his head. ''I'm not involved much with the department that handles adoptions. I deal more with kids in trouble.''

"So which route are you taking, Hailey?" Nicole ate the last of her dinner and pushed her plate away.

"Social services. I couldn't begin to afford the private-adoption thing. When I decided that I was going to adopt, I bought a little house over near Main Street. Real-estate agent called it a fixer-upper, but that was stretching the truth." She laughed. "It was more of a tear-downer, but by the time I'd figured that out, I'd already put money and energy into it. It's a real money pit, but I still love it. I've spent so much at Home Depot I'd buy shares if I had any cash left."

"You hire people to do the work for you?" Roy was wolfing down his dinner, enjoying every mouthful, but he was finding the conversation just as satisfying as the food. Hailey impressed him. She'd decided what she wanted out of life and then gone after it, full speed ahead.

"Don't I wish." She looked remorseful. "Nope, I can't afford to hire anyone. I wish I could sometimes. The first thing I'd do is get someone to redo my bathroom." Hailey shook her head, her curly red hair fanning out around her face. The overhead light struck sparks from it. "It's a total disaster area. The floor's rotting out, the bathtub needs resurfacing, the walls are peeling. I admit I don't know where to start on that project, but for everything else, I do the work myself—at least as much as is humanly possible."

"Did you take a course in carpentry?" Nicole was obviously just as interested as he was, Roy noted.

"Nope. I just bungle through. I've figured out how to put up drywall and I'm not bad at painting.

I've gotten pretty good at sanding. I've even done some minor electrical repairs.''

She sounded proud, and Roy thought she ought to be. He didn't know many other people, male or female, who'd take on what she had.

''I'm going to build a deck out back as soon as I get the money saved for the cedar,'' Hailey went on. ''Although the first priority is that darned bathroom.''

''But how do you know what to do?'' Nicole asked.

''Oh, I use instructional books and videos and watch repair shows on TV. And I ask the clerks at Home Depot—they're really knowledgeable. But a lot of it is common sense and trial and error.

Roy was fascinated and more than a little envious. ''I've always fantasized about buying a rundown place and fixing it up.''

Nicole shot him a surprised look. ''Have you, Roy? You never told me that. How come you've never done it?''

''Never had the guts.'' He smiled at Hailey. ''Would you do it again—buy the house, get into all the repair stuff—knowing what you know now?''

Her face was the kind that held no secrets. Her feelings showed in her expression, and she looked amazed that he would even ask. ''Absolutely. It's fun most of the time. I've gotten used to living in chaos and putting up with drains that overflow and toilets that don't flush, but at least it's a challenge you can do something about.''

Roy knew instinctively what she was talking

about. As a nurse, Hailey watched sick kids get sicker, knowing there wasn't much she could do about it. He often had the same feeling in his own work.

"It helps if you have buckets of money and lots of free time," she went on. "Neither of which I have, so everything's taking me a lot longer than it should."

"I'd love to see your house," Nicole said.

Roy was thinking the same thing, but he wasn't brave enough to say it.

"Really?" Hailey looked surprised. "Well, then, why not come over this Sunday. I'm off that day."

Roy accepted the dessert menu the waitress was handing him. "I'd like the berry compote with an extra scoop of ice cream, please. You two want anything?"

They shook their heads and he handed the menu back and turned to Hailey. "Can I come see your house, too?"

"Absolutely. Around ten. I'll make us all some brunch."

"Oh, Hailey, that's not necessary—coffee's just fine," Nicole began, but Roy interrupted her.

"Brunch would be fantastic. We'll *be* there," he said in a fervent tone, and wondered why the women looked at each other, shook their heads and then burst into giggles.

THE FOLLOWING DAY was Brittany's birthday, and Hailey had arranged a surprise for the girl. Brittany's mother and father, Susan and Tom Whitcomb, who lived in a small logging town on Vancouver Island, couldn't make it to Vancouver for her birthday, and Hailey knew Brittany would be missing her family.

Hailey had baked a huge birthday cake, iced it with purple icing and filled loot bags with prizes. She'd even hired a clown to come to the ward and present Brittany with her gifts and entertain the kids for two hours.

She knew she should have mentioned it to Margaret beforehand, but she also knew the older nurse would find some reason to veto the whole idea, so Hailey kept putting it off. She finally broke the news at one-thirty that afternoon, half an hour before the clown was due to arrive.

"I don't think it's wise to disrupt the entire ward and our routine in such a fashion." Margaret's round face got red and her small mouth drew into a familiar knot of displeasure. "And you should have told me long before this, Hailey. You can't just do things your own way all the time, you know. This is a medical center. Our first priority is taking care of our patients, not entertaining them."

"But making the kids laugh releases endorphins, it's a scientific fact that endorphins help us get better faster." It was a defense Hailey had almost worn out from overuse, and Margaret gave her a nasty, knowing look.

"I *am* the nursing supervisor, Hailey. I suggest you try to remember that once in a while, preferably before you make elaborate plans that have nothing whatsoever to do with nursing."

Fortunately a group of doctors came along just at

that moment, and Margaret, ever eager to please doctors, turned her attention to them.

Hailey sighed with relief. She was off the hook and the party was on.

The clown arrived shortly afterward. Hailey gathered all the kids into the large playroom, and Karen, who was also on duty, had helped her set up a table with the cake as a centerpiece. They made sure there was juice for everyone, and Hailey put the gifts she'd bought for Brittany alongside the stack that had arrived from her family.

The kids were beside themselves with excitement, and Hailey was excited, too. She loved birthday parties. And when she saw Brittany's thin face light with pleasure, she knew she'd done the right thing.

Hailey had brought David to the playroom. He was a somber little boy, but he had begun to smile on occasion and talk to her a little. He was still hooked to an IV, so Hailey popped him into an empty crib.

The clown was outrageous, and the kids laughed with delight. At one point, he went over to David's crib, and the other kids gathered around as he pretended to pluck candy out of David's ears and even out of his IV stand.

"Me, too, me, too," shouted four-year-old Joshua whose IV was pumping antibiotics into his system to counteract the infection he'd developed after an operation on his bladder.

The clown obliged, pulling a toy rabbit out of Joshua's IV stand.

The kids applauded, and when David laughed

aloud, tears came to Hailey's eyes. It was the first time she'd heard him laugh so heartily. That single reaction was worth all the work and organizing the party had taken, and Hailey's joy was compounded by the glowing delight on Brittany's face when she opened her gifts and found the entire collection of Stephen King novels, which Hailey had purchased at a secondhand bookstore.

Margaret came by only once to warn the nurses that four-o'clock meds had to be distributed along with dinner trays. "Laugh before dinner, cry before bed," she warned one little kid who was half-hysterical with giggling.

"Sour old bat," Karen whispered as Margaret flounced out.

The clown left, and Hailey and Karen took the kids back to their rooms. Hailey settled David down with a bottle of juice. His blood work showed that he'd soon be off the IV, and then he could join the other kids more often in the playroom.

Margaret tapped on the glass window, her face stern. Hailey knew Margaret's shift was over and wondered what she wanted. She went to the door and knew immediately that something was wrong. The supervisor's face was a triumphant mixture of blame and righteousness.

"Joshua's IV was somehow turned off during your party, and there's every possibility this could result in a life-threatening situation for him."

All of a sudden Hailey couldn't breathe.

CHAPTER SIX

"THAT CHILD missed his antibiotics because of *your* party."

Margaret spat out the words as if they were rotten. "Fortunately I checked and opened the valve again, but I'm sure you're aware of how serious this is, Hailey."

Of course she was. Her worst nightmare was causing harm to any patient. Her heart gave a sickening thud and slammed against her ribs.

"Is…is he okay?"

Margaret responded with her own question. "How could a thing like this have happened? Tell me that."

Miserable, guilty, worried sick, Hailey shook her head, trying to figure it out. "It must have been when the clown pretended to pull the rabbit from Joshua's IV," she finally said, and then she had the sense to glance at her watch. "That was only about a half hour ago, Margaret." A half hour without antibiotics wasn't a life-threatening situation in Joshua's case. For heaven's sake, what was she thinking?

That you've made what might have been a serious mistake.

An awful sense of foreboding washed over Hailey. Margaret had been waiting a long time for her to make such a mistake.

"That's your opinion. Mine happens to be quite different." Margaret's plump face was suffused with triumph. "I've called Joshua's doctor and asked him to come by immediately. I told him exactly what happened. And I feel I have no choice but to go to the association with this."

Hailey stared at her, speechless. Margaret was threatening to report her to the Registered Nurses Association of B.C. over this?

Incredulous, Hailey knew it was a first step in an effort to get her license lifted. She felt sick all over again, but she wasn't about to give Margaret the satisfaction of knowing that.

"Look, I'm terribly sorry for what happened, but I don't agree that the situation warrants an investigation. However, I'm sure you'll do what you feel you should, no matter what I say." Hailey managed an even tone, but her mouth was dry, her throat constricted. "Now, if you'll excuse me, I'm going to check on Joshua myself." She walked away from the older nurse, knees trembling. There was a linen closet off the hall, out of Margaret's sight, and she stepped inside and shut the door.

In spite of her show of bravado, in spite of knowing the situation wasn't as serious as Margaret was making it out to be, a little boy's treatment had been compromised because of her.

It was the worst thing that had ever happened to her. She felt overwhelmed with guilt and remorse.

She was trembling, and for a moment, hysteria almost got the better of her. But then her common sense took hold.

It was highly unlikely that Margaret could get her license lifted because of this one small mistake. The important thing was that Joshua was okay, that he'd suffered no ill effects.

She took another moment to compose herself and then went to Joshua's room. The little boy was on his bed, engrossed in Lego, trying to fit wheels on something he'd built.

"Hey there, Josh, how ya doin'?"

"Okay. I really liked that party, Hailey. Can I have one on my birthday?"

Hailey mustered up a smile and a wink. "We'll have to see. When's your birthday?"

He frowned and gave it some thought. "I think October."

"I'll bet you'll be home long before that, Josh. You're getting better and better every day." She checked him carefully. His temperature and pulse were consistent with what had been marked on the chart that morning, and as far as she could tell, he was feeling fine.

She checked and double-checked his IV, and Karen came in just as she finished.

"It's my coffee break—walk me down to the kitchen," Karen suggested with a wink.

As soon as they were out of earshot of the kids, Karen said in an undertone, "Did Margaret talk to you?"

"Yeah, she sure did. I feel terrible about what happened."

"*Nothing* happened." Karen blew out an exasperated breath and rolled her eyes. "That woman's trying to turn a molehill into a mountain."

"She's threatening to go to the association."

"*No way.*" Karen was horrified. "She has it in for you, you know that, but she's just grasping at straws. She'd never get to first base with a formal complaint." Karen shook her head in disgust. "It's obvious she doesn't enjoy her job, so why the heck does she stay?"

"You got me." It was a question Hailey had asked herself numerous times, with no clear answer.

"Anyway, don't let her get to you. I was there. I saw exactly what happened, and I don't know one person on this floor who'd support her. Hailey, we all know what a great nurse you are." Karen reached out and gave Hailey's arm a little squeeze before she disappeared into the coffee room.

Hailey felt marginally better, but the rest of her shift was still a struggle. Margaret had gone home, and it was a relief not to have her around. Hailey did her best not to let the kids see how down she was, but of course they knew, anyway. There was no fooling kids. The older ones did their best to cheer her up, telling her jokes and funny stories. The tiny ones offered comfort just by snuggling against her as she got them into fresh pajamas and administered their bedtime meds. As usual, she spent an extra half hour with David, reading him a book he especially liked about a farm.

By the time she got home, she was both exhausted and too nerved up to sleep. She'd bought a kit to replace the innards of the contrary toilet. The flushing mechanism had never worked properly. She got it out now and read the instructions, and for an hour, she struggled with it. The instructions were so complicated that her mind couldn't concentrate on anything else.

At last she turned the water back on and flushed the thing four or five times, thrilled when it worked perfectly. It was the only thing in the bathroom that *did* work. She looked around at the peeling wallpaper, the rusted old claw-footed, cast-iron tub, the drooping, water-stained ceiling. It was a disgrace, this bathroom. She'd have to fix it, and sooner rather than later.

She put away her tools and checked her phone messages. There was one from her mother, asking again if she'd called her sister. She'd totally forgotten, and for a moment she felt guilty.

What was it with Jean and Laura? Had they had a spat of some sort? They were so alike Hailey couldn't really see that happening, but she couldn't figure out any other reason for this thing her mother had about phoning Laura.

Hailey erased the message from the machine, but there was no way of getting it off her mind. Her mother was nothing if not persistent, Hailey thought despondently, and Jean would never give up on this until she made the call. It was ten past eleven, far too late tonight, and anyway, she was too upset from work to be objective.

She'd call first thing in the morning, she decided. She also had to buy some groceries. The weekend was coming up, and Nicole and Roy would be here Sunday for brunch.

After a bath, Hailey padded into the bedroom and pulled on her long white nightgown, fantasizing about what it would be like to make love with Roy Zedyck.

The man was so sexy. She shivered, thinking about his hands. He had good hands. Satisfying, that was how it would be. Spectacular. He was hot stuff, but he was also a caring, kind guy. From the little she'd seen of him, she thought he had his priorities in order.

He didn't seem to want fancy cars and designer suits. He wasn't obsessed with hockey or investments or golf, the way a lot of guys were. In his way, Roy was as single-minded and devoted to his job as she was.

The difference was that he was drop-dead handsome and could have any woman he set his sights on, whereas she—

Give it a rest. Hailey sighed and arranged her six down pillows all around her. She snuggled into her cocoon and pulled the duvet up, finishing her train of thought as her weary body relaxed.

Whereas she was…unusual-looking. She'd long ago stopped thinking of herself as ugly. She'd rationalized that she looked like Ingrid, and to call her beloved grandmother ugly was ludicrous. Ingrid's beauty wasn't the ordinary kind, but it was there, shining out like a beacon for anyone who cared enough about true quality to see. Sam saw.

Thinking about beauty brought her sister to mind, and the phone call she'd vowed to make in the morning. It was insane of her mother to think that Laura would tell Hailey anything. With both Laura's pregnancies, it hadn't been her sister who broke the news to Hailey. It had been Jean.

And when her niece and then her nephew were born, again it had been Jean who called Hailey to tell her the good news.

If Laura didn't share major happy things like pregnancy and childbirth with Hailey, she wasn't going to unburden herself about anything that was bothering her, that was certain.

IN THE MORNING, Hailey waited until after nine to make the call. By then, Christopher and Samantha would be off to school, and Frank would have left for his law office.

Hailey dialed and Laura answered, her deep, throaty voice the one thing she and Hailey had in common.

"Hey, sis, haven't heard from you in a while," Hailey began. "How are things going?" Best to keep this light and breezy, she figured.

"Hello, Hailey." Laura sounded weary and pissed off. "I'm okay, I guess. This thing with the cleaning service is getting me down. They were supposed to arrive at eight this morning and they're still not here. And Frank's partners are meeting here tonight, so of course he wants the house looking good." She sounded irritable. "They're just not reliable, these cleaning people, and this is the third service I've had this year."

Hailey rolled her eyes. What the heck was she supposed to say to that? Her cleaning service was lodged in her hall cupboard, mops and brooms and buckets she used herself.

"Ever thought of telling Frank to have the meeting someplace else?" As soon as she'd spoken, she wished she hadn't. Her brother-in-law was a pompous, controlling, patronizing jerk, but that was no reason to be sarcastic with Laura. "I've never seen your place looking anything but spotless," she amended, though she really didn't visit Laura's house very often.

"How are the kids?" she went on. And because she was feeling guilty, she added, "And Frank?" After all, she wasn't the one who'd chosen to live with him. And he did supply the standard of living Laura wanted. If things could make you happy, Laura should be ecstatic.

"They're fine, we're all fine." Laura didn't sound fine.

Hailey shook her head. Enough beating around the bush. She might as well just come out with it. Otherwise she and her sister would spend another twenty minutes talking about nothing, and she had a ton of stuff to do before she left for work.

"Mom's worried about you, Laura. She thinks there's something wrong that you're not talking to her about."

"I wish Mom would tend to her own affairs a

little more and leave mine alone,'' Laura snapped. ''I suppose she told you to call me?''

Was she really hearing this? Jean and Laura were usually in perfect accord.

''Yeah, she did. Twice, maybe three times now. She's worried about you, Laura. You're not sick or anything, are you?'' Sudden terrible images of breast lumps lodged in Hailey's head.

Laura's tone went way beyond annoyed to enraged. ''I'm perfectly healthy, thank you very much. The kids are the same. There's the doorbell—I'm going now. It had better be the cleaning service. I'll give you a call soon, Hailey. Bye.''

Hailey gaped at the phone. Unless Laura was suffering from a really bad case of PMS, Jean was right. Something was going on that she didn't want to talk about, something that made her grumpy as hell.

Well, as Ingrid was fond of saying, you could lead a horse to water, but you couldn't make him drink. Laura would spill the beans in her own good time. Or not. There was nothing more Hailey could do.

But the conversation stuck in her head all morning, and she grudgingly decided to make time to visit her sister over the weekend.

ROY AND NICOLE arrived at ten before ten Sunday morning in an old blue Toyota driven by Roy. Hailey was nervous at first, but her guests were so relaxed and admiring of her house and all she'd done that she started to enjoy herself. Nicole took one look at the backyard and exclaimed, ''Wow, mega potential. It's like an empty pallet. You're so lucky nobody's screwed it up.''

Hailey hadn't thought of it quite that way. ''It looks more like a bomb site.''

Nicole was poking around. ''Would you be insulted if I came up with some suggestions?''

''Are you kidding? I'd be eternally grateful.''

''Maybe we could eat first?'' Roy shot them a pathetic look, and Hailey laughed and led the way inside.

She'd been up since six, sweating over this production. She'd set the table in the dining room, which she hardly ever used, in front of the open windows. The August sun poured through the mullioned panes and the birds sang a cappella from the old cherry tree that shaded the area where she planned to eventually build a deck.

''Where'd you get all this scrumptious old china?'' Nicole touched a rose-patterned plate.

''From my grandma Ingrid. She decided to buy new stuff last year, and she gave me these.'' The dishes were mismatched bits of at least three different dinner sets, but they all had roses on them in one form or another. Hailey had put an old crocheted bedspread on the table and she'd used a small pitcher of lilies of the valley for a centerpiece.

''It looks beautiful.''

Nicole's approval was reassuring. Hailey poured cranberry juice and added ice and some of the white wine Roy had brought. She served the fruit salad and berry muffins, and the softly scrambled eggs and toast, and poured hot, strong coffee into thick mugs.

The last bit of tension fled as her guests devoured everything and asked for seconds.

After brunch Nicole went out to have another look at the garden.

Roy insisted on helping with the dishes, so Hailey washed and he dried. She brought him up-to-date on what was happening with David.

"He's off the IV." She rinsed a dish and handed it to him. "He likes going to the playroom with the other kids, and he's smiling a lot more now—talking, too. But he asks about his mom all the time." She scrubbed a frying pan, wondering what made Roy smell so good. She didn't think it was cologne. Maybe it was just good, clean, healthy male, up close and personal. "A woman came by to visit him, Cabral was her name. She said she was a friend of his mother's. No sign of her yet, I guess?"

Roy shook his head and reached for a dry dish towel, his shoulder brushing hers. The contact sent a small shiver down Hailey's spine.

"Nothing. The neighbor who found David thought she saw her in a car outside the apartment building one day, but she couldn't be sure, and by the time the cops got there she was gone."

"What's going to happen to him when the doctor decides he can be released?" It was a question that had been gnawing at her. "Now that he's off the IV, it won't be long."

"He'll go into foster care. I'm doing my best to find him really good foster parents, but the family I had in mind have an outbreak of chicken pox, and with David just out of hospital, that's not a good idea. There's always more kids than there are places to put them. I thought I had a line on a couple the other day, but another baby ended up with them, and they haven't got room for one more now.''

Hailey wiped at a stain on the counter, wondering if she dared ask the question that had kept her awake most of the previous night. She drew in a breath and let it out.

''Roy, I don't suppose there's any chance I could take him?''

CHAPTER SEVEN

HAILEY TURNED AWAY from him and started scrubbing the stove. She kept her head down, not wanting him to see how much his answer meant to her. "I know I'm not approved as a foster parent," she added in a rush, "but they just called me yesterday and said I'm fully approved to adopt now. Surely that's pretty much the same thing?"

He didn't answer right away, and the knot in her stomach grew tighter.

"You really care for David, don't you, Hailey?" He stopped drying dishes and leaned back against the counter, giving her his full attention. His voice was soft and the look he gave her was filled with understanding.

She nodded, embarrassed to have him see the silly tears that filled her eyes and threatened to roll down her cheeks.

"Yup, big time," she managed after a minute. "Which is why I can't bear to think of him getting shoved someplace where there's already too many kids, where he wouldn't be special, where—where nobody has time to read him the farm book at bedtime."

"You do understand that he's not available for adoption and may never be?"

She nodded again. She'd troubled over that one at length.

"If we locate Shannon, she can petition the court to have him back. She'd have to prove she was responsible, of course. And although it doesn't look likely, if relatives turned up, they'd have first claim on him." Roy reached out and touched her arm. "I guess what I'm trying to say is that fostering isn't a very secure position to be in when you love a child and want to keep him, Hailey."

"I know how insecure it would be." Hailey had thought of that. She'd raised all the arguments against taking him that she could dream up, but they didn't tip the scales enough to dissuade her. "I'd still like to try, Roy. If I don't try, I haven't any chance at all with him."

"That's true." He hung the dish towel on the wooden rack she'd installed beside the stove. "You're up against the system here. Being approved as a foster parent doesn't guarantee you any special child. You pretty much have to take whatever you get."

She hadn't thought about that. She gave him a stricken glance. "You mean I could get approved and still not get David?"

Roy nodded. "But there's also a chance you might. Once you're approved, of course."

"How...how long would that take?"

"We could probably get it through in three or four weeks."

"That long?" Her shoulders slumped. "He'll be discharged for sure before then. Where will he go?"

"Into an emergency receiving home, unless I can find suitable foster parents right away. And if I did, I'd be obligated to place him. Once he was settled, the ministry wouldn't see any reason to move him to your home."

She nodded, trying not to cry. She hadn't understood the complications.

Roy's voice softened. "I personally think you'd be the best thing that could happen to David, and I promise I'll do my best to hurry along your application, but doing the home study isn't my department."

"So it's not too likely I'll get him, that's what you're saying?" Her voice wobbled, and her heart felt as if it was swirling down the drain with the dishwater.

"Don't get your hopes up too high is what I'm saying. I'll see what I can do. I'd need to know, for instance, what your plans are for day care when you're working."

"I've already registered to use the nursery at St. Joe's." It was a relatively new service, and it was expensive, but it was ideal. Parents could see their kids during coffee and lunch breaks, and it was open twenty-four hours a day to accommodate shift workers. David would be just a short elevator ride away.

Hailey thought of Margaret and the complaint she was threatening to register with the association. "As long as I still have a job, that is," she added in a despondent voice. Maybe it wasn't the wisest thing to tell Roy that her job could be in jeopardy, but he needed to know. There mustn't be any secrets; this was too important.

"Problems at work?" He didn't sound disturbed at all, just interested.

Hailey told him in detail what had happened with Margaret Cross. "It was an accident, and certainly not life-threatening, but I feel like a jerk about it all the same. Margaret doesn't much like me. She'd do whatever it took to get me suspended."

Roy was quiet for several moments. He poured himself a cup of coffee from the pot and sprawled in a kitchen chair, one long leg resting on the opposite knee.

"I've noticed in my own work that it's the people who really care who come in for the most flak from supervisors. Would a letter stating what a marvelous and caring nurse you are help your case at all? Because I'd gladly write one and send copies to the entire nursing association." He took a swallow of coffee. "You're one of a kind, Hailey. Anyone with half a brain can see that the kids adore you."

"Thanks." She couldn't look at him. One of a kind, huh? She felt overwhelmed and shy and humble all at the same time. She knew she was a good nurse, but one of a kind? "I don't know if a letter would help or not, but it's great of you to offer." She managed a smile. "All donations gratefully accepted."

"Good. I'll write it. Can't do any harm. And, Hailey?" He stood up, coming close to her. "Keep your chin up, okay?" He used a finger to tilt it so she had to look in his eyes. For one amazing instant, she actually thought he might be going to kiss her, but then the kitchen screen door slammed open, and Nicole came in.

"Hey, you've got such potential in that garden, Hailey. You could have a pond at the south end and a rustic little bridge. And the old cherry tree is ideal for a tree house."

Roy had stepped back, and Hailey tried to think of what to say. She was flustered.

"I've always wanted a tree house," she lied. She'd never even thought of one before, but immediately she had visions of David, old enough to play in it. *Don't get your hopes up,* she reminded herself. "But it'll have to wait. You saw the bathroom." She'd winced when Nicole used it. "It's my big priority at the moment."

Nicole grinned. "See, that's the difference between us. If it was me, I'd do the garden and to hell with the bathroom."

"You'd just get me to do the bathroom for you," Roy said.

"I would, too." Nicole winked at Hailey. "He's really handy to have around. All you have to do is feed him."

"I'll give that some thought." She'd cook her fingers to the bone if there were any possibility.

"Well, when you get around to the garden, give me a call. I'd love to help." Nicole glanced at her watch. "God, it's nearly two. We've been here half the day. We should probably be going. I've got briefs to do for court tomorrow."

As they were leaving, Nicole gave Hailey a long, hard hug. "This was wonderful of you. I'm gonna have you over to my place really soon."

Roy reached out a long-fingered hand, but when Hailey took it, he unexpectedly gathered her into his arms and hugged her, just as Nicole had.

Hailey felt herself stiffen as her body pressed against his. Her heart hammered, and hot and cold chills went up and down her spine.

"Thanks for the great food, Hailey." Roy's voice rumbled into her ear, which was inches from his mouth. He held her a nanosecond longer than a thank-you hug required and then let go. "I'll be dropping by St. Joe's tomorrow. Are you working?"

"It's my days off. I'm on again on Wednesday." Maybe she could volunteer to work for somebody, though, if he was going to be there. Anybody?

"Maybe you could give me your phone number. I'll call and let you know what I can do about our discussion."

He was being discreet, even in front of his sister. Hailey scribbled her house and cell numbers down on the back of an empty envelope and handed it to him. Roy stuck it into his pocket as he and Nicole went out to the car.

Hailey watched them drive away, wishing they'd stayed the rest of the day. Nicole put out a hand and waved, and she waved back.

Get a grip, she warned herself. *Surely you're not stupid enough to spoil a budding friendship by developing some kind of adolescent crush on Roy, are you?*

Of course she wasn't. It was normal to feel lust for a healthy heterosexual male, she assured herself. She didn't have a thing for Roy Zedyck, not the slightest.

And that was such a lie it was a wonder her nose wasn't a foot long.

She walked through the house, restless, nervous…sexually aroused?

She had all of Sunday afternoon free. She could rip out the bathroom or sand the old wooden doors she was stripping of twenty coats of paint, or even go lie in the sun. Well, out of the sun. Freckles were already covering most of her face.

She didn't feel like doing any of those things, though. The day was a waste as far as work went, or play, either. She grabbed her handbag and keys and headed for the truck.

Might as well ruin what was left of a good day by going to see Laura.

ROY DROPPED Nicole off and went home, comparing his barren apartment with Hailey's house. Sure, he'd built bookcases and refinished an old round oak table, but that was as far as his decorating skills extended.

His place looked dusty and bare, as if nobody lived here most of the time. Well, he reminded himself, nobody did; he spent far more time at work than he did here.

Hailey worked long hours, too, but she had a knack for making a place feel welcoming and homey, and it sure wasn't done with expensive furniture. Her house was filled with plants and cushions and comfortably worn stuff she'd salvaged from secondhand stores, instead of expensive antique shops. It made a guy want to take his shoes off and put his feet up and relax. *With his arms around the hostess?*

Nicole had noticed he was attracted to Hailey— women picked up stuff like that right out of the air. How did they do it, anyway? ''She's a rare lady, huh?'' Nicole had said on the way home.

He'd agreed, trying not to sound too enthusiastic. He was also trying not to dwell on the sudden, urgent bolt of desire that had shot through him when he drew Hailey into his arms for that hug. It had taken him totally by surprise. Well, that wasn't exactly true. There'd been that overwhelming urge to kiss her a short while before.

''You should maybe think about asking her out.'' Nicole was watching his reaction; he could feel her eyes on him as he drove through heavy traffic.

''So now you've decided to be a matchmaker?'' He grinned at his sister and hoped he was deflecting her. He needed time to think this Hailey thing over before Nicole started probing.

''Maybe you need one. Maybe you need a little shove toward a woman who's got all the qualities you've listed as essential whenever we've talked about it.''

''And what qualities are those?''

Nicole ticked them off on her fingers. ''You said you want someone who's not materialistic, someone with the same value system you have, an earthy woman—read *sexy* there—who's more interested in social issues than in her wardrobe, and who's passionate about something besides a new car and her fingernails. And you did say once, remember, that you'd like a woman who wants a family more than a designer home. Well, toots, guess what? Hailey qualifies on all counts.''

"How do you remember all that stuff? And wasn't that your list, as well as mine?''

His sister wrinkled her nose and sighed. "Yeah, pretty much. Although I think I added that it would be nice if he read a book now and then, instead of just watching hockey and waiting for the swimsuit edition of *Sports Illustrated* to come out.''

"I dunno, Nick, that's really stretching the envelope, that thing about the swimsuit edition. I've got the date when it'll be on the stands marked on my calendar in red ink, and so does every guy I know. You don't think you're being totally unrealistic here?''

They'd laughed, and then he'd dropped her off at her condo, and now he was sitting at his desk, staring at the pile of files he'd brought home to work on. But it was hard to concentrate on anything but Hailey.

How, exactly, did he feel about her?

He liked her, he knew that for sure. He respected her. He liked the way she went about her life, with single-minded determination and a whole lot of guts. He admired the way she was with her young patients. He was amazed at what she'd done with that dilapidated house. And he couldn't stop looking at her legs today in those denim shorts she'd worn.

It was probably her legs that had caused the hard-on that forced him to sit down in her kitchen. The intensity of it had taken him by surprise, because he hadn't been thinking of her in sexual terms right at that moment. He'd thought he'd just been enjoying her as a unique and interesting person.

That's a crock, Zedyck. You've had a buzz on over her for a while now. You know damn well you'd like to take her to bed.

And what about this fostering thing? *Could be a big conflict of interest there, son. Remember the rule about never sleeping with a client?*

She wasn't a client, he reminded himself. David Riggs was his client. And there was no way he would ever recommend Hailey as a foster parent if he had the slightest doubt that she was the best person for the job. One thing for sure, he'd write the letter he'd promised her and make certain it got to the right people.

She loved that kid, no question about it. And God knew David needed all the love he could find—every kid did. It was a perfect match, an ideal placement. So why did he have the gut feeling that this whole thing was peppered with land mines?

His thoughts turned again to her hopes of fostering David. He knew that even if he pulled all the strings to make it happen for her, it was still unlikely. He also knew that the chances were overwhelming that she'd get her heart broken over the kid. Hadn't he seen it happen time and again, kids

yanked from one place to the next, regardless of
where they wanted to stay? As usual, Scotty Sieberg's round little face was there in his head, and
the familiar pain and guilt and sorrow filled his soul.
Maybe things would change now, but change never
came soon enough. He heaved a sigh and opened a
folder, trying to figure out all over again how he
could best balance out his conscience, his heart and
the ministry's rules to benefit yet another family in
desperate trouble.

"I WISH YOU'D CALLED first, Hailey." Laura wasn't
smiling. She was standing in the doorway of her
house, long, polished, chestnut hair pulled into a
stylish knot on top of her elegant head, wearing a
silver tracksuit that probably cost more than Hailey's
entire summer wardrobe.

"I'm really sorry, but I'm off to the gym," she
went on. "I can't cancel because this is the only time
my trainer could spare."

On Sunday afternoon? That didn't sound right.

"Well, would Sam and Chris like to come out
with me for a couple hours, then? We could go to a
movie. That new one's on, about the ice age."

"Sorry, they're not here. They've gone to visit
friends."

Talk about a cool reception. If the temperature
wasn't in the low eighties, Hailey would have shivered. "I see." At this rate, her niece and nephew
would be voting before she got to spend any time
with them. "Okay, I guess there's no point hanging

around waiting till you're done?'' Nothing like one last try at being a hero for her mother's sake.

Laura shrugged. ''I guess you can if you like.'' She sounded downright grudging. ''But I'll be about an hour and a half by the time I've showered, and then I have to pick up the kids and take them to the mall. They both need new runners and I'm looking for a decent fall jacket. I can't believe the poor quality that's out there.''

''I'll pass.'' The last thing Hailey wanted was to end up shopping with her sister, and she suspected Laura knew it. It meant trekking from one high-end store to the next, waiting while her sister tried on piles of clothing, being called on to give an opinion and make choices between one item and another, when everything Laura put on her long, slender body could only look spectacular.

''Maybe you could take the kids to a movie next Friday?'' Laura frowned. ''I'm not sure, but I don't *think* they have anything going that night.''

''Can't. I'm working nights next week.'' Hailey considered suggesting another day and decided against it. It would probably be easier to make an appointment with the mayor. ''Well, I'll be on my way. Enjoy your workout.''

The double garage doors were open, and as she got in her truck and drove away, Hailey noticed that Frank's black BMW wasn't there. It was Sunday. Wouldn't you think they'd be spending at least part of it as a family? Did they ever eat a family dinner together? Hailey had never been invited if they did. But then, what the heck did she know about how real families spent their time? The only thing she had to go on was her own life, and Jean and Laura had been on diets most of the time, so eating had been really low on their priority list.

Thinking about families made her feel lonely. Ingrid and Sam had gone to Vancouver Island for the weekend, so visiting them was out.

She must be really desperate, Hailey decided, to even think about dropping in on her mother.

CHAPTER EIGHT

JEAN HAD SOLD the house the girls had grown up in and moved into an apartment in Kerrisdale, an up-scale neighborhood on the west side of Vancouver. Hailey parked the truck behind her mother's building and buzzed the intercom.

Jean's voice over the speaker was tinny but welcoming. "Hailey, what a surprise. Come right up."

By the time the elevator stopped on the third floor, Hailey was already having second thoughts. Jean was going to grill her about Laura.

Coincidentally her mother was wearing a tracksuit similar to the one Laura had had on. They'd probably shopped for them together, Hailey realized. Jean's was navy blue, and Hailey thought for the billionth time how similar in appearance her mother and sister were. Apart from the obvious age difference, they could have been clones—tall, slender, high cheekbones, good boobs, that gleaming chestnut hair.

Jean had worked for years as a doctor's receptionist, and she took wonderful care of herself, exercising and having regular facials and manicures. Over the years she'd had a number of what she discreetly called "gentleman friends," and Hailey often wondered why her mother had never remarried. She'd been a widow for seventeen years and must have had plenty of offers.

Hailey took her sandals off at the door—her mother had white carpets—and Jean led the way into the kitchen.

"I was just going to make myself an early supper. Would you stay and have some with me?"

"Sure, thanks. Can I help?"

"You can wash and chop the stuff for salad," Jean said, getting the ingredients out of the fridge and handing them to Hailey. "I've got soup from the deli, and I was going to make a grilled cheese sandwich to go with it."

"Sounds good to me." It did, too.

There was a companionable feeling to helping Jean prepare the simple meal. To keep her mother's mind off Laura, Hailey asked about the elderly neighbor across the hall who kept stealing the newspapers.

They were actually sitting at the round glass-topped dining table eating salad before Jean got around to the subject.

"What is it with her, Hailey? I haven't seen her for over a week, and she doesn't confide in me the way she always has." Jean frowned and gnawed her lip. "If she weren't so young, I'd swear she was starting menopause."

Hailey had to laugh. "She's thirty-two, Mom. I dropped over there before I came here, but she was on her way to the gym. The kids were gone and Frank wasn't home."

"Oh, he's never home," Jean sniffed. "That's probably half the problem."

Hailey's jaw dropped. She'd never heard her mother say a negative thing about her revered son-in-law. *What's the world coming to?*

"Although maybe if Laura stayed home more," Jean added. "An empty house isn't very inviting to come home to."

Things are back to normal. What a relief.

"And if she's going to be this way about whatever's bothering her, then she'll just have to deal with it on her own," Jean declared, but Hailey could see she was really hurt, and she couldn't help feeling sorry for her mother. After all, Jean was missing her best friend.

"How's that adoption thing coming, Hailey?"

What was going on here? Jean was actually asking her something about her life, for heaven's sake.

"I got final approval just last week." Hailey debated mentioning David. She was pretty certain Jean would be against fostering; she hadn't been enthusiastic about adoption. Well, hell, might as well get it over with.

"But there's a little boy on the ward that I want to have as a foster child, Mom."

"A foster child? But I thought you wanted to adopt. I mean, couldn't they take him away from you if you were just his foster parent?"

No doubt about it, Jean had an instinct for the jugular.

"That could happen, but I'm willing to take the risk. He's the sweetest, best little boy, and I've fallen in love with him,'' she heard herself saying. What was wrong with her, telling all this to her mother? Jean was certain to burst her balloon.

But to her surprise, her mother didn't. She voiced Hailey's own fears, instead.

"I'd hate to see you take him and then have to give him up. I don't want you to get your heart broken.''

"Me, neither. But he doesn't have anybody who cares about him, and I can't stand that.''

Jean smiled. "You always were softhearted. I remember you bringing those kids home and feeding them.''

"The Polaski kids. I wonder what became of them?''

"They grew up and got into trouble. I always said they would. Tell me about this boy you're set on having.''

Hailey described David, adding, "There's been no sign of his mother or any other relative, even though the authorities are doing their best to locate them. I personally think the chances are pretty good that his mother is dead, which means that sooner or later he'll be available for adoption. But whatever the situation, I'm willing to take the chance. As long as the ministry approves it, of course.''

Jean looked skeptical. "That's a pretty big *if,* I imagine. Aren't there rules about foster kids having two parents? There certainly used to be.''

"I don't think they're as stringent as before.'' Hailey thought of Roy. At least she had someone on her side. She wasn't going to tell her mom about him, though.

"I'd think this over carefully, Hailey. You have to consider that at some point you'll marry and have babies of your own. I really don't think adopting can be the same as having your own. Why not just be patient until Mr. Right comes along?"

Well, at least they were getting back to normal here, Hailey thought with a sigh. Jean had been voicing that same opinion ever since Hailey first brought up the subject of adoption.

"There is no Mr. Right, Mom. I don't believe in that stuff, you know that. I'll just end up being forty or fifty without any kids that way."

"Well, I think you're being too hasty. And you know, Hailey, you just don't work at making yourself attractive. I've been telling you for years that you need to do something with all that hair. A good hairdresser could do wonders. And as slim as you are, you could wear clothes that accentuated your waistline, instead of—" she gave Hailey's loose, worn shorts and T-shirt a meaningful glance "—instead of sticking with this grunge look. It doesn't suit you."

Well, it had been nice while it lasted, but now they were definitely back on familiar ground.

The meal was over, so Hailey picked up the plates and took them to the dishwasher as Jean elaborated on a little boutique on West Boulevard that had some cute things Hailey really should see.

"Mom, I don't have money for clothes, and besides, I don't need any. I wear uniforms at work, and the rest of the time I'm working on my house. There's no point putting anything decent on to do that.''

''You should have something nice just in case.'' Jean wasn't about to give up.

When her mother got like this, there was no point arguing with her. Hailey thanked her for the meal, kissed her cheek and headed out the door.

She started for home, but halfway there she changed direction and drove to St. Joe's, instead. Supper would be over, and the nurses would be giving the babies their baths and getting them ready for bed.

Nobody would mind if she offered to do David. Her arms suddenly ached to hold him, and she parked and raced up the stairs, instead of waiting for the elevator.

He was in the playroom with a couple of the older children and a volunteer, squatting on his haunches in front of a plastic train set, his beloved Bonzo on the floor beside him. He was dressed in one of the red tracksuits Nicole had bought him, and his shiny black hair, longer now, curled angelically around his face. He looked up and his face broke into a huge, excited smile when he spotted Hailey.

''Hiya, Lee.'' He grabbed his dog and came trotting over to her. She reached down and picked him up, her heart swelling with love.

''So, big fellow, how you doin'?'' She pressed a kiss to his satiny cheek. ''You want to come for a walk with Hailey?''

''Walk.'' He nodded his head with enthusiasm. ''Walk with Lee.''

He was talking more and more. She set him down and took his hand, and slowly they walked up and down the corridors. Hailey greeted the other nurses, and they all remarked on how quickly David was improving.

She spent the next hour giving him a bath, splashing water with him, tickling his tummy and making him laugh. His sturdy little body was slowly beginning to fill out, losing the emaciated look he'd had when he was first admitted. Each smile, each giggle were precious gifts, and she savored them.

When he was in fresh blue pajamas, she carried him to the bookrack and let him pick one out for her to read. The one he chose was a Dr. Seuss book called, coincidentally enough, *Are You My Mother?*

Hailey had read it to children many times before, and she knew it by memory. But tonight, sitting in a rocking chair with the warm, fragrant child cuddled against her, the words took on new meaning. As the little bird in the story asked one animal and then the next if she was his mother, Hailey felt tears flowing down her cheeks.

She wanted so much to be David's mother. In her heart of hearts, she'd already taken on the role. Surely bureaucracy wouldn't prevent it?

''Mama?'' David pointed a tiny finger at the picture of the baby bird when he finally succeeded in his quest. ''You my mama?''

There was a plaintive note in his sleepy voice, and Hailey quickly put the book down and picked up another one, reading and singing nursery rhymes to him until at last he fell asleep, his downy head pillowed under her chin.

She sat cuddling him, wondering how long little kids remembered things. Would he always have some memory of the careless girl who'd been his birth mother, the girl who'd walked out of the apartment, leaving the door unlocked, and somehow forgotten or—*be fair here,* Hailey cautioned herself— was somehow prevented from returning to her baby son?

Kids forget fast, she reassured herself, carrying her sleeping bundle to the crib and gently putting him in it.

She couldn't remember things from when *she* was two, she recalled as she looked down at him and pressed one last kiss to the top of his head.

David would remember only the love she'd lavish on him. She'd make certain he had the happiest childhood she could possibly provide.

Please God, she whispered as she reluctantly made her way to the elevator. *Please, God, give me a chance to love this child the way he ought to be loved. I'll do such a good job. I promise I will.*

THE WEATHER the following morning was so lovely Hailey decided to work outside, instead of in. With a great deal of difficulty, she carried one of the oak doors she was stripping out to the backyard, laid it across two blocks of wood and set to it with sandpaper.

It was hard physical work, and it felt good. She

was wearing cutoff jeans and a sleeveless T-shirt, and soon she could feel the sweat running down her back. Her hair kept falling into her eyes, so she found two clips and shoved it back.

"Hi, Hailey. Nice day again, huh?"

Roy's voice made her jump. He'd come around the side of the house and was standing a few feet away by the time she noticed him. He was wearing tan slacks and a dark-brown short-sleeved shirt, and she couldn't help but be aware of how attractive he was—and what she must look like, covered in sweat and sawdust.

"Roy, hello. What are you doing here?" As soon as she'd blurted out the question, she realized how stupid it sounded, and her face burned. But that wouldn't matter, anyway, because the part that wasn't covered with freckles was undoubtedly beet-red from the sun.

"Sorry to just drop in on you. I did try to phone a few minutes ago, but there was no answer. Figured you were probably out here. I brought some forms for you to fill out. I want to get this application for fostering approved as quickly as possible. David's doctor told me this morning that he'll probably be released sometime next week."

Hailey's heart skipped a beat, and her mind went tumbling through a list of things she had to do before she brought David home—*if* she brought him home.

She set the sandpaper down and realized she was trembling. It was the thought of David, of course, but mixed in with it was an awareness of Roy, the breadth of his shoulders, the way his hair shone in the sunlight.

"Thanks." She rubbed her dusty hand on the seat of her shorts and reached for the brown envelope he was extending. "Come on inside. I'll get us a glass of lemonade." She had some she'd made from scratch cooling in the fridge, thank goodness.

"I can't stay long, I've got an appointment in a little while. But lemonade sounds great."

She led the way up the back steps and into her cool kitchen, and she wasn't sure if her skin was prickling from the sun or from knowing he was behind her. He sat down at the small kitchen table, as much at ease as if he'd spent far more time here than just one Sunday morning. She washed her hands and splashed cool water on her face, rubbing it dry with a clean kitchen towel.

"How did you manage to get that door outside by yourself? Those old oak doors weigh a ton."

"Us skinny gals are stronger than we look." She lifted her arm and made a muscle.

"I'm impressed. I won't challenge you to an arm-wrestling contest, that's for sure." His eyes crinkled at the corners when he laughed. They also went up and down her in an unconscious and very masculine survey, and she must have been hallucinating, because she thought she saw admiration in his expression.

She poured the lemonade, added ice and set his glass in front of him, then sat down and sipped her own. Was he experiencing the same heightened awareness of her that she was of him?

He opened the envelope and together they went over the questions. They were similar to the ones she'd already answered for the adoption process.

"I've never asked whether there's anyone special, anyone you're seriously dating." He was staring down at the forms, but she didn't think that question was on them. In fact, she knew it wasn't. She'd read them over.

"Not seriously or otherwise." She might as well be bone honest here. "I'm not dating anyone at all." Pride made her add, "At the moment."

She decided the silence between them was the kind books described as pregnant. Her heart was hammering against her ribs as if it planned to break them.

"Why?" he asked.

The simple query threw her. She decided to turn the tables on him.

"Why should I? Are *you* dating anyone?"

"Nope." He looked at her and gave a rueful grin. "I'm being a blundering idiot, though." He stopped smiling and said, "All I meant was, you don't prefer women, or anything like that?"

She laughed. She couldn't help it. He was so earnest, and his ears had turned red, probably from embarrassment.

"No. I'm definitely heterosexual." Not that sex had been a big issue in her life. The absence of it sure had—she had a good, healthy libido. She wasn't going to enlighten him about that, though. And she didn't dare have any expectations about where this conversation was going, because she had no idea how she'd handle it if—

"Then would you consider going out with me? Maybe to a movie or dinner or something?"

Glory be. He was asking her for a date.

CHAPTER NINE

HAILEY LOOKED at this handsome, smart, sexy, oh-so-desirable man, and something inside of her crumbled. She already had feelings for him, and she couldn't let them go any further. He'd break her heart simply by being what he was, making her aware of all her shortcomings, and she'd only just become comfortable with them herself.

But, oh, Lordie, it was tough. It took every ounce of her courage to look him in the eye and shake her head.

"Thanks, Roy, but I don't think so. I just don't have time," she lied. "I've got all I can do getting this house in some sort of order. And now that there's a chance I might get David, I've got a million other things to do, as well."

"I see. Sure. I understand."

It was gratifying that he seemed disappointed. They finished the paperwork and the lemonade and he left.

Hailey went upstairs and into her bedroom. She stood in front of the mirror, the only full-length mirror in the house.

The woman she saw was the same one she'd lived with all the days of her life. Tall, more scrawny than slender, with limbs that looked too long for her body. Her face was decidedly square, her nose generous, to say the least. Right now it was sunburned so that it shone as red as a stoplight. Her flaming hair stuck out every which way from the clips, and not in the artfully casual way Laura's did, with charming little curls here and there. And the sun had popped her freckles, billions of them.

She had nice eyes, though. And thanks to Jean and years of braces, her teeth were perfect.

But she was no beauty. So why would she want to be with a handsome hunk of a man who'd make her feel self-conscious about her looks? Not that he'd intend to, God no. Roy probably wouldn't even know how she felt. But she would. She wiped at the stupid tears that insisted on trickling out of her eyes and tried to tell herself she'd made exactly the right decision, but it wasn't easy.

Thank God Ingrid would be back tomorrow.

She needed a good healthy dose of Gran.

"HAILEY TURNED YOU down?" Nicole sounded incredulous. "Did she say why? Is she seeing anyone else?"

"She said not." Roy tried not to sound as let down as he felt. "She went on about having too much to do. I guess she *is* pretty busy." He didn't mention David; that was personal and confidential.

"That's weird," Nicole mused. "She's not gay. I'm sure I'd know if she was."

"She's not. I asked her."

"Nothing like being forthright. But something's

not kosher here, because I know she's attracted to you.''

''You do? How d'you know that?''

Nicole rolled her eyes. ''Women just know things like that.''

''So what do you figure I should do, matchmaker?'' He tried to keep his tone light, but it was difficult. Until Hailey turned him down, he hadn't realized quite how much he was counting on dating her.

''Be patient. If she won't go out with you, concentrate on being her friend. Friendship's good. You're just gonna have to work at this, Roy, and maybe that's a good thing. It's been too easy for you with women—you need a challenge.''

''Yeah, well, maybe I'll pass on the whole thing. My job's challenging enough for any five people. I don't need to go looking for more reasons to keep me awake at night.'' But even as he said it, he knew he wasn't about to give up on Hailey. ''How's it going with the airline pilot?''

''It crashed, big time. He confided that he was married and his wife didn't understand him. That has to be a common virus, don't you think?''

''I wouldn't know. No guy has said that to me lately.''

''You know, talking to you just isn't emotionally productive at times.''

''Sorry. I ought to have said, how did that make you feel?'' He thought of the little girl in St. Joe's who had asked him that.

''Lousy. I've decided to give men a rest for a

while. I'm not gonna date anybody until I figure out what it is in me that attracts alcoholics, deadbeat dads and misunderstood husbands. I'm gonna take a yoga class. That's supposed to make both your mind and your body flexible.''

"Don't women wear those tight things for yoga? You'll drive all the guys in the class mad with lust.''

"That's their problem. I plan to just concentrate on getting limber.''

Roy's cell phone beeped. It was Marty with yet another emergency that had to be dealt with immediately. One of their most reliable foster mothers, Maggie Kent, had just been diagnosed with chronic heart disease. Her husband, Arnie, wasn't able to cope, and other placements would have to be found for the four children in their care.

Roy's spirits sank. It wasn't going to be easy to relocate the kids. Two of them were brothers, both ADD, which made them harder than usual to place. He'd have to start making phone calls. He'd planned to visit David at St. Joe's, but that was going to have to be put off until tomorrow.

What had ever made him think he might have time for a relationship? It was probably a good thing Hailey had turned him down.

He couldn't quite make himself believe it, though.

"WHY DID YOU TURN him down?'' Ingrid shook her head and wrapped an arm around Hailey's shoulders, squeezing her tight. "You should have gone out with him. He sounds like a fine young man.''

"He *is* a fine man. Sexy, good-looking, fun. And

that's exactly why I'd end up getting my heart broken, Gran.'' It was so easy to be honest with Ingrid. It was so good to have one person she *could* be totally honest with.

"So you're attracted to him."

"Yup. Big time. I wish it wasn't so, but it is." Hailey sighed. "But he's too..." An image of Roy filled her heart and mind, and she couldn't even verbalize what she meant. "He's just too *everything* for me, Gran."

"Drop-dead handsome, right?"

"Yup."

Ingrid understood. "I thought at first with Sam that he was bound to be arrogant and stuck on himself because he looked the way he does. Plus, he was younger than me by a long shot, and those kids of his hated the ground I walked on. I was everything his last wife wasn't, which of course was why he was attracted to me in the first place, although I didn't know it then. But he wore me down. If this Roy is half the man you think he is, he won't take no for an answer. Just don't be so damned stubborn you ruin everything for yourself, honey. He'll ask you out again, and it won't kill you to go."

Hailey tried to figure out how she might feel about a second invitation. Hope and dread were inextricably combined. She glanced at her watch. She'd gotten ready for work early just so she could spend an hour with Ingrid before her shift started.

"Now just sit there and I'll put the music on and show you what I've learned in belly-dancing class. That'll take your mind off men." Ingrid hurried into the bedroom and came out wearing a long red chiffon skirt and a tie top that revealed several rolls of flesh around her bare middle. She fastened round metal clickers to each forefinger and thumb, put on a CD and struck a pose before she began to gyrate and sway to the music.

Hailey was able to smother her giggles, but only for a short time. Soon she was helpless with laughter as Ingrid swirled veils and swiveled her hips and clapped the zills, all totally out of tune with the music. What she lost in technique she made up for in enthusiasm, even attempting to get down on the floor and bend her body backward from the hips while swaying in a snakelike fashion.

When the music ended, Hailey couldn't stop giggling. She collapsed sideways on the sofa.

"So what do you think?" Ingrid was puffing, and although she hadn't succumbed to laughter herself, it was there, dancing in her eyes.

"It's...it's truly..." Hailey searched for a suitable word. "Gran, it's stupendous," she declared. "Have you danced like that for Sam?"

"Absolutely. It really turns him on." Ingrid gave Hailey a wicked wink. "He gets horny as hell watching me. It's worth every penny I spent on it."

Ingrid had always been frank about enjoying her sex life with Sam. Hailey couldn't help but feel a little envious.

"I'm going to have that dressmaker down the street make me some really sexy costumes."

"Gran, you're one of a kind," Hailey said. "Sam's so lucky to have you."

Ingrid beamed and nodded. "Damned straight he is. He knows it, too." She flung herself down on the sofa beside Hailey. "The best thing about getting older is you recognize your own worth, kid. Look, I'd like to meet this little boy you're so fond of. How about I come to the ward one evening this week and you can introduce me?"

"That would be super. Come tomorrow if you can. I'd love to have you meet him."

"It's a date. And when do you get days off again?"

"This Sunday, Monday and Tuesday. Then I'm working days again."

"Come for lunch Sunday. I'll make something Greek."

ALL THE WAY to St. Joe's, Hailey smiled at the memory of her grandmother belly dancing. Ingrid was so devoid of self-consciousness, so certain of her own worth. She'd told Hailey it had come with age, that as a girl she'd been insecure and awkward. Gran had described it as "not fitting in her skin," which expressed it perfectly, Hailey thought. Society put so much emphasis on physical appearance, and women grew up believing the hype. It was hard not to, with television and movies and their images of impossibly beautiful people. And in her case, having a mother and sister who were living examples of physical perfection.

That brought Laura to mind. Hailey hadn't heard from her sister since the aborted Sunday visit. Not that Laura was in the habit of calling daily or even weekly, but still...if Jean figured there was something wrong with Laura, then there probably was. And whether they were close or not, even Hailey was beginning to worry.

She sighed and made a mental note to call her sister one more time.

She was early for her shift, deliberately so, because she'd fallen in the habit of bathing David and rocking and reading to him, and if she got there well before seven, it didn't take any time away from the other kids.

God, she loved that little boy, and it was becoming more and more evident that David loved her back. He'd now come running to her the moment she appeared on the ward, chattering away, telling her garbled stories of things that had caught his attention, showing her pictures in books and toys that he'd taken a fancy to, dragging her by the hand to the rocking chair.

Hailey had always enjoyed coming to work, but these night shifts were especially pleasant, because by the time she arrived, Margaret had gone home. So far, nothing more had been said about the complaint the head nurse had threatened to make. Hailey hurried up to the ward, eager to see David catapult down the hallway toward her, calling, "Lee, hiya, Lee."

INGRID ARRIVED at St. Joe's the following evening, just as Hailey was preparing the meds. David had taken to following her from one room to the next, and he was quickly learning the names of the other patients.

"I'll bet this is the guy I've been hearing so much about," Ingrid said, smiling at him. "Are you David, young man?"

David went wide-eyed and shy. He ducked behind Hailey and held on to the back of her uniform trousers, peeking out at Ingrid.

"This is my grandma, David." Hailey picked him up, holding him on her hip.

"Mama?" He pointed a stubby finger at Ingrid.

"Nope, grandma. Can you say grandma?"

"Nope." It was becoming his favorite word, and he shook his head as both women laughed.

"You two go into the playroom and get acquainted—I'll be there as soon as I finish this," Hailey suggested. "Some of the kids are there already, waiting for a story."

"Well, I think I could manage that," Ingrid said. "You wanna come with me, David?"

He clung to Hailey and shook his head, but when she took him into the playroom, he was happy to sit on the sofa with Brittany, who always made a big fuss over him. She had a small stepbrother of her own at home, and Hailey knew that David helped fill the lonely gap that being away from her family left in the little girl's heart.

All the long-term kids knew Ingrid; she was a frequent visitor to the ward. Hailey introduced her to the others, and as she slipped out to finish her work, she heard Ingrid's husky voice beginning, "Once upon a time in a land far away called Sunny-

ville, a little girl lived with her mommy and daddy…"

For the next half hour Hailey settled a new patient
who'd just come up from intensive care, a seven-
year-old girl, Lauren Meadows, who'd been hit by
a car while riding her bike. She'd had surgery for a
fractured pelvis and dislocated shoulder, and she was
groggy and unhappy. Her mother and father were
with her, and Hailey soothed the child, gave her pain
medication and did her best to reassure Mr. and Mrs.
Meadows that Lauren would get the best care the
staff could provide. They made a point of telling her
that they were both lawyers, and Hailey was well
aware of the message they intended to convey. Parents were always frightened when a child they loved
was hurt or ill, and she'd grown accustomed to calm-
ing their fears and not taking offense when they re-
sorted to threats.

She was just coming out of Lauren's room when
Roy came striding along the corridor toward her.

"Just the person I wanted to see," he said with
the wide, welcoming grin that stirred all sorts of re-
sponses in her.

"I wanted you to know that I spoke with Dr. Larue today, and because I don't have a foster family
yet, he's agreed that David can stay here for another
few days. I'm very hopeful that by the time he's
ready to be released, the approval will have gone
through on your fostering application."

"Omigod, that's wonderful!" Hailey felt like
throwing her arms around him.

"Don't get your hopes up too high. There's always something that can come along and delay the whole process. It's a bureaucracy, remember.''

"I won't. I mean, I'll remember." She couldn't stop smiling. She knew this could never have happened without his help. "Oh, Roy, thank you."

"So where's the little guy? I glanced in his room, but he's not there."

"Follow me." Hailey led the way to the playroom, where Ingrid had just finished the story. Brittany and Elizabeth were quizzing her on details, but when Hailey and Roy walked in, the kids' attention was diverted.

"Hi, Roy," a chorus of voices greeted him. The kids were getting to know him.

"Ingrid Bergstrom, this is Roy Zedyck. Roy, my grandmother."

"Pleased to meet you." Ingrid got to her feet and smiled, holding out a hand for him to shake. "I understand that you're David's knight in shining armor?"

"I wouldn't go that far." Roy smiled at her, and Hailey saw right away that Gran liked him. But then, who wouldn't? As Gran herself was fond of saying, *What's not to like?*

"You and Hailey look a lot alike," Roy said.

"Thank you." Ingrid smiled with pleasure. "I've always been interested in social work," she said next. "I thought of going into it myself at one point."

Hailey lifted her eyebrows. As far as she knew, Gran had never given social work a thought as a career choice.

"It can be frustrating at times. And it doesn't leave a lot of time for a life of your own," Roy commented.

"I'd love to hear more about it. I'm having a luncheon on Sunday at noon. Why not come over and you can tell my husband and me all about the fascinating cases you must have."

The sneaky thing. Gran was arranging a setup. Hailey tried to catch her eye, but of course Ingrid didn't look her way. Surely Roy would see what she was up to. Hailey felt her face beginning to turn red with anxiety. How could Gran be so obvious? And, horror of horrors, would Roy think that Hailey had set this up, prompted Gran to invite him?

"Thanks, I'd like that. I'll be there." Roy dug a notepad out of his pocket and a pen. "What's your address?"

He scribbled it down, and Ingrid glanced at her watch. "I've got to fly—Sam will be wondering what's become of me." She hugged several of the kids, blew Hailey a kiss and gave Roy one of her most beguiling smiles.

"See you both Sunday and don't be late. I'm making eggs Benedict."

Hailey waited until Ingrid was gone and then turned to Roy.

"I'm sorry about that. I had no idea she was going to…"

He gave her a puzzled look. "Of course not, why would you?"

"Oh. I just thought… I mean… You know…" Her

face was redder than ever. She could happily have murdered Ingrid for this.

''That she was trying to set us up?'' The look he gave her sent hot shivers to her nether regions. And she sensed that he knew exactly how she felt. ''I could use all the help I can get. What's wrong with that?''

A buzzer sounded. Hailey had never been so glad to hear a summons. *Everything, you beguiling idiot.*

''Well, then, I guess I'll see you Sunday.''

It would serve him right to find out that Gran was the world's worst cook.

CHAPTER TEN

THE LETTER WAS WAITING for Hailey when she got to work Friday evening.

The return addressee was Registered Nurses Association of B.C. With sickness gnawing at her gut and fingers that trembled, she tore open the envelope and drew out the single sheet of paper:

This is to inform you that a complaint has been filed against you. The Association will be sending Louise Cornell, a nurse consultant, to investigate immediately.

Margaret. A feeling of outright hatred for the older woman came over Hailey. What had she ever done except try to perform her job to the very best of her ability and attempt to make her small patients' difficult lives a little easier?

It took every ounce of determination to laugh and tease the kids, to read to them, to spend her coffee break with Brittany, who was going through another series of chemo, and to explain to Mr. and Mrs. Meadows that Lauren was absolutely not being ignored. The little girl was proving to be a tiresome patient, expecting attention every moment and throwing tantrums when the nursing staff didn't respond immediately to her buzzer, which rang non-stop all day. The Meadowses weren't easy to reassure, and when they finally left, there were baths to give, meds to administer, kids to coax into bed.

When a quiet time finally came in the middle of the night, Hailey spent it standing beside David's crib and gently stroking his soft, dark curls. He slept soundly, flat on his back, one arm curled around Bonzo.

David and her hope of fostering him seemed the single bright spot in her life at the moment, and her heart ached to take him home and show him the crib she'd refinished for him, the room she'd painted egg-yolk yellow, the toys and little pants and shirts she'd found at a thrift shop. None of those material things mattered to him in the slightest, she knew; babies needed only copious amounts of love, good food, diaper changes on a regular basis. But she was determined to supply this child of her heart with all the things that would add to his enjoyment of life. He'd already had enough bad things happen to him.

She tucked the blanket closer around his small form and wondered with just a trace of irritation whether he'd ever stop clutching that battered stuffed dog.

WORRYING ABOUT the investigation made it hard to sleep, and by the time Sunday and Ingrid's luncheon arrived, Hailey felt drained and exhausted. In an effort to lift her spirits, she put on a sky-blue sundress that Jean had given her for her birthday. It fitted snugly around her narrow waist, and Hailey felt the flared skirt disguised her equally narrow hips.

Roy's blue car was already parked outside the house when she arrived. Feeling nervous, Hailey went inside.

Sam came over and put his arms around her, giving her a warm, welcoming hug and a kiss on the cheek. "You look beautiful in blue," he declared, which Hailey felt was stretching the truth much too far, especially when Roy gave her a long look and then gallantly agreed.

Ingrid's version of eggs Benedict was every bit as awful as Hailey had anticipated. Runny and a peculiar grayish color, the concoction was virtually inedible. She watched Roy doing his best to swallow the generous helping Ingrid heaped on his plate, and she couldn't help but feel sorry for him.

"Have some toast, Roy," Sam urged. He and Hailey had been lucky enough to receive small portions of egg, and they were old hands at filling up on toast and marmalade.

But as always, the conversation and laughter made up for the culinary failure. Ingrid got Roy talking about his work, and she and Sam and Hailey listened, fascinated, as Roy related funny and heartrending stories about his job.

It was Ingrid who asked, "What made you decide to go into social work in the first place?"

"I started out in sports medicine," he said. "I played football and it seemed a logical progression. But then I listened to a guest lecturer, a social worker, and I decided to change course." He was quiet for a few moments, and when he spoke again, he looked straight at Hailey, as if he wanted her to know what he was about to say.

"But there was more to it than that. I think it had to do with my being adopted," he began slowly.

Hailey found herself unable to tear her gaze away.

"I was adopted as a newborn, and my adoptive parents were already in their mid forties. They were dairy farmers in the Fraser Valley. I was an only child. I always knew I'd been adopted. Mom and Dad are very honest and they told me how lucky they were to have me, considering their age. It was a private adoption, arranged through the family doctor. I knew they loved me, but they were the sort of people who don't believe in making a show of their emotions."

Hailey knew that Sam and Ingrid were there in the room, but she had the strangest feeling that she and Roy were alone.

"I grew up longing for brothers and sisters and parents who were—well, younger, but looking back, I see that it was a matter of attitude more than age. Mom and Dad lived a regulated life. There weren't any relatives—they'd both come here from Czechoslovakia, leaving their families behind. I didn't invite kids home—Mom had strict rules about things. She was older than my friends' mothers, she dressed differently and talked with an accent, and I didn't want the guys to make fun of her. Dad was a good farmer who didn't believe much in higher education. He wanted me to work with him after I graduated from high school, but I wanted to go to university, so there were lots of hot and heavy clashes between us. Mom supported me, and it caused trouble between them. I felt responsible. They did the best they could, but I know they never really understood me.'' He grinned at Hailey. ''Typical teenage angst, huh?'' He paused for several moments, and Hailey and her grandparents waited in silence, sensing that the story wasn't complete.

''Then when I was seventeen,'' he went on, ''I got a call saying that my birth parents wanted to contact me. I didn't want to hurt Mom and Dad, but I knew I had to meet them. Ellie and Stephen Hepburn had been childhood sweethearts. She got pregnant with me when she was fifteen. They both came from high-achieving families, and both sets of parents insisted I be given up for adoption. They went away to university on different sides of the country, but when they were in their twenties, they met again and married. They had five other kids—three girls, two boys.'' His smile was bittersweet. ''Just goes to show you should be careful what you wish for, because suddenly I had all these sisters and brothers, and I didn't have a clue how to fit in with them, even though they were—''

He stopped and abruptly corrected himself. ''They *are* all totally accepting of me. But they grew up in this boisterous, outgoing household, see, where the emphasis was on academic achievement. I try hard, but to this day I can't really be a part of them. Nicole is the only one I'm truly close to, although I see them all a fair amount. They include me in every family get-together. But my loyalties really lie with the Zedycks, the parents who raised me.''

''They're both still alive?'' It was Ingrid who asked, although Hailey was wondering the same thing.

Roy nodded. ''They're in their early eighties, in a retirement home now, but they're both still mentally sharp. Mom's had the flu, but she's fine again. I talk to them almost every day. I helped them sell the farm three years ago, when it got to be too much for them. Dad was still disappointed that I didn't want to take it over.'' He lifted his cup and sipped coffee that had to be cold.

Hailey got up and took the cup from him, dumping the cold coffee and refilling it with fresh from the pot. She took her time, giving herself a chance to regain her composure, because Roy's story had touched her heart. Tears burned behind her eyes.

It was very clear that he'd never felt he belonged, either with his adoptive parents or with his birth family. It was a situation she could relate to, although she'd had Ingrid, who was her rock. A rush of love for Gran brought a fresh surge of tears, and she had to wipe her eyes and blow her nose on a paper towel before she could return to the table.

But when she did, Ingrid was pulling another of her sneaky moves.

''Isn't today the last day that movie's showing, Sam? The one about the wedding that you promised you'd take me to see?''

Sam started to shake his head, but Ingrid must have kicked him under the table, because he looked at his watch and sprang to his feet. "We just have time to catch the matinee if we leave right now."

"You don't mind doing the cleaning up, Hailey? You know where everything goes, honey, and I'm sure Roy will give you a hand. Sorry for being rude, but I've waited forever to see this movie. Thanks for coming over, both of you. We'll do it again really soon. Now where the heck is my hat?"

And just like that, they were gone.

Hailey shut her eyes and blew out an exasperated breath. When she opened them, she caught Roy laughing.

"Your grandma's a babe."

"My grandma's sly and treacherous and sneaky as hell."

"I like her style. Shall we get this stuff cleared away?" He started scraping the generous remnants of the eggs Benedict into the garburator. "I don't mean to be rude, but what the heck *was* this stuff, anyway?"

Hailey started to laugh and couldn't stop.

"What?" Roy looked at her with a puzzled expression.

"It's just that Sam and I have asked that question about Ingrid's concoctions more times than you can count. She has the best of intentions, but the truth is, Gran can't cook worth a damn, and the funniest thing is she doesn't know it."

"Well, I'll be the last one to tell her. The company beats the food any old day." He opened the dishwasher and started to load it. "I enjoy being around you, Hailey. I'd like to do more of it, lots more."

Hailey swallowed hard. She opened the fridge and carefully put the eggs and milk in. She'd been giving a lot of thought to what Gran had said about being so stubborn she ruined everything.

"I enjoyed today, too." Now, that wasn't so hard. And it was ambiguous enough that he could read something into it or not, just as he chose. She took the dishcloth and wiped the counter. "We seem to spend a lot of time cleaning up kitchens together," she said.

His voice was soft and low, intimate. It reminded her that they were alone in the house. "I don't suppose that means you might reconsider and step out of the kitchen with me on a real date?"

Gran said he'd ask again. God, Gran is smart.

"I might if you get around to asking me." She'd meant her reply to be light and teasing, but her chest was tight and her voice didn't sound right.

He didn't seem to notice. He didn't say anything at first, which scared her, but then he took the dish towel she'd slung over her shoulder and carefully dried his hands. He reached out and touched her hair, just a single, gentle touch with the palm of his hand.

"I wanted to see if it would burn me," he said.

She dared to meet his eyes. He was looking at her in that intense way that made it hard to breathe, as if he liked what he saw.

"Will you have dinner with me, Hailey?"

She drew a shaky breath and blew it out again.

"Okay." *Idiot.* Surely she knew more enthusiastic

words than *okay*. She tried again. Her hands were shaking. "Yes, I would…like to have dinner with you." She tipped her head to the side and looked straight at him. It took all her courage, because, Lordy, he was gorgeous. "When?"

"Now?"

She frowned and shook her head, bewildered. "But we only just finished lunch. It's two in the afternoon."

"I know. But I'm starving. Those eggs didn't do it for me." He grinned and managed to look abashed. "And I guess I'm also scared that if I give you time to think about it, you'll change your mind."

She swallowed over the lump in her throat. He was making it clear he really wanted to spend time with her. And Lord knew, today she didn't want to be alone. In the back of her mind was that letter, hanging over her like a thundercloud.

"Okay, then. I guess that's what we'll do." What was wrong with her vocabulary today? "To tell you the truth, I'm sort of hungry myself."

This time his grin was huge. "Are we done here?"

She glanced around. "Yup. Clean and shining." She brushed off her sundress. "I'm not dressed very fancy." *As if he couldn't see that.*

His eyes raked her body and sent heat shooting to private places.

"You look pretty fancy to me. How about Chinatown? We can take my car. I'll bring you back here for yours."

"I love Chinatown."

"Settled, then." He reached out and took her hand. His was broad, the palm surprisingly rough. What did he do to get calluses on his palms? she wondered.

And going to Chinatown at two in the afternoon couldn't be classed as a date, could it?

But she was dead wrong.

It turned out to be a real date, with white tablecloths and hovering waiters and wine, and even a spray of lilies in a vase. She might have been nervous if she'd had a chance to anticipate, but the way it had happened made her relaxed, instead.

Over a leisurely meal in the comfortably elegant and almost empty restaurant, she watched his mouth as he ordered, and she felt giddy and delighted when he reached across and took her hand in his. She should have been nervous and ill at ease, because she hadn't done this dating thing a whole lot. But instead, being here with Roy felt as natural as breathing.

She even got around to asking him about the calluses.

"Oh, I've been refinishing a table. My dad taught me woodworking when I was a little kid. It was his hobby. Like most farmers, he was pretty good at a lot of different things."

She felt suddenly defensive. "You must have been pretty horrified by the stuff I've refinished."

"Are you kidding? I was blown away by what you've done. I like working with wood, but I haven't been doing it. You have, and it's pushed me into getting back into it.''

''I'm glad.'' She was surprised and pleased by the compliment. ''That house boggles me sometimes, though,'' she admitted with a sigh. ''There's so much to do and so many things I don't know how to fix.'' And today she felt as if she'd never have the energy to tackle anything again.

''You could let me help.'' Before she could refuse, he quickly added, ''Please. It would be relaxing and fun and different. Granted, I don't have a lot of free time, so if you're concerned about me being underfoot all the time, don't be. But I do have a few hours here and there that I'd like to spend helping you. Those doors you were working on the other day, for instance. I'm a pro at sanding. And the bathroom—I could help you redo the bathroom, put in a new subflooring, new drywall. Then you could have the tub refinished.''

The bathroom. It was petty to be seduced by a bathroom, but the automatic refusal that had been on her lips died. Hailey could hear Gran whispering in her ear about cutting off noses again. What the heck, if he wanted to help her, why not let him? Her back and bottom were raw from that darned tub.

''Okay.'' Had *okay* become her new favorite word? ''Yes, please.''

''When can I start?''

''Whenever you want.'' She offered him a fortune cookie before taking one for herself.

''How about now?''

This guy didn't waste time. And the universe was

on her side, because the paper inside her cookie said, *Much good change is heading your way.*

He read his fortune, grinned, and handed it to her. *New endeavors will bring great pleasure.*

"Okay." She was doing it again, the *okay* thing. Being around Roy turned her brain to pabulum. She'd turn into a mindless blob with a one-word vocabulary that could get her into real trouble.

But this was free labor. She just had to keep thinking about the bathroom and stop wondering what he'd be like in bed.

CHAPTER ELEVEN

BY SEVEN THAT EVENING the ceiling and walls in the downstairs bathroom were stripped to the rafters. That was the good news.

The bad news was, Roy had taken off his shirt at some point, and his chest wasn't what you'd expect from a guy whose work was mainly head stuff. Roy's chest was broad and matted with enticing dark curls, and he had muscles that Hailey hadn't had a chance to fully appreciate when he was wearing clothes.

"We could do the drywall and the subflooring next weekend if you want," he suggested, wolfing down the vegetable omelet and hot biscuits she'd put together for their supper. He'd washed his face and hands, but there was still plaster dust in his thick dark hair. He was going to have females attacking h   n the streets when he started turning naturally g   She had to control the urge to reach across the table and brush the dust away. She could smell honest male sweat, and she'd worked closely enough with him for the past three hours to know that he used lemon-scented shampoo.

"Only problem is, I may have to drop everything

and go to work if an emergency comes up. It's one of the hazards of my job."

"Well, count yourself lucky. I may not have a job to go to after this week," she blurted. She'd actually forgotten about Margaret and the association until right now.

He looked at her and frowned. "Cross carried through on her threat?"

Hailey explained about the letter, cursing herself for bringing it up. Guys didn't want to know about your problems.

But Roy listened closely. "What's this woman's name again, the nurse consultant they're sending?"

"Louise Cornell."

He reached across the table and took her hand. "It's a stupid thing to say, I know, but try not to worry too much about it. I guarantee it's not going to affect your job."

He couldn't possibly know that, but just having him say it made her feel better. And to her immense relief, he didn't dwell on the issue.

Instead, he reached for another biscuit, bit into it and sighed with pleasure. "These are the best I've tasted since I left home. I didn't think anyone could make biscuits the way my mom did."

She felt ridiculously pleased. "I'm glad you like them." She couldn't help but wonder if all his appetites were as large, but she put the thought hastily out of her head. *Don't go there, Bergstrom. Here there be dragons.*

The one thing she knew for sure was that her dratted bathroom was way too small for the two of them

to be in there at the same time. She'd been clearing
away debris from the floor when he'd turned quickly
and nearly knocked her over. His arms had come
around her and she'd stopped breathing.

Their eyes had locked and for a prayerful instant
she'd thought he was going to kiss her. His body
tensed, her pulse raced, her breath came back short
and shallow.

And then she'd come to her senses, taken one defensive step back, and he'd dropped his arms. She
felt as if she'd been teetering on the edge of a ravine.

And now she could kick herself for taking that
one fatal step.

Was she going to grow old regretting the things
she didn't do?

AS HE DROVE HOME later that evening, Roy was
wondering exactly the same thing. Why the hell
hadn't he kissed her when the opportunity presented
itself? She was right there in his arms, and there
were hot sparks in those golden eyes of hers that
made him think she wanted to be kissed. But he'd
hesitated that one split second and she stepped away,
and the moment was lost.

He was an idiot. Well, he amended, he was an
intelligent idiot, because he *had* managed to convince her that having him around once in a while
wasn't such a bad idea.

That bathroom was going to be an absolute bitch,
but it had its advantages. It was a really small space,
and she was going to have to be in there giving him
a hand. And he might be an idiot, but he was also a

quick learner. There'd be another shot at kissing, and the next time he'd be faster than a speeding bullet.

In the meantime he intended to write that letter he'd been planning, saying just how fantastic a nurse Hailey was, and he'd fax a copy of it to the nurses association, to the attention of this Cornell woman. He'd do it tonight, before time got away from him again.

HAILEY WASN'T DUE BACK at work until Wednesday, but Tuesday at nine in the morning the phone rang.

"Hailey Bergstrom? This is Louise Cornell, the nurse consultant for the association."

Hailey's stomach cramped. She tried to get some idea of what Cornell was like from her voice, but all she could sense was professional friendliness and detachment.

"I know you're off, but I wondered if you'd mind coming in this afternoon to talk with me? These matters cause a lot of anxiety, and for that reason I'd like to get this settled as quickly as possible. I've spoken to the others who were involved in the incident, and now I'd very much like to speak to you."

Hailey swallowed hard and agreed to come in at two.

The only bright spot she could see in the day was that she'd get to spend time with David. Whatever happened, holding him, telling him stories would be solace.

LOUISE CORNELL was comfortably plump, dressed in a gray business suit with a pink silk blouse. Her

hair was nut-brown, cut short in a style more prac-
tical than fashionable. She had kindly brown eyes
and a crooked smile that helped quiet the butterflies
in Hailey's belly, and she asked to be called Louise.

She invited Hailey to describe exactly what had
occurred, and she didn't take notes or seem to do
anything other than listen attentively.

Hailey did her best not to sound defensive or to
underplay what had happened. She'd gone over the
events so many times in her mind that retelling them
was easy. When she was done, Louise nodded.

"Our policy is to try as often as possible to see
that matters are worked out in a nonconfrontational
fashion between the people involved. Now, I'm
wondering why this matter couldn't have been discussed and settled between you and your supervisor."

Hailey swallowed. She had to be very cautious
here. "I did attempt that, but Margaret was very, um,
upset."

"I see." The brown eyes didn't miss much. "Do
you have any objections to having her join us now?
And also the hospital administrator?"

"Not at all." Hailey braced herself as Louise
paged them both. Rational discussions weren't possible with Margaret, everyone knew that. Melissa
Clayton-Burke, the hospital administrator, was noted
for being sensible, honest and supportive, but this
still could turn into a fiasco. *Watch your temper,* she
cautioned herself.

Within five minutes Margaret marched in, back
like a ramrod, in what Hailey considered full battle

dress. She was wearing her cap, a dress uniform so white it was blinding, and her perfectly polished white nursing shoes. She was from the Old School, and she was Right. Everything about her trumpeted that conviction. And when she looked at Hailey, her eyes glittered and her small, pinched mouth wore a self-satisfied little smirk.

She sat as far away from Hailey as she could get, which was a relief.

Melissa came in on a wave of energy and a swirl of navy silk shirtdress. Hailey had always liked Melissa, who was noted for being a no-nonsense administrator. She'd been a nurse herself, working at St. Joe's before she went into administration, which endeared her to all the nurses because they knew she understood their job. And on a totally irrational level, Hailey liked her because her hair was almost the same violent shade of red as her own.

"As I've explained to each of you," Louise began, "I'm wondering why this whole matter couldn't have been discussed and settled without involving the association. Our entire aim is to take away the hierarchy traditionally associated with nursing and replace it with openness and honesty. Now, Margaret, could you maybe explain why it wasn't possible to reconcile this entire thing with Hailey, and if that didn't achieve positive results, why you didn't go to Melissa?"

Margaret looked stunned, and it was a long moment before she found her voice. "Well, as I told you before, there's no point in even *trying* to talk to Hailey." She sneered. "Goodness knows I've tried in the past, but *she* has a degree and of course she knows *everything*.''

Hailey could feel her face burning at the personal nature of the insult, and she wanted to hit Margaret across the mouth, but she managed not to say anything in her own defense. It was a wise move, because Margaret wasn't finished. There was outright malice in her tone when she burst out, ''She refuses to dress in a professional manner, and she's insubordinate. When she's on shift, the children are out of control, and she encourages them to be cheeky and defiant. They won't obey the rules, and neither will she.''

Obey the rules? Insubordinate? Hailey had a hysterical urge to giggle, but she quelled it. Margaret sounded like a drill sergeant in the military, instead of a supervising nurse on a pediatric ward.

Melissa and Louise studiously avoided looking at one another, and with a surge of hope, Hailey wondered if, like her, they were feeling that Margaret was voicing complaints that sounded both antiquated and ridiculous. Nursing had changed, and the woman had refused to change with it.

''I've interviewed all the staff on the pediatric ward,'' Louise said in a neutral tone. ''And everyone seems to agree that Hailey does her job extremely well. I also have a letter from a worker with Social Services, Roy Zedyck, commending her for her cooperation and devotion to a patient in the care of the ministry.''

Hailey's face flamed. Roy had written the letter just as he'd promised. She felt humble and grateful and indebted to everyone who'd defended her, but knowing *he'd* gone to such trouble for her sent an irrational bubble of happiness shooting through her.

"The staff, including the child's attending pediatrician, agrees unanimously that the incident you reported was not at all serious," Louise said to Margaret. Her tone was still kind, but noticeably cooler than it had been. "Everyone agrees that the child's care wasn't compromised in the slightest. I think we should just drop this entire matter. Thank you all for your cooperation."

Margaret's face was vermilion. She was breathing audibly through her nose, and sweat beaded her forehead. Her mouth was tied in a tight little knot, and she didn't say anything or look at anyone. She got to her feet and marched out of the room. The door sighed shut behind her.

Louise and Melissa chatted breezily about a meeting that was coming up soon.

Hailey breathed a sigh of relief that seemed to originate in her toes, then she stood up and extended her hand, first to Louise, then to Melissa. She was still trembling, but it didn't matter now if they knew how scared she'd been.

"Thank you both so much," she said in a fervent tone. "This is such a relief to me."

Louise left, and Melissa said, "It's gratifying to have a nurse of your caliber here at St. Joe's, Hailey. Before you go, I wonder if I could have a word with you."

Now what? "Sure."

Melissa sat down again and so did Hailey.

"I worked with Margaret years ago, on geriatrics," Melissa began. "And I had many of the same difficulties with her that you're having. Like you, I felt angry and frustrated."

Hailey nodded. No point denying that was how she felt about Margaret.

"One of my patients knew her well. She'd been a friend of Margaret's mother, and she gave me some insights into Margaret's life that helped me understand her much better, which I'm going to share with you. I'd like you to keep this strictly confidential, however."

More mystified than ever, Hailey agreed.

"When she was in her twenties," Melissa began, "Margaret fell in love with a married doctor. She had a baby with him, a girl she adored. The girl drowned when she was three in a neighbor's backyard pond. The doctor blamed Margaret for not watching their daughter closely enough. He ended the relationship, and Margaret came close to a breakdown. She moved back in with her mother, and my patient intimated that Mrs. Cross was difficult in the extreme. She developed Alzheimer's five years ago, and died just last summer. Margaret nursed her at home right up to the end."

Hailey knew Margaret had nursed her mother, but she hadn't known any of the other stuff. Grudgingly she said, "I guess she's had a hard life."

"Yes, she has. Knowing about it helped me understand her, and understanding helped me be more patient with her." The unspoken assumption was it would also help Hailey. "I felt you should know."

"Thanks, Melissa."

The office where they'd met was just one floor down from pediatrics, and as she got on the elevator, Hailey knew that the last thing she wanted to do was run into Margaret. She still had a big load of resentment against her, though what Melissa told her had put a dent in it. She could understand, just a little, why Margaret was the way she was.

But David was up there, and she needed to see him. She'd just do her best to stay out of the head nurse's way.

Karen was at the nurses' station, along with two of the aides, and thank heavens, Margaret was nowhere to be seen. Feeling relieved, Hailey went over to them.

"She's gone for lunch," Karen said in a hushed voice. "She looked like a volcano about to erupt and didn't say a word to anybody about what went on. We figured that probably meant it hadn't gone her way. Spill the beans—we're all dying to know."

If Melissa hadn't confided in her, Hailey would have reveled in telling them about Margaret getting what amounted to a reprimand. But now she just couldn't do it.

"Well, I didn't get suspended," she said.

The other nurses cheered.

"And you guys all went to bat for me," Hailey went on, looking at each of them. "Thank you. More than I can say."

Karen waved a dismissive hand. "We told the truth, that's all. I'm glad it turned out the way it should have. But what's the score with Margaret? What did the rep say to her?''

Hailey opened her mouth to tell them, then again stopped herself. Melissa had managed to make Margaret far too human. ''Nothing much, but I guess it just didn't turn out the way Margaret thought it was going to.''

''Sore loser. Serves her right, trying to cause trouble over nothing.''

Though she was grateful for their loyalty, Hailey felt a little pang of sympathy for Margaret. It must be tough to be her, alone and childless, with memories that haunted you. She almost wished Melissa hadn't told her all that stuff. It was way easier to just out-and-out hate Margaret.

''Thanks again, all of you. I'm heading down to see David.''

The nurses exchanged quick glances, then Karen said, ''His mother finally turned up. She's down there now. I tried to call you on your cell to let you know, but it was turned off.''

For a moment the world teetered.

CHAPTER TWELVE

"How...how long has she been here?" Hailey could hardly get the words out.

"Twenty minutes or so."

"Does Roy know?" Her throat was dry, and her heart was hammering. "Did you call him?"

Karen nodded. "First thing I did was call Roy. He was out in the suburbs—he's on his way in now. He said to make certain she doesn't try to take David anywhere, that we should call security and have them stand by. I did that, and Mavis is down there with her, keeping a close eye on what's going on." Mavis was a security guard they all knew and liked.

"I'm his primary-care nurse. I'll go talk to her." Hailey headed down the hall, feeling angry and betrayed all over again. She'd known this was a possibility, but because so much time had passed, she'd begun to assume that Shannon Riggs would never turn up. Things were going so well without her.

Hailey paused in front of David's room. The door was open, and she could see the girl holding David. Her bleached-blond hair was pulled back in a ponytail from a face plastered with too much makeup, and her skin was stretched tightly over bones that jutted out like a cadaver's. She was wearing jeans and a long-sleeved white T-shirt with a patterned vest over it. The clothing hung loosely on her emaciated body, and David looked too heavy for her to manage easily. But his plump arms and legs were curved around her body, and his face was buried in her neck. The girl's arms were wrapped around him, clutching him to her.

Jealousy, hot and bitter, flowed through Hailey's veins. It took every ounce of her self-control to walk into the room and say in a reasonably steady voice, "Hello, I'm Hailey Bergstrom, David's primary-care nurse. You must be Shannon Riggs."

Shannon nodded without really looking at Hailey, but David's head popped up over her shoulder, and the smile he gave Hailey was nothing short of radiant.

"Lee, Mama come."

"I see that. Hi, sweetheart." She managed a smile for him, but the words almost choked her.

Mavis was standing by the other crib. "If you're going to be in here, Hailey, I'll wait outside the door." She gave Hailey a wink and walked out.

Hailey stood frozen, trying to quell the awful urge to tear David out of this teenager's skinny arms. She didn't deserve him; she'd left him alone and helpless; he'd almost died because of her. What right did she have to come here now, to take him in her arms? She'd forfeited her rights as a mother.

"Mama." David used both hands to pat Shannon's face in a tender gesture that almost broke Hailey's heart, because he'd patted her face that very same way and made her heart melt with love for him.

"I see you still got Bonzo, Davie." Shannon's voice was that of a child, light and soft and tentative.

"Bonzo." David pointed to his crib, where the battered toy lay on his pillow. "My dog."

"I got him that for Christmas—he won't go to sleep without it," Shannon said to Hailey, as if that was news.

And he almost slept forever with only that cheap, dirty stuffed toy to comfort him, thanks to you. The words burned in Hailey's throat and she ached to shriek them aloud.

"He looks so good." Shannon planted a kiss on David's cheek, and Hailey felt nauseous. "My beautiful boy, aren't you, Davie?"

"He is beautiful, and he's feeling better now." Hailey's voice was brittle, and she knew she was breaking her own rule about talking about a child within earshot of that child, but she couldn't help herself. "He was pretty bad when he first arrived, you know, dehydrated and unconscious. He'd been left all alone, with no food or water, for three days. He couldn't cry anymore, he was too weak. He arrested in the ER, he was in intensive care for the first while, and things were touch-and-go. He's a very lucky little boy." *In spite of you.*

Shannon's face contorted and she swallowed, once and then again. She turned away, so her back was toward Hailey. David waggled his fingers over her shoulder, and Hailey forced another smile and waved back at him.

The door opened and Roy came in. He smiled at Hailey.

"Shannon, I'm Roy Zedyck, David's social worker, and I'd like to speak to you, please. Would you give the baby to Hailey and come with me?"

Shannon turned slowly, her brown eyes filled with panic. David's eyes were the same shape as hers, Hailey noted, but otherwise he didn't resemble her at all. She stepped forward to take him, but Shannon moved away. There was raw terror on her face, and her arms tightened convulsively on David.

"Do I have to? Can I come back and visit with him again?"

"Of course you can, but I have some questions for you to answer just now."

"But I can come back, can't I? I can see him after?" Shannon sounded about ten years old. Hailey hardened her heart against an unexpected, unwanted stab of pity.

"Yes, you can."

Hailey moved close and tried to take David, but although Shannon released him, he started to shriek and cling to her with all his strength.

"Mama, Mama, *Mama*..."

In the end Hailey had to wrestle him from her. Shannon was sobbing as she walked away, and David fought with fists and feet to get out of Hailey's arms and follow her. He was stronger than she'd suspected, and for half an hour, Hailey tried everything she knew to comfort and quieten him, but he wouldn't stop sobbing. He fought her, and each time she put him down, David raced toward the locked door of the ward, shrieking, "Mama, Mama!"

Exhaustion finally took over and he fell asleep, but not before Hailey was exhausted herself. She sat and rocked him in the rocking chair, his limp, hot little body shuddering with the aftermath of sobs.

At last she got up carefully and put him in his crib. She kissed his sweaty head and tucked Bonzo in close beside him.

Roy was waiting for her at the nurses' station, his face somber.

"He finally calmed down?"

Hailey shrugged. "Not really. He just cried himself to sleep."

"Can we talk for a few minutes?"

"Sure." There were people everywhere, nurses and visitors and patients, so she led the way to an empty room and closed the door so they'd have some privacy. She felt drained and frightened and furious. She turned toward him, hands on her hips.

"So what's going to happen now, Roy?" Hailey couldn't keep the anger from her voice. "She just walks in and takes over?"

"Of course not. She's a minor—she'll be detained in juvenile hall until a judge hears the circumstances. She has a lawyer from Legal Aid, and she's going to meet him after she sees David."

"And how long will all that take? For the judge to decide?"

"Not long. Probably tomorrow morning."

"And then what?"

Roy rubbed a weary hand across his forehead and through his hair.

"I can't say for sure, but she'll likely be released. Apparently the woman who sponsored her before brought her here today, Tonya Cabral. She'll undoubtedly give evidence on Shannon's behalf. She told me before that she considered Shannon a good mother to David."

"That makes me *sick*. Shannon ought to go to jail. They should throw away the key." The muscles in Hailey's arms were throbbing from struggling with David. He'd banged a small fist into her eye, and it was stinging, but the worst damage was to her heart. It felt bruised and torn from hearing those endless, shrieking, desperate sobs, the wailing for a mommy who didn't deserve the name.

"Will she be able to do this to him again?" Hailey asked. "Come and see him, upset him this way?"

"Yes." Roy looked at her, and she could see the weary resignation in his eyes. "Yes. My guess is she'll be granted supervised visits."

Rage and utter frustration were taking the place of weariness. "Even…even though it makes him half-crazy? Even though she…she deserted him? Even though he's too little to understand what's going on and so he feels abandoned every time she comes and then leaves him this way?"

Roy sighed and nodded. "Legally, she's still his mother."

"But she's worse than an animal. No animal would deliberately desert their young the way she did.'' Hailey knew her voice was rising, but she didn't care. "He's just a baby, Roy. She has no right to walk back into his life this way and make him so unhappy. It's…it's…'' She was losing it. She could feel the hot tears starting to stream from her eyes. "It's *barbaric*. It's…it's not *fair.*''

His face was etched with weary lines, and his eyes were sad, but she didn't want to see that. She wanted him to agree with her, to get angry, to do something that would prevent Shannon Riggs from tearing David's life apart this way.

But he stayed calm. "You're right, it's both of those. But in your job and in mine, we have to live by the rules.'' He stepped forward and his arms came around her, hard and warm. "I'm sorry.''

She pushed him away. "Don't touch me. Don't—''

"You wanna hit me? If it'll make you feel better, go ahead.''

For one insane second, she did want to. She wanted to smash her fist into something, to release the terrible tension.

Instead, her tears turned to sobs, and that made her even madder. She hated losing control that way. She shut her eyes and tried to regain it, but choking sobs ripped through her, anyway.

"Ah, Hailey.'' He sighed. "Let it go, c'mere and just let it go.''

She struggled, but he wrapped his arms tightly around her again and maneuvered her over to a chair. He sat down in it and pulled her onto his lap, and she gave up and let herself collapse against him.

He was big and strong and comforting, and it had been a train wreck of a day.

Gradually the sobs quieted and she became aware of his smell, his warmth. She was also aware that her nose was running, and she'd slobbered all over his green shirt.

Then she remembered how blotchy her face got when she cried. She probably looked a mess. She *knew* she looked a mess. Oh, to heck with it. She never looked that good even at the best of times, but right now she didn't give a holy hoot.

Instead, she breathed a resigned sigh and let her head rest on his shoulder just one moment longer than necessary, and then she started to get to her feet. Someone could barge in here at any moment.

"Stay." He held her close with one arm and shifted her slightly, digging in his pocket and coming up with crumpled tissues.

"I think these are only slightly used."

So what if somebody barged in—too darned bad. Sometimes a person had a perfect right to bawl her head off. She sat where she was and blew her nose in the tissues, thinking she was far too large a woman to perch on a man's knee. It was dangerous for all sorts of reasons. But she couldn't seem to make herself move.

He touched her cheek with a finger. "Better?"

"Much." She ducked her head to hide from him the damage to her appearance. She did care, after all. "Thanks."

"My pleasure." There was a gruffness to his voice. He lifted a hand to thread his fingers through her hair, cupping her skull and forcing her to look at him. He was awfully close.

''Dammit, Hailey. I keep wanting to do this, but it never seems the right time.'' And then his mouth, hard, hot and hungry, was on hers.

Sleeping passions sprang to life in her, sudden and shocking. She resisted for a split second and then, helpless against the sensations that swamped her, she opened to him, tasting, exploring, kissing him the voracious way she'd dreamed of doing.

After a time they got too enthusiastic. Their teeth banged together and she reared back, but he simply angled his mouth for a better fit and drew her close again, and she sighed and slid her arms around his shoulders, wishing she could slide her hands under his shirt and feel his skin. He rubbed his hands up and down her back, and she wished they'd find her breasts, but they didn't.

The kiss lasted longer than it probably should have for a first kiss, and still it was way too short. She finally pulled back a little, although it took every ounce of willpower she possessed.

They were both breathing hard, and she could feel his erection against her bottom. It sent wild signals coursing through her, along with a sense of jubilation. So her hormones weren't the only ones raging. It was reassuring to know he was feeling some of what she was—horny and needy and starved for what could come next, what should come next, if they weren't at St. Joe's behind a door that didn't lock.

"Dammit, Hailey, I want you." The words were raw and vital and exactly what she wanted to hear.

"Me, too."

He pulled her close and kissed her again, a fast, hot, frenzied kiss. "If we were anywhere but here…"

But they weren't. What if one of the kids on the ward walked in? And since when did she want to tear off her clothes and jump on a guy just because he'd kissed her?

This was what sexual abstinence did to a person. It turned a perfectly functioning brain to cotton fluff. But gosh, he could kiss like nobody's business. And she wanted to throw herself on the narrow bed and drag him down with her, not bothering to take their clothes off. She wanted him to…

She struggled to her feet and straightened her dress.

He got up, as well, and clasped her by the shoulders, looking deep into her eyes. His were filled with tenderness and amusement and ferocious heat.

"I hope you don't start thinking I took advantage of you when you were down."

If only.

She managed a facsimile of a grin. "You weren't the one sitting on *my* knee."

His grin was lopsided. "I should be so lucky."

"I should go."

He glanced at his watch and shook his head. "Me, too. I'm later than usual. But first, I do have some good news for you. For some reason I almost forgot what I wanted to tell you. I got a call this morning saying you've been approved as a foster parent—in order to expedite, they agreed to use the home study done for your adoption application. It's my call now about where David goes, so of course you can take him home. Dr. Larue is going to check him over and release him tomorrow morning. I'll leave the proper forms at the desk.''

''Omigod.'' Hailey brought her hands to her face and then lost control entirely and threw her arms around him in a ferocious hug, squealing, ''Oh, that's wonderful. Thank you, Roy.''

But then she thought of Shannon, and the way David had sobbed and struggled to follow her. Abruptly she let go of Roy. ''But she'll be able to visit him? His...'' It was hard for her even to say the word... ''His...mother. Shannon Riggs will be able to see him?''

He nodded. ''Yeah, she will—after she sees a judge. My guess is she'll be allowed supervised visits.''

Outrage and resentment rose again like steam. ''Supervised by whom?''

''By a child-care worker.''

''At my house?'' The thought of Shannon coming to her house made her want to vomit.

''No. It'll be at one of the group centers or the office. The ministry believes that in most cases it's best not to have the foster parent involved.''

The ministry was right. It could lead to murder. ''And this worker will take him there?''

''Yes. She'll pick him up from your house and

return him when the visit's over.'' He was studying her closely. ''Do you have a problem with that?''

''No.'' Of course she did, but she didn't want to rock the boat here. She detested the thought of a stranger taking David anywhere, much less to see the woman who, in her estimation, had no right to call herself a mother.

But he was going home with *her,* and for right now, that was enough. There were a million things she needed to do, like notify the nursery downstairs that David would be attending, give them a list of her shifts, pick up diapers and extra milk and fresh vegetables, make some soup and finish fixing his room, and—

''Hailey?'' Roy was smiling at her.

She looked at him, and something deep inside of her slipped sideways, caught and held in a place she didn't want to go.

She didn't want to feel this way about him. Damn and blast and murder. She didn't want to look at him and start having fantasies about happy-ever-after. She wouldn't—she just wouldn't. But wishing and the force of will couldn't make it go away.

''Hailey? Why are you looking at me like that?'' He raised a quizzical eyebrow.

It was all she could do to speak. ''Like…how?''

He shrugged and frowned. ''Scowling. Almost like you're fuming mad again. I'm sorry about the visitation thing. There's absolutely nothing I can do about it. It's policy.''

''I know that.'' But she *was* furious with him. She wanted to smack him one, hard, just as she'd wanted to before. Why had he done this—come into her life and made her start hoping that there could be the kind of romance she'd long ago given up on?

At least he didn't suspect why she was mad. That was some comfort.

"I'm not angry at all," she lied. "I'm just over-whelmed. Too much has been happening. I'm thrilled about taking David home, but I didn't eat this morning. I guess I need to have some lunch or something."

Hunger he understood. "C'mon, I'll walk you down to the cafeteria and buy you a sandwich. I wish I had time to take you somewhere special to cele-brate, but we'll go out another time."

When they passed the nursing desk, Karen came rushing over.

"There you are. I'm so glad you're still around. Hailey, we're having a problem with David."

Hailey stiffened. "What's wrong?"

"He woke up a few minutes ago, got out of his crib and went over right by the door and sat down on the floor." She motioned with her chin. An aide was sitting on a chair by the door with David on her lap.

"He insists on being there. He won't budge even a foot from it, and every time someone comes in, he thinks it's his mother. He has a tantrum if we try to move him." Karen rolled her eyes. "Margaret says he's to be put back in his crib and a cover will be put on it if he tries to get out again. Can you believe that? She's down in the drug dispensary at the moment, but she'll be back soon." She shot Hailey a helpless look. "Poor little fellow."

Hailey's eyes were on David and the woman holding him. The aide had dragged the chair right up to the door and was sitting there with David on her lap. He was clutching Bonzo and watching the door with an intensity that seared Hailey's heart.

"I'll take care of him," she said fiercely.

She hurried over to David, Roy close behind her. Hailey knelt and stroked David's flushed cheek, keeping her voice light and playful.

"Hey, little guy, want to come with Hailey to the playroom?"

He glanced at her and shook his head. His eyes went back to the door.

"I'll take him." Hailey lifted him in her arms, feeling the tension in his body. He stiffened and pointed wordlessly at the door.

"Yeah, sport, I know. You want to stay here so you can watch for her."

"Mama." His face puckered and the word came out on a choked sob.

Hailey had to struggle to keep her own tears back.

She sank into the chair with David on her knee. Roy stood beside her for a moment, then leaned over and pressed a kiss to David's head.

"Hang in there, sport. Hailey, I'm going to get you a sandwich. I'll send someone up with it. And I'll call you a little later and see how this turns out."

He left, and shortly afterward a woman from the kitchen arrived with two tuna sandwiches, a box of chocolate cookies and a carton of milk. Hailey nibbled at the food as she talked to David, trying to distract him, trying to get him to agree to move further than three feet from the door.

But each time she tried, he stiffened and struggled to escape from her arms.

Margaret came marching down the ward and stopped beside them, her hands on her hips. "And just what is going on here, may I ask?"

Her voice was icy cold, and the look she gave Hailey was overflowing with venom.

Hailey kept her voice low. "He's upset and I'm trying to soothe him."

The older nurse harrumphed. "That child belongs in his crib. Anyone can see that he's overwrought and needs a nap. I've already instructed housekeeping to send up a cover to contain him."

The very idea of trapping a child in a crib was monstrous. The urge to lash out at Margaret was overwhelming, but Hailey struggled for control. David didn't need adults hollering all around him. Margaret didn't need to be hollered at, either—she just needed to do something besides nursing.

"A cover won't be necessary, honest. I'll stay with him until he goes to sleep."

"And I suppose you'll also make sure he doesn't climb out during the night and disrupt the entire ward? Do you plan to spend twenty-four hours a day here, Hailey? Because if that's your plan, then obviously there's no need for the rest of the nursing team. We all know you could run this ward singlehanded, don't we? The rest of us might just as well go home."

CHAPTER THIRTEEN

HAILEY HELD ON to her temper. Barely.

"David is my responsibility, Margaret. I've been approved as his foster mother, and I'm taking him home with me tomorrow morning." Her voice was shaking, her efforts at control no longer possible. "And if I hear that you've put any sort of cover on his crib or upset him in any way, I promise you, you'll answer not only to me, but to the association and the ministry and...and the newspapers and anyone else I can think of who would sympathize with a helpless child. Is that clear?"

Margaret's face turned from scarlet to magenta, and for an instant Hailey wondered if she might be about to have a coronary. But she turned without another word and marched to the nurses' station.

David had started to wail again during the confrontation, and Hailey got up and tried to walk with him, needing to release her own welter of emotions before they blew a hole in the top of her head. Why did Margaret have to push her so hard? She'd tried to stay reasonable, she really had.

David became hysterical if they moved more than a few feet from the door, so at last Hailey gave up and simply sat down again with him cradled on her lap. She spent the time singing and telling him stories, talking to the other kids that came by, feeding him when the aide brought his tray, changing his diaper when it needed changing. She'd have to just outwait him, she decided. Sooner or later he'd give up his vigil or fall asleep.

But hours passed, and bedtime came and still he fought sleep. Every so often, he pointed at the door and said in a soft, plaintive voice, "Mama?"

Hailey thought her heart would break each time he did it.

Finally, finally his head nodded, and then he gave in, his body going limp and his breathing becoming steady. She held her breath as she carried him to his crib and gently put him down.

Weary to the bone, she still had to stop at the desk and talk with the other nurses. She wasn't sure if Margaret had left orders to cover the crib or not.

It turned out she hadn't. The grapevine had been thorough, and the other nurses all knew Hailey was taking David home with her in the morning. They congratulated her and agreed that it was the best thing for David. And they all said they were happy for Hailey, because they knew how long she'd waited for a baby.

But there was also concern about Shannon.

"Too bad she ever showed up," Karen said. "He's been doing so well."

Hailey was too angry with Shannon Riggs even to speak about her.

"I hope he stays asleep, and probably by morning he'll have forgotten her," Karen suggested.

Hailey wasn't so certain. She had a bad feeling about the situation. She considered staying, bedding down in the room beside him, but she had so much to do at home.

"Don't worry, we'll keep a close eye on him tonight," Karen promised.

"Be sure to call me if there's any problem," Hailey said.

SHE HAD TONS of shopping to do, and she hated shopping.

It was after nine by the time she stopped in front of her house. At first she didn't recognize Laura's red van parked across the street.

But she heard the voices from the backyard as soon as she got out of the car—her sister's cautioning tone and then Christopher, her nephew, laughing.

Mystified, she walked around the house.

Laura was sitting on the back steps, one arm around Samantha. Christopher was in the rabbit pen, playing with Skippy. What on earth were her sister and the kids doing at her house at this hour? And why in heck had Laura chosen one of the worst possible times to pay her a visit?

"Hey, you guys." Hailey braced herself as Sam jumped off the step and threw herself into her arms.

"Auntie, where were you? We've been waiting *forever* for you to get home. We went for a burger and came back and you *still* weren't here."

"Sorry, dumpling, I didn't know you were coming." Hailey kissed the little girl and then went over to Laura.

"So, just when you decide to come visit, I'm out shopping," she said in a light tone, but alarm bells were going off in her head. Something was up. Laura's eye makeup was smeared, and her eyes were bloodshot, and it looked as if she wasn't wearing any lipstick. Hailey hadn't seen Laura without lipstick since the day her sister turned thirteen and was finally allowed to wear it.

Sudden fear sent Hailey's pulse rocketing. "Is Mom okay?"

"Mom?" Laura sounded distracted. "I guess so. I dunno. Why are you worried about Mom?"

Hailey didn't answer. Well, at least that wasn't it, she thought as relief spilled through her. But there was still something fishy here. "Come on inside, all of you," she suggested, unlocking her back door and leading the way in, switching on lights. "It's getting too dark to sit outside. We can have herbal tea. Maybe the kids would like grape juice?"

"Should we bring our stuff in from the van, Mommy?" Samantha asked.

Stuff? What stuff? Hailey was more confused than ever.

"Leave it where it is for now."

"Maybe you guys could go out and bring in all the groceries from my car," Hailey said. She handed them the keys and they raced out.

Laura sank into a chair.

"My head is splitting." She sighed. "I've had the most horrendous day."

Hailey hadn't exactly had a terrific day herself,

but she decided not to mention it. She put the kettle on and waited, but her sister didn't say any more.

"What's going on, Laura?"

"I've left Frank."

Hailey was stunned. She stared at her sister and then pulled a chair close to her and took her hand.

"God, I'm so sorry. I had no idea. How come?"

"Because he's having another affair." Laura's voice was resigned.

Shock waves rippled through Hailey. "*Another* affair?"

Her sister gave a weary shrug. "Oh, it's a long story. He started right after we were married. There's probably more women than I know about, or care to know about. But this time he brought her to the house. The kids were at soccer practice and I guess he thought I was at the gym." Raw pain made Laura's voice tremble. "They were in the bedroom—in our bed, on *my* Porthault sheets. I walked in on them. Seeing him there with her…well, before I could ignore it, but this time I just couldn't."

Needing to hide her shock and revulsion, Hailey got up and made the tea.

"I just blew, Hailey. I walked out. I can't stand it anymore."

Hailey couldn't understand how her sister had stood it as long as she had.

The kids came in laden with bags, and Hailey took a packet of peanut-butter cookies and two glasses of milk into the tiny parlor where she kept her television.

"You guys can watch anything you like."

''We want your video about that lady who lived at Tara.''

The original *Gone With The Wind* was the only video she owned. It probably wasn't the best choice for seven- and nine-year-olds, but it was long and it would keep them occupied. Hailey plugged it in.

Back in the kitchen, she asked the question that was bothering her.

''How come you didn't leave before?''

''I threatened a couple of times. He's a lawyer. He told me I'd lose everything—the house, my car, even the kids. He's smart—he could probably do it.'' She gave Hailey a look, and for the first time her voice was angry. ''And if I left him, where would I go? What would I do? It's not as if I have a career to fall back on like you.''

There was resentment in Laura's voice, which surprised Hailey. She'd never thought her sister wanted anything to do with a career.

Laura patted her hair. ''And I'm used to living a certain way. It's horrible to think of...of having to count every penny and worry about bills and all that stuff.''

Hailey nodded, but she thought how much she would prefer counting pennies and worrying about bills to living with a philandering, arrogant bully.

Laura's anger suddenly gave way to more tears, and they rolled freely down her cheeks. ''I know I sound awful, thinking only about money, and I know the law would make him support the kids,'' she sobbed. ''But I've seen what happens to some women when he defends their husbands in a divorce proceeding. One of the partners divorced his wife last year. Frank handled the case for him, and the poor woman's working in a supermarket now. I saw her last week. She said her legal bills ate up most of the settlement she finally got, because her ex took her to court over and over. And Frank told me she got off easy compared with what would happen to me.''

Rage, hot and wild and sudden, burned its way through Hailey's veins. It was small consolation to learn that Frank was the creep she'd always suspected him of being.

''We'll just murder him and bury him in the backyard and avoid the whole court thing.'' She said it to lighten the atmosphere, but she actually felt like doing it. How dare that…that puffed-up waste of human skin treat her sister this way?

''I've thought about it.'' Laura sniffled, and Hailey found tissues and handed them to her. ''Mom doesn't know, so please don't say anything to her, okay, Hailey?'' Laura's voice was imploring. ''She'll just figure it's my fault.''

''Your fault?'' Hailey was astounded. ''How the heck could she ever think this was your fault?''

''She will. You know how much she likes Frank. I've tried sometimes to talk to her, but she doesn't want to know anything bad about him. She brags about him to the people she works with, how much money he makes, what a nice house we have, the fancy stores where she and I go shopping.''

It was pathetic, but Hailey knew it was true. Jean got a lot of mileage out of her son-in-law the lawyer.

And Frank played up to her, gave her an allowance each month, flirted with her. The way Jean simpered and ate it up made Hailey cringe.

"But she's going to have to know sooner or later." An awful thought struck Hailey. "Or are you— God, Laura, you're not planning on going back to him, are you?"

Hailey could see by the way her sister averted her eyes and flushed a deep red that she'd guessed correctly. Horror and pity jostled for space as she realized just how much Laura was willing to put up with.

Laura was studying her cup and still wouldn't meet Hailey's eyes. "I just thought maybe... Please, Hailey, could the kids and I stay with you until I sort of get over being so...so mad at him?"

How the dickens could anybody get over such betrayal? But she couldn't say that to Laura.

"Of course you can. As long as you like." But Hailey's heart sank. She was bringing David home tomorrow, and she'd so looked forward to being alone with him, to having him get used to her and the house. Now there'd be all these other people around. And, God help her, she'd even fantasized about her and Roy up in her bedroom...

"Thanks, Hailey." Laura blew her nose and got to her feet. "If you'll show us where we'll be sleeping, I'll get the kids settled. They're sort of hyper. I just told them we were visiting you for a sleepover. I didn't know what else to say to them."

Sometimes Laura was exasperating. "I think you're going to have to be more honest with them, and with Mom, too. I guarantee the kids already know more than you think. Does Frank know where you are?''

''No, I don't want him to know. And that's why I don't want Mom to know just yet. She'll tell him, and I...I just can't deal with him right now, or her, either. The kids don't go back to school for another two weeks. I'll get it sorted out by then.''

Two weeks. Hailey thought about her own life and felt resentful as hell, and then guilty for feeling that way. But this was going to cause any number of complications for her. It was going to mean lying to Jean, because the phone would start ringing as soon as she figured out that Laura wasn't at her own house. It was going to be tough on David, having a whole houseful of new people to get used to. It was going to be tough on her, as well, but as usual, Laura hadn't given that a single thought.

How many more things could go wrong today?

For the next hour, bedlam reigned as Hailey did her best to accommodate her guests in the two empty upstairs rooms. Fortunately it was summer, so at least it wouldn't be cold up there, but she didn't have beds. She did have bedding, thanks to Ingrid, who'd cleaned out her linen closet and given Hailey what she didn't need.

Hailey managed to borrow an inflatable mattress from a neighbor for Laura's room, and fortunately, in the back of the van, Laura had the foam mattresses that the kids used for camping. So everyone at least had a bed of some sort.

Compared with their luxurious rooms at home,

Hailey's upstairs bedrooms were primitive in the extreme, but Samantha and Christopher seemed to think it was an adventure, especially when Hailey smuggled marshmallows and lemonade up to them while Laura had a shower.

"Why is there a baby's bed in that little room beside yours, Auntie Hailey?" Samantha asked.

Laura hadn't even mentioned it.

"Because tomorrow I'm bringing a little boy here to live with me."

The two of them stared at her with huge, questioning eyes.

Christopher said, "How old is he? Can I play soccer with him?"

"He's two, so he's a little small for soccer. But he'll grow."

Samantha frowned. "Where are you getting him from? I thought babies were supposed to grow in your tummy. We grew in our mummy's tummy."

Christopher rolled his eyes. "Don't be such a dope, Sam. Some kids are adopted, that's what Auntie's gonna do. She's gonna adopt him, right, Auntie?"

"Right." She refused to think of the complications that might interfere with that procedure. Instead, she told them all about David, being honest but not dwelling on the fact that his mother had gone away and left him. The kids zeroed in on that, of course, and they had dozens of questions. Hailey had to think carefully before answering them. There was no fooling kids. If Laura thought these two had no idea what was going on she was in for a rude awakening.

When they'd run out of questions, she was so tired she could hardly get to her feet. She kissed them good-night, took a deep breath and went down to talk to Laura.

Her sister was sitting on the living-room sofa in maroon satin pajamas. She was smoothing some exotic-smelling lotion carefully onto her skin, and she looked disgruntled.

She scowled at Hailey. "Whatever happened to your downstairs bathroom? It looks as if a truck went through it. I hope your workmen are coming to fix it tomorrow."

Your workmen. Laura definitely lived in a different world. Hailey explained about the renovation and Roy's offer to help her with the bathroom. "I have to do it a little at a time. Neither of us has much time off and money's an issue. There's a company that will come and refinish the inside of the tub, but I wanted the walls and flooring repaired first."

"I'd do the bathtub. I've got scratches from the darned thing." Laura, fixated on the bathroom, didn't even ask about Roy. She didn't show the least sign of curiosity or interest at this hint of a man in her sister's life.

Feeling disappointed—it might actually have been fun to talk to Laura about him—Hailey went on, instead, to tell Laura about David. She knew her voice reflected the excitement she felt when she described him and said that she was bringing him home the following day.

But Laura just went on buffing her nails. "Mom said something about you getting too involved with some baby at St. Joe's. I guess I wasn't really paying much attention."

Hailey swallowed hard. It wasn't the first time Laura had acted as if her life was unimportant, but under the circumstances, her sister's attitude not only stung, it made her furious. This was obviously her day for losing her temper, Hailey thought, but she'd listened and sympathized with Laura over her marital problems, hadn't she? Was it too much to ask that her sister be just a little bit excited about the idea of Hailey becoming a foster mother?

She tried to tell herself that this was a difficult time for Laura, that she ought to cut her some slack. But it had always been the same between them—the events in Hailey's life took second place to whatever was happening with Laura. And she felt more and more resentful and bitter. Now that her sister was going to be around for a while, Hailey was going to have to get this out in the open.

She took a deep breath and with remarkable restraint, considering how angry she was, said, "It kind of hurts my feelings that you're not interested enough to even pay attention to what's going on in my life. After all, it's a pretty big thing for me, getting a baby."

"Well, it's a pretty big thing for me, walking out on Frank."

Hailey blew up. "Have you ever, just once in your entire selfish existence, considered that anybody else has a life except you? That other people have problems and…and things that make them happy or sad? You're my only sister. I'm trying to share something deeply personal and important with you here. Don't you even care?''

''Of course I care.'' Laura sounded petulant. ''It's just that your life has always been so easy.''

''Easy?'' Hailey figured her mouth had dropped open enough to show her tonsils. ''What the heck is easy about living alone, being in debt, working your buns off and deciding to be a single parent?''

At least Laura had stopped filing her nails. At least she was paying attention. She frowned at Hailey as if she truly didn't get it.

''But things have always been easy for you, Hailey. You got top marks in school, you knew what you wanted to do and went ahead and did it. Like this house—you didn't even ask anyone's advice.'' Laura sighed and then blurted, ''Damn. I've always been sort of jealous, I guess. I was never as smart as you, and I just couldn't do stuff on my own the way you did. I knew that getting married to Frank was what Mom wanted for me, and I thought he'd take care of me, so…''

Hailey was nearly speechless. ''You were *jealous?* Of *me?* But you're so beautiful, and I'm not. I always figured…I mean, you and Mom are so alike. Both of you made such a big issue about clothes and looks, and you were a unit. Oh, I know Mom loves me, in her way, but I've always thought you didn't really have much use for me. That you were ashamed or something.''

''Ashamed? Of you?'' Laura looked shocked and

then stricken. "God, Hailey, I remember when you were born. You were my baby sister and I couldn't wait for you to grow up so we could play together. I was so proud of you. Then when we got into our teens, our interests were so different. And then I got pregnant, and Mom said I had to marry Frank, and since then...well, I've tried hard, but I can't make it work."

For Hailey, one shock was following hard on the heels of the next. "I didn't know you were pregnant when you got married."

"Mom was furious at me. I lost the baby at five months. She said it was a blessing."

"Omigod. I remember when you had the miscarriage, but I thought you were only six weeks or so."

Laura shook her head and wiped the back of her hand across her eyes. "In spite of everything, I really, really wanted that baby."

"I'm sorry, Laura. I guess this is totally insensitive of me, landing all this stuff on you when you're down."

"I'm sorry, too. I guess it was just as insensitive of *me,* not paying attention to what you were saying."

"Yeah, it was. But then, you never do." There was no point lying about it. Hailey braced herself. Laura had a temper, too, and she'd probably explode now, pack up the kids and leave.

Instead, she said, "So who's going to take care of your baby while you work?"

Hailey explained about the nursery at St. Joe's. "I wish I could afford a nanny, but that's out of the question.'' She'd stewed about taking David to yet another strange place, but there really was no choice.

"While we're here, the kids and I could take care of him, if that's okay with you.'' Laura looked wistful. "I love babies.''

"That's great of you to offer.'' Hailey thought it over. "He's gonna be upset at first. He may cry a lot, be hard to handle.'' Hailey shuddered, remembering how he'd screamed today. She told Laura what had happened, and this time there was true compassion in her sister's eyes.

"Poor little guy. The kids are old enough not to mind sharing me. I could give him lots of attention. They'd help me with him. You know I'm good with kids, Hailey.''

"Of course you are. That's something we have in common.'' It was the first time she'd really thought much about what she and Laura had in common. She'd trust her sister with David. "Thanks, Laura. I'd really be grateful if you would, especially since I'm going back on nights. This way he can get used to his own crib and his own room before I have to take him to the nursery.''

She didn't get into the fact that some social worker she'd never met might be picking him up and taking him to see the irresponsible child who'd birthed him. She'd tell Laura about that tomorrow.

The phone rang, and both of them tensed. It might be Jean. Or it might be Frank. Hailey almost let the machine pick up, but on the fourth ring thought better of it, remembering she'd asked the nurses at St. Joe's to call if there was a problem with David.

"Hailey?" It was Roy, and her face flushed with pleasure.

Laura guessed she wanted privacy. She made her way upstairs, waggling her fingers in a silent goodnight.

"I'm sorry for calling so late. There was an emergency and I just got free."

"That's okay, I wasn't in bed or anything." She closed her eyes, letting the deep timber of his voice remind her of what it felt like to have him kissing her. But then her eyes sprang open again.

"There's nothing wrong with David, is there?"

"Not that I know of. I haven't had any calls about him. I wanted to know how you made out with him today."

"It was really bad. I was there all afternoon, but he finally cried himself to sleep." It was such a relief to be able to tell someone, to know that Roy understood how heartwrenching it had been for David—and for her.

"I'm sorry." He sounded it, and frustrated, as well. "The worst part is, there's not a damned thing I can do about it. Shannon's his mother—the judge will give her visiting privileges."

"You've seen other kids in this situation. How does it affect them in the long term?"

He was quiet for a moment, and when he answered, his words were guarded. "The ministry feels that in most cases, it's less damaging for the child to see his parent than not."

Her hand tightened on the phone. "But the kids don't understand. They don't know why the person they know as Mommy keeps on appearing and disappearing. Wouldn't it be better if—''

''There aren't any easy answers.'' His tone contained both anger and resignation. ''There are areas of my work, as I'm sure there are with yours, where I have to uphold policy even when I don't agree. I have to make myself believe, and most of the time I do, that we *are* helping, that what we do has value, that my job is worthwhile.''

Chastened, Hailey remained quiet.

''Dammit, Hailey.'' She heard him heave a sigh. ''I didn't call to give you a lecture about policy. Truth is, I didn't call just about David, either. I wanted to hear your voice.'' His tone deepened. ''I've been thinking of you all afternoon. You're really good at sitting on laps, you know.''

She felt herself blushing. What the heck was a girl supposed to say to that? She was *so* bad at this flirting thing. Why hadn't Laura taught her?

''I liked it.'' She only knew how to tell the truth. ''I've been thinking about you, too.'' She had. In some deep part of her, separate from everything else that had gone on during this long, chaotic day, she'd held on to the memory of that kiss.

''Hey, that's such a relief.'' She heard him take a long breath and then release it. ''We should talk about where we're going with this, Hailey.''

Where they were going? Alarm bells went off inside her. She figured she knew all too well where *she* was going.

Down a dead-end road with a broken heart at the bottom.

CHAPTER FOURTEEN

"THE TRUTH IS, you're driving me nuts," Roy said. "I want to know you, Hailey. On every level."

There was heat in his voice and no mistaking his meaning. Waves of feeling swept over and through her as her imagination careened down delicious paths.

"I'm going to hand this case over to Larissa the moment she's back from bereavement leave, because I don't want any business complications to interfere with our relationship, Hailey."

So now they had a relationship? Man, this was going fast. She wasn't sure how she felt about anything except that she wanted him something awful. She couldn't help that. She couldn't help the fear, either. She really didn't want a broken heart for Christmas—if this "relationship" lasted that long.

He broke the long silence. "Hailey, speak to me. Am I out in left field here all by myself? I know I'm pushing, probably too fast, but I need to know how you feel about me, because if the feeling isn't mutual, I'll just slit my throat or something. It's your call."

This was her chance. This was her opportunity to

get the hurt over with before it had a chance to turn into agony.

She opened her mouth to tell him yes, he had to back off, and no, she had no feelings for him whatsoever, but her traitorous tongue betrayed her. It didn't have a single thing to do with the bathroom repairs, either, she was pretty sure of that.

She heard herself croak, "It's mutual." *You maniac, what are you saying? It's not enough you're taking on a kid, and your sister's moved in for an indefinite time, and your mother's going to be royally pissed off at you, and your supervisor hates your guts. Now you need a guy in your life, as well?*

He made a sound in his throat, of pleasure and relief and anticipation. "Thank you," he growled. "I was beginning to think I'd have to chain you up somewhere and do nasty things to your body until you changed your mind."

That scenario played itself out fast and hot in her brain, and she shifted on the chair.

"I don't suppose you'd come out for a coffee with me, would you?"

"Now?" She glanced at the clock. It was ten past eleven.

"It's late, and I know you've had a long, tough day. It's unreasonable and thoughtless and selfish as hell of me to even ask. So will you?"

It was absolutely out of the question. She'd been up since dawn, she had a million things still to do— and there was a loneliness and hunger in his voice she was all too familiar with.

Maybe she wasn't as tired as she thought. "Sure.

I'll come for a quick coffee. I'd ask you to come here, but I have houseguests.''

"Thanks." He packed a lot of feeling into one little word. "I'll be there in ten minutes.''

IT ACTUALLY TOOK HIM only eight. He'd been heading toward her neighborhood the entire time he talked to her on his cell. If that wasn't optimism, he didn't know what was. He did know that he had to see her, and his reasons were totally selfish.

The day had escalated from the scene at St. Joe's with David screaming for his mother to the usual merry-go-round of meetings, questions and minor emergencies, most of which left him out of sorts, feeling frustrated with the system. He'd eaten dinner alone, driven around for an aimless hour and a half and then dialed Hailey's number because she was good and honest and real, and the kiss he'd shared with her that afternoon had been the best thing he'd done all day. He also needed to talk to someone rooted and sane and healthy. And sexy—sexy didn't hurt.

He hadn't meant to blurt out the things he had, hadn't planned to put her on the spot that way about her feelings. He'd taken one hell of a chance, laying it on the line. And she'd scared him half to death when she'd hesitated for that endless moment.

The rational part of his mind demanded, *What do you think you're doing, Zedyck?* But the part that had him on automatic pilot replied, *Damned if I know, but it feels right.*

He pulled up in front of her house and got out of

the car, but before he could make it halfway up her walk, she'd slipped out the door and was coming toward him.

There was a streetlight nearby, and he could see she was wearing jeans and a yellow T-shirt. Her long arms and legs reminded him of the half-grown colts he'd played with as a boy on the farm. Her wild hair stood out all around her head, and all he could see of her face was the flash of white teeth when she smiled.

"I'd ask you in, but my sister and her kids are staying with me."

"I didn't expect to go in." He waited until she was a single step away before he gathered her in his arms for what he intended to be a warm hug and ended up as a kiss that spiraled out of control. She felt pliant and soft in his arms, and he wanted to make love to her more than anything in the world.

He sniffed in the unique fragrance of her hair and skin, a mix of shampoo and the antibacterial soap they used at St. Joe's. It was more arousing than any fancy French perfume. Maybe he'd just kidnap her, take her to his apartment, strip her naked, explore that long body with his hands and tongue—

"I can't stay out long, Roy. I need some sleep, because I'm picking up David in the morning."

Timing, timing, timing. It was a lot like location, location, location.

He'd have to put his raging hormones on hold until the timing was right.

When he opened the car door for her, the overhead light brought her features into focus. He looked at her, and his breath caught. God, she was beautiful. Her beauty was in the strong lines of her face, the angle of her jaw, the way her ears lay flat against her skull. It was in her generous mouth, in her smile, in the way her body moved, in the endearing awkward folding of her long legs, the vulnerable slenderness of throat and waist.

Shaken, he started the car and drove slowly along the deserted urban streets, aware that she was staring at him.

"Bad day?"

He was about to deny it, but instead, he told the truth, that this was one of those times when he doubted the job, himself, the system. He'd never been able to share the details of his days with anyone but his sister Nicole. Other women hadn't wanted to know about pain and betrayal and, sometimes, death. But Hailey was a nurse; he instinctively knew she'd understand.

"Some days I feel as if all I'm doing is putting a Band-Aid on a festering sore," he admitted. "I feel like smashing something by the end of the day."

"I felt that way today, with David and his mother." She reached over and put a hand on his arm and squeezed in sympathy and understanding. "I felt helpless and furious listening to him scream for her that way."

"How the hell do you deal with it?" He had his own techniques—running until he was exhausted, visiting his parents, reassuring himself that there was good as well as evil, in the world, and that the good outweighed the evil.

"When battered kids come in, I used to get so worked up about it I felt physically sick," she said. "An older nurse noticed and talked to me about it. She pointed out that all that anger wasn't hurting the people I was aiming it at. They weren't even aware of it and probably wouldn't care if they were. It was only hurting me and draining my energy, and, in turn, diminishing the level of care I could give the poor little kid. It still makes me sick and angry when kids are deliberately hurt, but I've learned to get past it, to focus on the positive things I can give, instead of the negative stuff I can't control."

"Makes sense. You're a smart lady." He wasn't so sure he could succeed with the idea, but it gave him a new outlook.

"Nope. I know the formula, but I can't seem to apply it to Shannon Riggs, or Margaret, either. You saw how mad I was today."

"But you got past it."

"Not before I exploded at Margaret."

"How did it go with her? At the meeting."

"How did you know about that?"

"When Karen called to tell me Shannon was there, I asked her to get in touch with you, and she said you were already at St. Joe's, in a meeting. I surmised the rest."

"They dropped the complaint."

"Good. There shouldn't have been one in the first place."

"Thank you for the letter you sent on my behalf."

"My pleasure." Just being with her was pleasure,

in so many different ways. "So what made you lose your temper?"

"Margaret threatened to put a cover on David's crib to keep him in there."

"Wow. I thought stuff like that went out with the Dark Ages. Understandable you'd be mad."

"Not smart, though. Losing your temper doesn't get you anywhere. It feels good at the time, but it doesn't win the war. And I've always had a bad temper."

They laughed and then were silent, and even that was comfortable. He pulled up in front of a late-night café and they went inside.

Over coffee and servings of the mile-high coconut pie the place was famous for, they talked about books they'd read, movies they hadn't seen—they'd both been too busy all summer to get to the theatre—and their work.

Hailey told him about Brittany and the other kids on the ward she'd come to love, and he did the same. Their jobs were similar, and tragedy was sometimes the outcome with the kids they cared about.

"If you're at home next weekend, I'll come over and work on the bathroom," he offered.

"My sister would be grateful," she said. "For some strange reason, Laura wasn't impressed with that tub tonight."

"Is she visiting from out of town?"

"Nope." Hailey took a bite of her pie, then added, "She lives on the west side. She and her husband are having some marital problems, and she

and my niece and nephew are staying with me while
they sort them out.''

"I hope it works for them.'' He saw too many
broken homes, too many kids cast adrift as a result
of divorce.

She shot him a look. "I don't. She's married to a
prize prick, and I hope she comes to her senses and
divorces him. Trouble is, he's got her intimidated
because he's a bully, as well as a lawyer.''

"Does she have a lawyer?''

Hailey shook her head. "Do you think Nicole
would mind if I gave Laura her number? She needs
to talk to somebody unbiased and knowledgeable
who'll tell her that what her husband says is a
crock.''

"Nicole wouldn't mind at all. And if she's too
busy to take Laura's case, my extended family is
crawling with lawyers. Want me to give Nick a call
tomorrow and tell her Laura might be coming?''

"Please. Her last name's Quiggly.''

"Laura Quiggly.'' He folded the napkin and put
it in his pocket.

"I can't be sure Laura will even make an appointment, but thanks. Again.'' She grinned. "You seem
to be making a career out of helping me out. My
bathroom, that letter and now this.''

Roy couldn't think of a better way of spending
his time. He reached out and placed his hand over
hers.

It was long past midnight when they climbed
back in the car and he drove her home. He walked
her to the door. They hadn't spoken of what he'd

said to her on the phone, but it was there now, between them.

"Thank you for coming out with me," he said formally.

"Anytime, anyplace." Her grin flashed in the moonlight. "Although I'll be cursing you in the morning when it's time to get up. I want to bring David home as early as I can, before Margaret gets any more perverted ideas. Maybe you'd like to come by and see how he's making out," she suggested. "You could meet my sister and my niece and nephew."

He'd rather have her alone, but he'd take whatever he could get.

"I'll come by in the evening, if that's okay with you."

"Come for dinner. I'll get Laura to cook."

"You really know the way to a man's heart."

"Introducing you to all my relatives?"

"It's an age-old custom."

When he dipped his head to kiss her, there was no hesitation on her part. Her arms came around him, and her mouth was ripe and soft and eager, and he felt heat and suppressed passion in every line of her body. He wanted her then with a need that had him trembling before he reluctantly released her, pressing one last kiss to her swollen mouth before he let her go.

Her breathing was as rapid as his. "Good night, Roy."

"'Good night' isn't what I want at this moment,

but it's gonna have to get me through." He kissed her again, softly, with regret, and watched as she went in the house.

ALL THE LIGHTS were out, and Hailey slipped in the door, closing it quietly behind her.

"Sneaking in, huh?"

Hailey jumped and gasped when Laura's voice came out of the darkness.

"Sorry, I didn't mean to scare you. I couldn't sleep, and then the phone rang. Your machine took the message. Where'd you go at this hour, anyway? And who was the guy?"

"Just out for coffee." For an insane moment, she felt like a teenager sneaking in after making out with her guy. "That was Roy Zedyck, the social worker handling David's file." She wondered whether Laura had seen them kissing and decided she must have. The front window looked out on where they'd been standing.

"Good guy? Bad guy? Dangerous guy?" There was something wistful in Laura's voice.

"Good. Dangerous, too. For me, anyway. You'll meet him. I asked him for supper tomorrow night. I thought maybe I could talk you into making something?"

"Lasagna? I make great lasagna."

"Perfect." Hailey pushed the button that would play back her messages, and her heart caught in her throat when she heard Mary, the nurse who was on the peds ward tonight.

"Hailey, Karen said you wanted us to call you if

there was any problem with David. His temperature spiked and he's vomited three times in the last hour. I called the resident and he came and had a look at him, left an order for a suppository if the vomiting doesn't slow down. We're giving him a bath now to bring his temp down. We're taking good care of him, so don't feel you have to race over or anything, but I figured you'd want to know."

Of course she did. She had to go. David needed her.

Laura had been standing beside her, listening.

Hailey grabbed her purse from the table and her keys from the hook by the door. "You might as well crawl into my bed, Laura. I'll probably be at St. Joe's the rest of the night."

Laura tried to look regretful, but she couldn't quite manage it. "I'm sorry about David, but I have to admit I'm glad about the bed. That floor is not exactly the softest thing I've ever tried to sleep on."

Hailey was thinking about David, but she had to grin at her sister. "You are one spoiled lady. Ever hear about the princess and the pea?"

"Yeah, but didn't she marry a prince? I missed out on that deal—I got the frog, instead."

At least Laura still had a sense of humor. Hailey remembered about Nicole and dug her business card out of her wallet. "If you decide you wanna dump the frog, this is someone to go see. She's a friend of mine, and she's also Roy's sister. I'm pretty sure she's really good at what she does."

It was encouraging that Laura even accepted the card.

"See you in the morning," Hailey said, and then

felt warm and fuzzy all over when, for the first time in years, her sister grabbed her close and hugged her tight.

AT ST. JOE'S, Mary was sitting beside the door holding David, wrapped in a big blue blanket. His hair was damp and his face flushed, and when he saw Hailey, he held out his arms and whimpered.

"Hey, punkin, what's up with you?" She scooped him into her arms and kissed his hot cheek.

"Hailey, you shouldn't have trekked out here in the middle of the night." But Mary looked relieved. "Sick as he is, he won't stay in his crib. He climbs out and comes to the door and lies down on the floor. It makes me want to cry."

Hailey had been thinking about it on the way in.

"Why don't we just move his crib out here for the time being? I'm taking him home first thing in the morning, as soon as Harry Larue signs the release. I'll stay till then, anyway. No point in driving home and coming back. We can move the crib back before Margaret comes on shift."

Mary's forehead wrinkled in thought and then she nodded. "Let's do it. I'll go get it now—that way at least he might sleep. Being held all the time isn't very restful, for him or for us."

The crib made the difference. Hailey rocked David until he was sleepy and then laid him in it. He turned his head so he could see the door, clutched Bonzo to his cheek and finally fell asleep.

Hailey spent what remained of the night on a cot in a room nearby. Drained and exhausted, she awoke with a start at seven, when the new shift of nurses arrived. Incredibly enough, David was still sleeping, bottom in the air, head facing the door.

In the staff washroom, Hailey showered quickly, hoping the hot water would take away the muzziness in her head. She kept a change of clothes in her locker, and David was awake by the time she'd changed. He was cranky and restless, refusing fluids. Karen took his temperature.

"It's still way up," she said.

"Look at this." Hailey was changing his diaper.

A sprinkling of angry red spots peppered his round belly.

"There's more coming out on his neck, as well. What do you think, Karen? Chicken pox, measles?"

"Nobody else seems to have symptoms," Karen said. "We're gonna have to move him into an isolation unit."

Although she knew it was necessary, Hailey felt totally defeated. Whatever this was, it was doubtful Harry Larue would sign any release for her to take David home today. And unless things had changed overnight, David was going to scream and fight when they moved him, and that was going to challenge his immune system even further.

"We'd better get it done before Margaret arrives," Karen suggested.

The move went exactly the way Hailey had thought it would.

As soon as he was away from the door, David started screaming and climbing out of his crib. Hailey held him and did everything she could think of to distract him, but ten minutes later, he was still screaming and she was beginning to panic. Margaret would be coming on shift soon and undoubtedly would insist on either restraints or a cover on the crib. And now David's entire face and body were covered in red spots.

Hailey fought the idea, but there was only one thing to do.

She rang the call button, and Karen came.

It hurt to say the words, and her voice was harsh. "Get hold of Roy and ask him to bring Shannon Riggs here. And have him tell her she has to stay right here with David until he's better."

It took the better part of two hours. Harry Larue arrived, and his jovial face puckered into a frown when he saw David, who was still sobbing intermittently and refusing any liquids.

Hailey held David down while Harry examined him. The rash was a mystery, neither measles nor chicken pox. Harry thought it was likely a food allergy, but that didn't account for the fever or vomiting.

"We'll keep him here for another twenty-four hours," he decided. "I know you were looking forward to taking him home, but I'd like to see him feeling really well again before he leaves."

When Harry left, David refused to eat and drank only a quarter of his bottle of juice, no matter how much Hailey coaxed.

Margaret came by and looked in, but to Hailey's relief she left without commenting.

Hailey was rocking David and her back was to

the door, but she knew by the sudden stiffening of his body the exact moment when Shannon arrived.

"Mama." There was a husky catch in his voice. He was hoarse from crying, but he managed to smile at Shannon. His arms went out to her, and for just an instant, Hailey wished with all her heart she'd never laid eyes on either of them.

CHAPTER FIFTEEN

SHANNON LOOKED as if she hadn't slept much. Her eyes had huge dark circles beneath them, and her hands were visibly trembling when she held them out to David, who almost leaped into her arms, snuggling his face into her shoulder. He strung together a series of words, indecipherable except for *Mama*.

Hailey held out the bottle of apple juice and the tray with his uneaten cereal and fruit. "See if you can get him to eat and drink something," she snapped. "He needs nourishment."

"What's wrong with him? What are these red spots?"

"The doctor thinks maybe an allergy."

"He's never had any allergies." Shannon offered the bottle to David and he took it and began to swallow in great gulps. His eyelids fluttered and closed, and he knotted one plump fist in Shannon's T-shirt.

Hailey went to the nurses' lounge. She made toast and ate a slice, but her stomach was roiling. When she returned to David's room, he was asleep in his crib and Shannon was sitting in a chair, one leg drawn up beneath her, a paperback novel in her hand.

"He ate everything and then he went to sleep."

Shannon gave her a defiant look and gestured at the empty food containers and bottle.

"I want to talk to you. Come outside for a minute." Hailey led the way out into the ward and around a corner to a visitors' waiting room, which was empty. She turned and faced Shannon.

"I wonder if you have any idea what you've done to David, how seriously you've damaged him." She kept her voice low and conversational, but the overwhelming emotion she felt made it quaver.

Shannon's eyes grew big and she held up a hand, palm front, but Hailey wasn't about to stop now.

"He was brought into emerg after being alone for three days. Your son was too little to even reach a water tap and get a drink, much less find any food. He had blisters on his bottom from feces, and he'd cried until he had no voice left to cry with. He was unconscious when they brought him in, and in another few hours, maybe a day, he would have died. When he came to, you were the person he asked for, over and over." She kept her gaze on Shannon's face. Her sallow skin had turned greenish white, and tears swam in her eyes.

Angry as she'd ever been, Hailey felt only satisfaction at confronting Shannon. "As if it wasn't enough to desert him, you waltzed back in here yesterday, after he'd adjusted to us, to being here, and when you left, he screamed for hours. He kept an all-night vigil at the door to the ward, Ms. Riggs. He grew hysterical when we tried to move him, and he developed a fever and that rash and wouldn't eat.

The doctor can find no physical reason for it, so we can only assume it's emotional.''

Shannon was crying now, mouth open, sniffling like a child. She rubbed her shirtsleeve over her eyes and runny nose.

''I love David.'' Hailey knew she sounded fierce now. ''I've been approved to foster him, and I want to take him home and take care of him the way he deserves, the way *you* didn't care enough to do. But before that can happen, he needs to rest and relax and get well again, and he can't do that unless you stay here with him. He's only two—he doesn't understand why you'd desert him.'' She added in an icy voice, ''Frankly, neither do I, but you're the one who has to live with what you've done to him.''

''You...you shouldn't talk to me this way,'' Shannon whined. ''I took good care of him. That was the only time—''

''Once is all it takes, isn't it?'' The impotent rage Hailey felt toward this girl spilled out in sarcasm. ''Do you think you can possibly manage to give him your attention for maybe a couple days and nights, so he has a chance to get out of here?''

Shannon's face was stricken. ''You want him—that's what this is about. You want my baby.''

Savage now, Hailey said, ''Someone has to want him and love him and care for him, don't you think?''

Crying in earnest now, Shannon turned and ran from the waiting room, and for a few moments Hailey felt vindicated. She'd said what she'd been feeling and thinking, and she told herself that Shannon deserved to hear it. But then she began to regret her outburst.

Shannon was right—she did want Davie. But was her own need interfering with her role as a caring professional? She was an adult, and Shannon Riggs was only a teenager, a sad, skinny kid far too young to have a child. The words Hailey had used were harsh and judgmental. Would she have been more understanding if she weren't so personally involved?

"Damn." Hailey walked up and down the corridor, trying to shake the guilt and shame that clung to her like a bad odor. She wasn't thinking straight. She was still pacing when she heard her name called.

"Hailey Bergstrom." Margaret came sailing toward her like a heat-seeking projectile, nostrils flaring, breath huffing in and out. "I know you feel you're above reproach, but this time you've gone too far."

Margaret was in a rage, and the dislike she felt for Hailey was evident in her scathing look. "How dare you take it upon yourself to upset that child's mother in such a fashion? I won't have such unprofessional behavior from a nurse on my ward."

Hailey's instinctive reaction was to turn her back and walk away. She didn't need this on top of everything else. But a tiny, nagging voice was telling her that this time, however galling she might find it, Margaret was right.

"You will apologize to her," the head nurse ordered. "She's in the child's room."

Didn't Margaret ever ask, instead of ordering?

"Okay. I'll apologize. What I did was wrong."

It was almost worth humbling herself just to see the shock on Margaret's face. She'd obviously expected an argument or a flat-out refusal.

"I'll go do it right now."

Hailey walked down the hall to David's room. She opened the door to find Shannon huddled on the chair, knees up, forehead resting on them. When the girl looked up and saw Hailey, she lifted her chin defiantly, but her face was still wet with tears.

Hailey gestured for her to come out into the hall so David wouldn't be disturbed. Shannon did so, but with visible reluctance.

"Look, I'm sorry for what I said," Hailey began. This was hard to do, but she knew it was the right thing. "I was way out of line. He needs you badly right now, and I was wrong to upset you."

Shannon went on the offensive. "Yeah, well, he's my kid, just remember that, Bergstrom. And *nobody's* gonna take him away from me." There was a manic tone to her voice. "Maybe you'll have him for a few weeks. I can't do anything about that until I go through rehab and stuff. I can visit him, though, the lawyer said so. And I'll get him back because I'm his *real* mother. He'll remember me."

She shot Hailey one last burning look, then spun on her heel and went back into David's room.

That was what she got for trying to do the right thing, Hailey fumed as she hurried out of the hospital, found her truck and headed home. The girl's words bothered her. How likely was it that Shannon would get custody of David again? Not very, Hailey consoled herself. She had both Shannon's track record and Roy's support on her side. There was no way a judge would hand David back.

With all that had happened, she'd forgotten about Laura and the kids. It was a shock all over again to see the red van in front of her house, hear the kids laughing in the backyard. She felt mean, but this was one day when she really wanted the house to herself.

Well, she was having a run on not getting what she wanted, wasn't she?

Sam and Christopher, wearing perfectly coordinated shorts and tops, were outside playing with Skippy. They came and greeted her with hugs and questions about where the baby was.

Weary and depressed, Hailey explained.

Laura was in the kitchen, boiling pasta and sautéing onions and fresh tomatoes for the lasagna. She had a dish towel pinned around her middle to protect her narrow, green twill skirt and matching sleeveless blouse, and her hair and makeup were flawless.

How did anybody manage to look like that before ten in the morning?

She glanced at Hailey. "You look wrecked—you mustn't have slept at all. And where's your little boy?"

"You look your usual gorgeous self, and he's with his useless birth mother at St. Joe's." Sick to death of explaining, Hailey did so once again.

"Well, sounds like you did the best you could," Laura said. "And he'll be coming here soon, so why don't you use the time to get some sleep? You won't get much afterward. That bed of yours is actually quite comfortable."

"Thanks, I've noticed." Hailey collapsed in a chair. Every bone in her body ached right along with her head. "I'm going to have to sleep awhile, all right. I'm suicidal when I'm this tired."

Laura added spices to the tomato sauce. "It'll be quiet here—we're going out. The kids have soccer camp and then swimming lessons, and I have errands and an appointment with the hairdresser. I have to leave in a few minutes and we probably won't be back until after five today. Could you put the lasagna in the oven at four? I made a chocolate cake—it just needs to be iced. It's on top of the bread bin. And the salad greens are washed and in the fridge."

In spite of the cooking, the kitchen was cleaner than it had probably ever been.

Hailey said, "You are amazing. You wanna stick around for a couple of years? I've always wanted a wife."

"I'd rather have one than be one." Laura dumped tomato paste into the sauce. "I'm thinking of calling that lawyer."

"So do it."

"There's just one little problem."

"You mean besides having to sleep on my floor until you win the house away from Frank?"

"There's that, and also the fact that I'm pregnant."

"Omigod. How far along?" Hailey sat up and gaped at her sister.

"Six weeks."

"Does Frank…?"

Laura shook her head. "Nope." She blushed and paid more attention to assembling the lasagna than was necessary. "The thing is, I don't think it's Frank's."

CHAPTER SIXTEEN

HAILEY'S WORLD was turning bottom side up.

"Then whose baby is it?"

"Michael Bjorn's. The kids' soccer coach."

Hailey's head was spinning. "Married?"

"Divorced."

"So…are you in love with him?"

Laura nodded, but she looked miserable.

"Does he know? About the…" Hailey gestured at Laura's flat belly.

"Nope. And I'm not going to tell him."

Hailey closed her eyes and blew out a breath. "I hate to break this to you, but it's not something you can hide for very long."

"If he knows it's his, he'll insist I divorce Frank and marry him. I don't know whether I want to be married to anybody. And I don't want to *have* to get married a second time, either. Besides, if Frank finds out this baby isn't his, it'll give him all the ammunition he needs to crucify me in court."

"Does Michael have kids?"

Laura shook her head. "They couldn't have any. He wanted them."

So this would be his first. Hailey whistled. "You're in a major mess, big sister."

"Yup. That's why I don't want Mom to know." Laura glanced at the clock and covered the lasagna pan with aluminum foil. "I'm also gonna be late. Don't forget to put this in. See you at dinner."

When she left, Hailey sat for a while, too stunned and weary and overwhelmed to go up to bed. Her world, her life had been predictable for so long—the job she loved at St. Joe's, visits with Ingrid and Sam, much rarer ones with her sister and mother, work on her house.

Now, in the space of a couple of weeks, a bomb had gone off and everything had changed. She'd gone head-to-head with Margaret, she'd found out her sister wasn't at all what she'd believed her to be, and she'd fallen in love, not just with a baby, but also with a man. Most astounding of all, the man actually seemed to have feelings for her, as well. For the time being, at least.

It was too much for her overtaxed brain to process. She got up and, one step at a time, climbed the stairs, stripped off her clothes and fell into bed.

SHE AWOKE to the telephone ringing. She fumbled for the phone beside the bed.

"It's me," Laura said. "I'm calling because I won't be coming back for dinner tonight. The kids are having sleepovers with their friends, and, um, I'm...well, I'm with Michael."

"Okay." Hailey's groggy brain worked its way slowly around all that.

"You sound half-asleep. Have you put the lasagna in yet?" Trust Laura to remember the lasagna.

The doorbell rang.

"Not yet. I just woke up."

"Well, you should. It needs to cook for an hour."

The doorbell rang again, more insistently this time.

"Okay. Look, I have to go. Someone's at the door."

"I'll see you in the morning, then."

So Laura was planning a sleepover of her own. Hailey pulled on the gray shorts and blue T-shirt that were flung on the chair and staggered downstairs.

"Did I get the wrong day?" Roy was standing at the door smiling at her. In one hand he held two bottles of wine in a plastic bag and in the other a bouquet of pink roses.

ROY COULD SEE she'd been asleep. Her cheek was creased from the pillow, and her eyes were still heavy-lidded. Her hair was flat on one side, and she obviously wasn't wearing a bra under her rumpled shirt. Her legs were long and brown and enticing. She looked sexy and disheveled, blinking at him with those sleepy tiger eyes.

"Nope, it's okay. It's the right day. I just... Darn, I fell asleep. What time is it, anyhow?"

"Six. The exact time you said to come for dinner."

"Oh, yoiks." She wrinkled her nose and then yawned. "Come on in. Laura and the kids aren't going to be here, and I haven't put the lasagna in the oven yet." She took the wine when he handed it to her. One bottle was white, the other red. "Could you put those roses in something and then open one of these and pour yourself a glass while I go to the bathroom?'' She handed the wine back to him and pointed. ''The glasses are up in that cupboard.''

''Why don't I put the lasagna in, as well?''

''Sarcasm, sir?'' She grinned, which was what he'd aimed for.

''No, absolutely not. Would you believe starvation?''

''I should have guessed. In that case, go right ahead, knock yourself out. There's probably an apron in one of those drawers. Oven's supposed to be at 350. Salad greens are washed and in the fridge. Garlic bread just needs heating.''

He did everything, because she was gone a long time. He was setting the table when she came back, and he could see she'd had a shower. Her face was shiny clean and her hair curled in damp red ringlets around her ears.

''Sorry I was so long. I called St. Joe's to find out how David is.''

''And?''

''He's feeling better. He's asleep. His— Shannon is still there. She's staying the night.''

''For his sake, that's a good thing.''

She nodded, but he could see how much the situation troubled her.

''You look wonderful.''

''Thank you.'' She'd put on a loose green summer dress that left her arms and shoulders bare and stopped well above her knees. She hadn't bothered with shoes, and he was pretty certain she wasn't wearing a bra, which he thought was a great idea.

"You're really good." She looked around, taking in the lasagna in the oven, the salad on the counter, the two wineglasses he'd filled. He'd stuck the roses in an empty glass jar from the top of her cupboard and placed them in the middle of the table, along with a candle he'd found on the windowsill.

"I've flipped through a couple of women's magazines in my time. I know how these things go." He handed her a glass of red wine.

She sipped and made an appreciative sound in her throat. "That lasagna won't be done for an hour." Was that a seductive look she was giving him, or was he hallucinating? "What should we do in the meantime?"

He knew what he wanted to do. "We could work on the bathroom." And that wasn't it.

"I thought of that, but I don't feel like it."

What he did feel like doing wasn't something he wanted to verbalize. *Show, don't tell, Zedyck.* Reaching out, he took the wineglass from her and set it on the counter. The easy way she came into his arms told him that their minds just might be on the same wavelength.

She tasted of wine and toothpaste. The sound she made in her throat was of pleasure and greed, and when he deepened the kiss, she pressed herself against him, from breasts to eager hips. The blood left his head and pooled in his groin in a flood of wanting.

"I like how you kiss." This time she was the one

who tilted her head, found his lips, traced them with her tongue. "Do it some more."

"I need to touch you." He had to feel her skin, hot and bare against his hands, or die. He gripped and lifted the hem of the short dress, moving his palms slowly up the back of her thighs. Delicious surprise made him pause an instant and catch his breath when he realized she wasn't wearing panties. Her rounded bottom was firm and silky bare against his hands.

The implicit invitation sent a sexual rush through him, and the way her body trembled made him want to take her right then and there, on the kitchen counter, on the floor, on the table.

"Hailey, I want you."

"I want you, too." Her voice was shaking. "Right now. Let's go upstairs."

"Can't wait that long." Much closer was the couch in the living room. Or the rug. Or the tile on the hall floor—he was beyond caring.

Holding her against him, kissing her every step of the way, he walked her backward through the hall, and when the backs of her knees hit the sofa, she tumbled down, taking him with her.

The dress slid off over her head, and there was enough light to see that her breasts were perfect, small, rounded, pink-tipped. Her body was long, golden, inviting, and she was shivering. The temperature had to be in the high eighties, so it wasn't ego that made him think she was as hungry for him as he was for her.

She looked at him and whispered, "Take your clothes off. Hurry."

It took all of ten seconds for him to get naked, grateful for the condoms he'd optimistically slid into his pants pocket.

He kissed her, greedy for mouth and breasts, throat and earlobes, belly and beyond—every part of her his lips could reach. They were too tall for the sofa, so he maneuvered them down to the rug, dragging along the cushions to pillow their heads.

The phone rang, and they both ignored it.

He told himself to go slowly, but the way she moved and moaned when he kissed and stroked her drove him way beyond slowing down.

She arched against him, and his fingers slipped into liquid, throbbing heat. And she climaxed like that, so quick and hard he couldn't restrain himself any longer.

"Hailey. God, you're so hot." He wound his fingers into her hair and slid into her, and the convulsions that rocked her seconds before began all over again, only this time he was right there with her.

THE CARPET WAS ROUGH against her back, but she didn't care. She didn't care about a darned thing, and it was the best feeling in the world.

Stretching, she drew the musky, delicious smell of their lovemaking deep into her lungs, then snuggled more deeply into Roy's arms. Her head was on his shoulder, their legs intertwined.

He had great shoulders. He had great everything. She loved the hair on his chest, the roughness of his beard scraping against her in places where her skin was soft. Her body was limp and warm, and sensitive nerves were still sending aftershocks of pleasure shooting through her.

This wasn't love, she tried to tell herself.

"It's just endorphins," she said aloud.

"Endorphins, huh?" His voice was thick and sleepy and unbearably sexy.

"This fantastic feeling after sex—it's just the endorphins in your bloodstream." Not that she believed it, of course.

"Hardly the most romantic explanation I ever heard."

She could tell by his voice that he was smiling. She wondered how long he'd go on smiling if she told him the truth about what she was feeling. From everything she'd read, and what she'd heard from the women she worked with, guys got really nervous when a woman said the L-word after sex.

He sniffed and sniffed again. "What's that smell?"

"That's just us. It's— Omigod, it's not. It's the lasagna. If I let that burn, Laura's gonna kill me. She made the whole thing from scratch." Hailey struggled out of his embrace, clambered to her feet and hurried to the kitchen. She grabbed pot holders from the drawer, then opened the oven door too fast and swore creatively as heat scorched tender parts of her anatomy.

"That's a great word. Seems to me we used it differently a few minutes ago." He was right behind her. "Is it burned?"

"It may not be, but I am. Maybe it just spilled over, and that's what's burning. I hope so, anyhow." She lifted the pan out with great care, holding it far away from her naked body as she settled it on a hot pad on the counter.

She turned and looked at him, and started to giggle.

"You haven't got a stitch of clothes on." All of him was spectacular, but she particularly liked his bum. Nurses saw lots of bums, so she had ample grounds for comparison.

"Neither have you." He was giving her a heavy-lidded look that made her doubly conscious of being buck naked.

"Are you hungry?" The way to a man's heart, et cetera, she thought. "I'm famished." Her stomach rumbled as if to prove the point.

"I'm always hungry." But the look he was giving her suggested that it might not be for food.

"Okay, let's put some clothes on and we can—"

"Uh-uh." He put a hand on her arm and she stood still.

"No? No what?" Her heart sank. He looked serious.

Picking up one of the wineglasses, he used two fingers to smear red wine on her nipples. She stopped breathing.

Then he leaned closer, not touching her with anything but his tongue, and licked it off.

It was the most imaginative thing anyone had ever done to her, and she could see it excited him as much as it did her. There were advantages to being naked.

He must have thought so, too, because he said, "You're beautiful the way you are. Don't put any clothes on."

She digested that. "You mean...you mean you want us to eat lasagna in our birthday suits?"

"Yup." His eyes were challenging. "Dare you."

She thought it over for a moment. There were curtains on all the windows. Nobody was likely to come to the door. What the heck—how many chances had she ever had to be kinky?

"Okay." She found the wine bottle and refilled their glasses. She was going to need all the false courage she could swallow to carry through with this, but it would sure give her something to remember.

The phone rang, and she ignored it. The machine could take the message.

With extreme caution, she loaded their plates with lasagna and salad, and they sat down. She was very glad she'd made soft cushions for the wooden chairs. She was glad, too, of the generous tablecloth. All that showed when she was sitting were her shoulders and her breasts. Which was bad enough, because in terms of size, they weren't anything to write home about. At least there wasn't enough of them to droop onto her plate.

The thought of her nipples resting in the lasagna made her laugh, and although he didn't know what it was about, he laughed, too. Or maybe he did know; she was beginning to realize that Roy Zedyck had depths to him you'd never suspect.

He'd had his way with the clothes thing. She'd go for the head trip.

"How come you're still single, Roy? It's obvious you really like kids." *And you're gorgeous to look at and have a repertoire in bed that any sex-minded woman would love to come home to.*

He could have deflected the question, turned it into a joke. She half expected him to, but instead, he frowned, and she could tell he was trying hard to give her an honest answer.

"I'm not exactly sure why. You're right. I'd like a family of my own, but it's just never happened. In my early twenties, I remember wanting to meet someone and settle down. I still feel that way, but maybe I've gotten too selective. Too picky. I've heard it gets worse the older we get."

As far as she knew, "selective" meant looks and personality and compatibility and libido and plain old kindness. Those things were always on the lists the single nurses made to detail what qualities they wanted in a partner. The married ones made lists of the things they didn't want, which as far as she could figure out were pretty much habits of the guys they were married to, including such things as smoking or chewing tobacco and farting in bed.

"Picky how?" It wouldn't hurt to have him detail all the things she couldn't provide, would it? Well, it might hurt some, but it would be good to know exactly why this wasn't going to work.

Damn, it was hard to carry on a sensible conversation across the table from that bare, furry chest and those great shoulders. To say nothing of what she knew was hidden by the tablecloth. She had to give him credit, though. He was giving this conversation thing his best shot.

"Last time around it was a difference in values. She wanted the good life, fancy car, big house, trips to the latest vacation hotspot. A social worker's salary doesn't allow for those kind of extras, and even if it did, I'm not interested in living that way."

Neither was she. "That's one of Ingrid's favorite truisms—money doesn't buy happiness." All she had to do was think of Laura to appreciate that.

"Ingrid and my mom went to the same school of *isms*." He smiled and forked up another mouthful of lasagna, chewed it and swallowed.

"What else?" This wasn't too helpful. He'd obviously been involved with pretty shallow women. God, he had nice forearms. Hands, too. She shivered, remembering where those hands had been.

"The other sore point's been my job, the amount of time it demands, the unpredictable hours. And women have a valid point there. It's tough to be with someone who doesn't work a regular nine-to-five day. Not that I need to tell you about that."

"I've thought sometimes of getting on steady days, but I sort of like shifts. I get to see the kids at bedtime, in the morning and during the night." And she'd never had a guy around long enough to complain about her hours, anyway. "So who ended them? Your relationships."

He shrugged. "Me, I guess. I could see it wasn't gonna work, so I got out early."

"Before the women had a chance to?" This was good info, she told herself. She'd know what to expect. She might not know when, but it was still good to know what was in store. The lasagna stuck in her throat. "Have you ever been in love?" *Hell, yeah, Bergstrom, just psychoanalyze the guy right out the door.* But these were important questions. "The kind of love where you wanted to get married and have kids? You must have had lots of opportunities."

He took a slice of garlic bread and shook his head. "Not as many as all that. I've dated a fair amount—all of us have by the time we reach thirty-six. But love, I dunno. I *thought* I was in love twice, the happy-ever-after kind. But the first woman couldn't make up her mind between me and someone else, and like I told you, the second one wanted a different lifestyle. Both times it was pretty obvious it wouldn't work." She could see he was getting uncomfortable, and then he turned the tables on her.

"What about you, Hailey? How come you're not married? I've seldom seen anyone more suited to having a houseful of kids."

She had nothing to lose by being honest. Maybe it had something to do with sitting here naked. "I used to think it was because I wasn't beautiful." It was hard to say out loud.

He looked as if he wanted to protest, and she was glad when he didn't. Facts were facts.

"But then I got it through my head that lots of women who aren't technically beautiful fall in love and get married,'' she went on. ''So I had to dig a little deeper than that.''

''And?''

''And I think that in psycho-jargon, I have big issues with abandonment.''

He looked surprised, and then slowly nodded. ''Because of your dad dying when you were so young?''

He was quick, this guy. But then he'd probably had to take his share of psych courses to get his degree, just as she had.

She nodded. ''Other things, too. My mom and my sister are really alike, and even though they didn't mean to, they sort of excluded me while I was growing up. They had a club that I didn't understand and certainly didn't belong to.''

''Ever been in love?''

''Yup.'' Boy, this naked thing was intimate, all right. People at nudist camps mustn't have any secrets at all. ''Once. I was in training, and he was a second-year med student.''

''What happened?''

''He let me take care of him for six months and then he dumped me for a lab tech.''

''What a jerk.''

''Yeah.'' And she was abandoned again.

''Didn't you get right back on the horse?''

''Not really.'' You couldn't call Norman Patino a real, honest-to-goodness attempt. ''I decided to skip B and go straight to C. Skip the husband part and go for the baby, instead.''

Roy had finished his second helping of lasagna.

Just as she stood up to take their plates to the sink, someone rang the front doorbell. A second later she heard Jean hollering, "Hailey? Hailey, are you in there?"

"Omigod." Hailey dropped the plates and one of them shattered on the tile floor. "Quick, get some clothes on. It's my mother."

Roy was right behind Hailey in the race for their clothing, strewn across the living-room carpet.

CHAPTER SEVENTEEN

HAILEY PULLED ON her dress to the persistent dinging of the doorbell, searching frantically for her panties until she remembered she hadn't been wearing any.

Roy was yanking on his shirt and zipping up his jeans. She saw his blue briefs on the rug and kicked them under the couch.

"Okay?" He reached out and smoothed her hair.

"Okay." She turned his shirt collar right side out, then went to the door and opened it.

"Hi, Mom." She sounded chirpy. She hated chirpy.

"Hailey, where were you? I've been ringing forever. Were you in bed?" Jean glanced past her and must have seen Roy. "Oh, sorry. I didn't realize you had company."

"Come on in." It was the last thing Hailey wanted, but there weren't a lot of choices here. "This is Roy Zedyck, David's social worker," she babbled as Jean stepped inside. "We were just having dinner—" Hailey stopped herself and drew a sane breath. "Roy, my mother, Jean Bergstrom."

"Pleased to meet you, Mrs. Bergstrom."

"Call me Jean. Nice to meet you, Ron."

"Roy."

"Sorry. Roy."

"Come and sit—" Hailey realized too late that all the sofa cushions were on the floor and did a swift right turn toward the kitchen.

"Come and sit in here."

Of course Jean had noticed the cushions. How could she miss them?

But she was running true to form. She didn't seem to be noticing much of anything, which for the first time ever was a blessing.

"We were just having dinner. Would you like some lasagna, Mom?"

"No, I— Good Lord, Hailey, did you break something?"

She'd steered her mother into the kitchen, forgetting about the pieces of crockery scattered over the tile.

"Sorry, watch where you step. I dropped a plate." She bent and scooped up pieces and tossed them into the garbage, feeling like a nitwit.

Jean bent down and helped her. "You'll have to get the tiny bits with a wet paper towel," she instructed, and Roy tore off a wad and held it under the tap. Now all three of them were down on the kitchen floor. Hailey had a hysterical urge to giggle, and she wondered if her mother could tell she had no underwear on.

She smoothed her dress down and got to her feet, and Jean followed. Roy stayed down, meticulously swooping the wet paper towel over the tile, getting every last splinter.

"Sure you won't join us?" Hailey gestured at the table, where the remains of the salad were wilting and red-wine splotches stained the tablecloth. It didn't look very inviting.

"I can't stay. Is there something wrong with your phone, Hailey? I called twice."

"We were busy. Talking." Damn, that sounded so defensive. She was twenty-nine years old; she had a right to a sex life. But her skin didn't get the message, because she could feel herself turning crimson.

Again, Jean didn't seem to notice. Sometimes there were advantages to having a mother who was oblivious to your life.

"Hailey, do you have any idea where your sister is?"

Jean's question caught her off guard, although she ought to have expected it. Why else would Jean drive all the way to her younger daughter's house on a weekday evening?

Hailey glanced around in a panic, wondering if any of the kids' toys were in evidence, but thanks to Laura's housekeeping skills, there was nothing in sight except what was left of the lasagna.

"No, I don't." She *didn't* know, not in the literal sense; Laura hadn't told her where Michael lived. Hailey prayed that Jean wouldn't ask if she knew what Laura was doing.

She didn't. "Well, Frank's worried sick about her. Apparently she left him a note saying she was taking the kids away until school started, but she didn't say where she was going. And she never said a single word to me. I can't believe she'd just go off without telling me. I think she's having some sort of breakdown.''

Jean sounded hurt and angry and worried, but Hailey didn't cave in. She'd promised Laura, and under the circumstances it seemed safest to say as little as possible.

It dawned on her that Roy knew Laura and the kids were staying here. He was looking at her and she could see the puzzlement on his face.

Damn her sister, anyway. Now the man was going to think she was a practiced liar.

''Tea, Mom? Coffee? A glass of wine?'' Hailey felt like taking the bottle and downing it, and then opening the other one for good measure. ''A piece of cake?'' It still wasn't iced, but what the heck.

''No, I should be going, although I haven't a clue who to try next. You don't suppose Frank's sister might know where Laura's gone.''

''I doubt it.'' Jean must really be desperate. She knew Laura had always despised Frank's sister. Suddenly Hailey felt sorry for her mother. ''I'm sure that wherever she is, she's just fine, Mom. Maybe she just needed to get away for a while.''

Jean gave her an incredulous look. ''Away from *what?* She has everything a woman could want right at home.''

There was nothing Hailey could say to that without incriminating herself and Laura. After several endless moments of strained silence, Jean said, ''I'd best be going. Nice to meet you, Ron.''

"And you, Joan."

"Jean." She gave him a look.

When her mother was safely out the door, Hailey threw herself into a chair, grabbed handfuls of her hair and shrieked as loud as she could.

Roy waited it out, but not surprisingly, looked more confused than ever.

"What the heck was that all about?" he said when she ran out of breath. "Why don't you want your mom to know that your sister's staying here?"

She had to tell him the truth, but she needed chocolate to get through it. Hailey retrieved the cake from the top of the bread bin, cut two huge slabs and plunked them on plates. Then she poured glasses of milk.

She handed him his. "I didn't get around to making any icing."

"You're fired. And could you take your clothes off again? It makes the food taste so much better." He took a bite and looked at her with an expectant expression. "Well?"

"Can't. I only do naked when I'm eating lasagna."

"We'll just have to have lasagna three times a day from now on."

Hailey noticed the projection, but she wasn't going to make too much of it. Besides, she had to unravel her family's tangled knots for him.

"My mother should have married Frank, instead of making Laura do it," Hailey began. Then she filled in all the details about Frank the louse, and Laura the victim and Jean the facilitator. The only part she didn't mention was that Laura the slut was pregnant, and probably right this moment having wild sex with her son's soccer coach.

"My sister's a little like one of those women you fell in love with," she concluded. "She's always had love and possessions and money all mixed up."

His eyes were intense, watching her. He'd finished the cake, and he set the plate on the counter and reached over and took hers away.

"You'd never make that mistake," he said, pulling her into his arms. His voice was gravelly, coming from deep in his chest. "You'd be very good at love, Hailey. You're exceptionally good at sex."

She didn't want to try to figure out why he was saying that. The words were enough. She moved into his arms, and this time they actually made it up the stairs to the bedroom.

"HAILEY, WAKE UP." Laura was shaking her arm. "I brought you a coffee."

It took her a while to open her eyes.

"Thanks." The bedside clock said nine-forty-five. Shocked at the time, Hailey sat up. "Did anybody phone from St. Joe's?"

"I don't think so. There weren't any lights blinking on your machine. I just got here a while ago, and I have an appointment with Nicole at eleven. Could you watch the kids for me for a couple of hours?"

"Sure." Hailey's body felt boneless, and her voice seemed to come from far away. The memory of the night before sent pleasure scooting through her sluggish veins. Roy had left, reluctantly, at three-fifteen. He had to work today, and it had taken him several tries to finally make it up and out the door, and then she'd fallen into a sleep as deep as a coma.

Sex was exhausting. Sex was delicious. Sex was addictive. Sex was self-perpetuating.

Get real, honey. It's not the sex, it's the man participating.

"I need to talk to you. Want an omelet for breakfast?"

"Sure, I'll be right down."

"It smells like a bordello in here. Where do you keep the clean sheets?"

"Hall cupboard. And how do you know what a bordello smells like?"

"My vivid imagination." Laura giggled and left, and Hailey gulped the coffee. When her brain started working a little, she picked up the phone and called St. Joe's.

Karen was on duty, and she assured Hailey that David had slept all night. Shannon had stayed with him, on a cot in his room. His rash seemed to be disappearing, his temperature was down, and he'd started eating again.

"Looks like he's on the mend."

Hailey agreed. Galling as it was, she knew that with emotional relaxation often came physical healing. Having Shannon with him was obviously helping David, and it was David's well-being she had at heart, wasn't it?

"She's giving him a bath just now. Harry should be in soon. I'll call you and tell you what he says."

Karen added, "You're gonna have a time with that little guy when you take him home, Hailey. He's really fixated on his mother."

Hailey felt annoyed. She didn't need Karen to remind her of that.

"I'll come by this afternoon and see him," she promised.

By the time she'd showered and dressed, Laura had a vegetable omelet, toast and sliced oranges ready for her downstairs. The kids were throwing a ball in the backyard.

"You cleaned up in here." Hailey remembered that there'd been a huge mess in the kitchen last night, and she and Roy hadn't given a single thought to cleaning it up.

"You guys obviously had bigger fish to fry. I tidied the living room, too." With one finger, Laura held out Roy's blue briefs. "He was in a hurry. What did he wear home?"

"Pants, I guess. Thanks." Hailey took them and stuffed them in her shorts pocket. "Mom came looking for you."

"Damn. I hope not right in the middle of—" Laura pointed at the underwear.

"After. We were eating lasagna, but we still had no clothes on. It was really good, by the way."

"I assume you aren't talking about the lasagna."

"That, too." It felt weird and wonderful to be this open with her sister.

"And?"

"I didn't tell her anything. But she's seriously

worried about you. You're gonna have to talk to her.''

"I will—today. After I see Nicole. I had a long talk with her on the phone yesterday and I liked her, so I made this appointment.''

"What have you decided to do?''

"Leave Frank.''

"And?''

"And I don't know.'' Laura blew out a breath. "I had a big fight with Michael. I told him about the baby, and now he insists I move in with him, which I'm not going to do. I'm not going from one man straight to another just because it's convenient. I need time to figure out what *I* want.''

"Good for you.'' Hailey knew she didn't sound all that enthusiastic, because although she applauded Laura's bid for independence, there was the small matter of the baby coming, the kids she already had, the lavish lifestyle Laura was accustomed to and the fact that she'd never held down a paying job in her life.

"You know you're welcome to stay here as long as you like.'' That was a lie, because Hailey really wanted her place to herself now that she and Roy had started eating in the nude and using the bedroom. Maybe she could fix up the basement, instead of the bathroom.

"Thanks, but Nicole says she'll get an order for me to move back into the house. She says a judge will decide it's easier for one person to find a place to live than three, and the kids need to be in familiar surroundings.''

"That's good." Hailey felt a guilty stab of relief.

"She said the first thing Frank will do is cancel the charge cards, which she thinks is actually a good thing, because it'll help me learn to budget." Laura rolled her eyes. "Whatever that is."

Hailey nodded enthusiastic agreement. Budgeting was a skill Laura really needed to learn, no doubt about that.

"All the debts Frank and I have will be divided equally, so that way my share of the proceeds will be greater. And she's going to get an order so that I get support right away. She also said that I should get the kids counseling, and it wouldn't hurt for me to get some, too."

Maybe that was what *she* needed, Hailey thought glumly. Maybe counseling would take away her urge to murder Shannon and kidnap David.

And what about Roy?

She didn't need counseling for that. She knew what she wanted with Roy. It was called happy-ever-after love, and it only happened in fairy tales.

"I just called the bathtub doctor and gave him the charge-card number. I might as well make good use of it before Frank finds out."

"What bathtub doctor?"

Laura beamed. "The one that's coming to refinish your tub. Honestly, Hailey, some things a person can put up with, but that tub isn't one of them. You know the expression 'no skin off my butt'? Well, it's not true."

"What about when Frank sees the bill?"

"It'll be a lot less than the bill for a fancy hotel,

which is where I'd be if I weren't here." Laura's logic was scary. "And I'm not living with him anymore. I want a divorce. I want my house back." But now Laura looked less sure of herself.

"Maybe he could move in with Mom."

They giggled, but Laura quickly turned sober again. "She's gonna have a seizure when I tell her all this. Hailey, please come with me this afternoon when I go to talk to her?"

"Gosh, I'd love to, but I think I'm gonna be sick this afternoon." On a scale of things to do, going with Laura to her mother's rated somewhere below making a luncheon date with Margaret.

"Please, Hailey. Don't make me beg."

"I have to go to St. Joe's first and see how David's doing."

"Mom's working today and the kids have karate at six. That would mean we'd only have to listen to her for an hour before we had to go pick them up. And then I'll buy us all dinner at that new place on Tenth."

"Bribery." But Laura looked so anxious that Hailey relented. "Okay. But no punching."

"I'll make it up to you, swear to God. I'll babysit anytime. I'll wash your stinky sheets and retrieve your lover's underwear." Laura looked at her watch and got to her feet. "Gotta run. I'll be back by one-thirty. The kids like leftover lasagna—it's in the fridge."

Laura left, and before Hailey could finish her toast, the phone rang.

She picked up, and Roy whispered, "This is an obscene phone call."

"I've always wanted one of these." His voice reminded Hailey of the night before, and she felt warm and happy and giddy.

"If I said you had a beautiful body, would you hold it against me?"

She giggled and then groaned. "That's not going to get you anywhere in the obscene-calling sweepstakes."

"Darn, and it's worked so many times before."

"Try harder."

"I just talked to David's doctor. Harry says he's releasing him tomorrow morning around eight, as long as he continues to improve."

"I'll be there to get him."

"Would you like to have dinner with me tonight, fully clothed, in a restaurant?"

Damn. Why had she ever given in to Laura?

"Can't, although I'd love to." She told him why.

"Best of luck with Joan. Tell her hello from Ron."

Jean wasn't going to adore Roy the way she had Frank, Hailey decided as she hung up the phone.

"Auntie Hailey, can you come out and play ball with us?" Christopher stuck his head in the door.

"Sure thing, I'll be right there." Having her niece and nephew around was definitely the upside of this whole affair. She remembered just in time to take Roy's briefs out of her pocket before she went outside. She stuck them in her handbag. She'd find the right moment to give them back to him.

She played with the kids and fed them lunch, but her mind was only half on what she was doing. She kept thinking of Roy, and when she wasn't thinking of him, she thought of David. Laura came back at exactly one-thirty.

"How'd it go with Nicole?"

"Great. I'm dying to tell you about it, but I'll wait till we have more time. Right now you need to go see how that baby of yours is."

Hailey drove off, thinking about the change in her sister. A week ago it wouldn't have crossed Laura's mind to put Hailey's needs first.

Adultery and divorce were making Laura a much nicer person.

CHAPTER EIGHTEEN

SHE HURRIED to David's room. He was on the floor, playing with a train set, and Shannon sat cross-legged beside him.

"Afternoon," Hailey said, forcing a friendly smile in her direction. "How's it going? This big boy looks lots better today, isn't that great?" She saw David's vitamin preparation on his lunch tray. "He needs to swallow this. Want me to do it?"

Shannon just gave her a blank stare for an answer, so Hailey turned her attention to David. "How's my sweet pea today?"

He grinned at her and waved a train engine in one pudgy hand. "Train, Lee," he greeted her, and then made a choo-choo sound Hailey had taught him.

"Clever boy, open wide for Hailey." She emptied the medication dropper into his mouth and then bent and gave him a kiss on the top of his head.

"I can do that," Shannon said. "He doesn't need you slobbering all over him. You stay away from him when I'm around." She whipped him into her arms and turned so that her back was to Hailey.

It was all Hailey could do to control her temper, but she managed. She waved goodbye to David and hurried out, seething with anger.

At the nurses' station, Mary and Judy greeted her.

"David's spots are gone and he's eating everything in sight," Mary said. "Gotta give that mother of his credit—she's been good for him these last couple of days."

Hailey didn't want to hear that. "I'm gonna have a cup of tea." She headed into the nurses' lounge, and by some miracle, it was empty. All of a sudden she felt tired and hungry and sad and lonely for Roy.

"I wonder if I could have a word with you, Hailey?"

From behind her, Margaret's voice sent her spirits down into her shoes.

"Sure. Would you like a cup of tea?" Hailey dropped a bag into a mug of water and stuck it in the microwave.

Margaret shook her head. "It was suggested that I communicate directly with you, Hailey," she began. "So that's what I'm attempting to do."

Hailey rescued her tea and blew on it, hoisting the bag up and down. Maybe it was better when Margaret just yelled at her. This new format was sort of scary. She tried to keep in mind what Melissa had confided, because she had the definite impression that in the next few moments she was going to need all the compassion and patience she could muster.

"You said you've made application to foster David Riggs."

Danger signs started flashing in Hailey's head, and she took a sip of tea to calm herself. "I said I'd been approved."

Margaret sniffed. "Your treatment of his mother yesterday was both rude and intolerable."

"I know, and I apologized to her."

"I've spent considerable time with Ms. Riggs. She's only a young girl, and she's having a difficult go of it. She's now enrolled in a drug-rehabilitation program and her lawyer is making application to the courts to have her son returned to her."

That was pretty much what Roy had said would happen, so it wasn't news, but the tea wasn't sitting well in her stomach. Hailey dumped it down the sink.

"That won't happen for quite a while, Margaret," she said carefully. "There's a fair chance it won't ever happen, because Shannon Riggs is an addict and the odds of her staying clean are slim at best."

"On the contrary, Shannon's lawyer has requested an immediate hearing, because it's obvious that David doesn't thrive unless he's with her. It's also obvious that Shannon loves that child dearly." The smug expression on Margaret's face told Hailey that something bad was coming. She braced herself.

"I've written a letter attesting to the fact that she's done a good job of mothering her son during his stay here in St. Joe's, and I said that I feel David needs to be with his natural mother. I faxed a copy to the *Province* newspaper, as well."

Outraged, Hailey opened her mouth to say that Shannon had been on the scene for all of two days, but then a picture flashed into her head of David sitting at that damned door, waiting for his mother, then another picture of him clinging to Shannon's neck. She hated to acknowledge David's feelings for his mother, but they were a reality.

Margaret wasn't finished.

"*And* I have also spoken to a supervisor at the ministry and given him my opinion."

So this was Margaret's way of getting back at her. Hailey was furious. How could she find it in her heart to feel sorry for this bitter woman who delighted in making trouble? She wanted to lash out at her, but instead, she forced herself to think.

What possible impact could Margaret have on something that was already decided? Hailey was fully approved, David was feeling well again, and Roy had said she could take him home tomorrow morning. It took immense self-control, but she managed to remain silent.

Margaret wasn't finished. "Also, I've been watching you and Mr. Zedyck, Hailey. It's perfectly obvious to me that the two of you have more than a professional relationship, which I don't think is suitable under the circumstances."

It was taking superhuman energy to keep her lip zipped, but again Hailey managed it. She needed to hear everything Margaret had to say.

"It certainly indicates to me that Mr. Zedyck was anything but impartial in recommending you as a foster parent." Margaret sounded triumphant. "I included my feelings about that in what I said."

Hailey was shaking, but if she showed how angry she was or started to defend herself, Margaret would win this confrontation. *Stay cool, Bergstrom.* It was an effort to keep her voice steady, but somehow Hailey managed.

"You're entitled to your opinion, Margaret. But that's all it is, just an opinion." She met the other woman's hostile eyes head on. "Now, is that all? Because I really should get going."

She turned and walked out, trying not to hate Margaret, trying to convince herself how sad it was that a colleague should be so vindictive. It was a tough task, especially when fear was eating at her gut.

How much damage could Margaret really do? She had no idea.

She had to talk to Roy. She needed him to assure her that Margaret was simply out of her little mind, that no one would pay the slightest attention to her rantings.

Roy's cell phone wasn't turned on, and when she called his office, a secretary said he was in a meeting and couldn't be disturbed.

Hailey left an urgent message asking him to call her, and then, not knowing what else to do, went to meet Laura at their mother's apartment.

THE REPORTER was brandishing a microphone, and she caught up with Roy at two-fifteen, just as he left his office. He recognized the woman—middle-aged, a chain smoker, prematurely wrinkled, whiskey-voiced. She'd covered the Sieberg trial, and she was one of the few members of the press who'd managed to get the facts straight, which was the reason he stopped and talked to her now.

She was doing a follow-up on the abandoned-baby story, she explained. She'd just spoken to Shannon's lawyer, who said that the young mother would be petitioning the court for custody, and she wanted to know Roy's opinion on giving the baby back to her, considering the Scotty Sieberg tragedy.

Roy had begun to hope that the media weren't going to turn David into news. He tried to think of the best way to downplay the circumstances.

"Every situation is unique and individual." It was a litany he'd learned to use with reporters. "In this case, we'll take a careful look at what's in the boy's best interests, as we always do."

"Is there any truth to the allegation that you and the child's foster mother are involved in a personal relationship, Mr. Zedyck?"

Her words caught him totally off guard, just as she'd counted on.

"Where did you hear that?" He did his best to sound incredulous.

"From a reliable source at St. Joe's. Is there any truth to it, Mr. Zedyck?"

Roy managed to smile at her. "You don't seem to realize that the child isn't *in* foster care at this moment. He's still a patient at the hospital. Now, I'm late for a meeting. I'd suggest you direct any further inquiries to my supervisor, Marty Grossman."

Feeling as if he'd been broadsided, Roy hurried past her. The moment he was in the car, he dialed Marty's number and told him exactly what had just occurred.

"They talked to me ten minutes ago, same drill,"

Marty said. Roy could hear the tension in his voice. "I also got a call from the head nurse in pediatrics. She's insisting that the boy becomes emotionally disturbed when he's away from his mother. And Shannon Riggs's lawyer is kicking up a fuss, requesting an immediate hearing, claiming that it's impossible for you to be impartial in this case because of your bias against the natural parent in the Sieberg trial. What this boils down to is that the Riggs' girl has herself a smart lawyer who's leaking things to the papers, and if we don't move quickly, we'll be in the midst of a media circus."

"You haven't asked me if I'm having a personal relationship with the woman who's approved to foster David." Roy's voice was hard.

"I don't intend to, Roy. I know you well enough to know that you'd never allow any personal relationship to affect your decisions about your work. I told that reporter so in no uncertain terms."

"Thanks, Marty." He'd been prepared to offer his resignation; the fact that he didn't have to brought a feeling of intense satisfaction and a surprising surge of joy. He'd been having doubts about his job. It had taken this to make him see that he was doing what he wanted and needed to be doing.

"Any suggestions as to what we ought to do to avoid a feeding frenzy with the press, Roy?"

"There's only one thing to do. We need to have a protection hearing on this case immediately. The lawyer's insisting on one, so we'll go along with what he wants."

Marty sounded uncertain. "You know the judge

pretty much rules on whatever the social worker on the case recommends. You sure about what your recommendations will be?''

''Not at this moment. But I guarantee they'll be honest, and in the best interests of David Riggs.''

''That's good enough for me,'' Marty said. ''Let's see if we can get this done today.''

SITTING IN JUDGE JENKINS'S chambers late that day, Roy wished to God he was a liar. Across from him were Shannon Riggs, Tonya Cabral and the young male lawyer from Legal Aid.

''We're here to determine what is best for David Riggs, who is currently in the care of this court,'' Jenkins had stated a few moments earlier. ''Ordinarily this hearing would take place at a later date, but it has been brought to the court's attention that there are mitigating circumstances, one of which is that the child, David Riggs, is suffering extreme emotional stress resulting in physical illness as a direct result of being separated from his mother. We've heard statements attesting to the fact that Ms. Riggs is enrolled in a drug-rehabilitation program, that she intends to fulfill her role as a responsible parent to David, and that she had adequate living accommodations for herself and her son, arranged by Ms. Cabral. Ms. Riggs has the full support of Ms. Cabral, and in a written deposition, Ms. Margaret Cross has given her opinion that during David's hospital stay, Ms. Riggs has proved to be a caring and attentive mother. Now, if we could hear your thoughts on this matter, Mr. Zedyck?''

Roy had known this moment was coming and dreaded it. He'd listened carefully to everything that had been said. He'd heard the lawyer's accusations that he should be withdrawn from the case. Judge Jenkins had told the young man in no uncertain terms that such a suggestion was ludicrous and out of place. Roy had appeared before the judge many times before, and it was heartening to know that the respect he felt was mutual.

In his mind's eye, Roy could see the little bedroom Hailey had prepared, the crib, the teddy bear on the dresser. He saw her honey-gold eyes, filled with light and love, and the way her mouth lifted in that crooked, goofy smile whenever she saw David.

He looked across at skinny, tattooed Shannon Riggs, with her earful of rings and her arms covered with long sleeves in spite of the warmth of the day. Any rational human being would agree that David belonged with Hailey.

But the most important person in this entire mess wasn't here to speak for himself. David had to rely on Roy to decide what was best for him, what would make him happy and allow him to develop the way a healthy little boy should. In that regard, Roy knew he had no options.

"It's my opinion, Your Honor, that David Riggs must remain in the care of the ministry until his mother proves she can carry through with her resolution to be drug-free and responsible as a parent. She hasn't proved that yet."

Shannon's face crumpled and she put her hands over her eyes. The young lawyer shook his head and looked cynical.

"However," Roy continued, feeling as lousy as he'd ever felt in his life, "David Riggs is a child who undoubtedly belongs with his mother. I've personally witnessed his distress at being separated from her. He obviously suffers severe physical and emotional trauma, and my strong recommendation would be that he live with Shannon Riggs, closely supervised by the ministry, and that Ms. Riggs receive as much support as the community and court can provide."

Judge Jenkins ruled in direct agreement with his recommendation.

When it was over, Shannon came over to him and extended her hand.

"Thank you," she said in a quavery voice. "I'm going to take good care of him."

"See that you do." Roy shook her hand and left without speaking to the others.

He knew what he had to do next, and he dreaded it. He had to phone Hailey and tell her what had happened here.

Two things had become clear to him today. The first was knowing absolutely that he wanted to go on doing his job.

The second had come to him when he recommended that Shannon Riggs be allowed to take her son home with her.

He was in love with Hailey. He hadn't recognized it until now because he'd never really been in love before.

And now he was going to have to break her heart.

FOR HAILEY, the confrontation with Jean wasn't any easier than the one with Margaret, but at least it was

Laura on the hot seat, instead of her. She sat beside
her sister on her mother's gray silk couch and kept
quiet as the two of them butted heads.

"You've taken leave of your senses," Jean declared when Laura told her she was divorcing Frank.
"You're spoiled, that's what's wrong. You've had
it too easy." Her lips drew together, and Hailey
could see fine lines on her mother's face, like tiny
cracks in smooth icing. "And what about Samantha
and Christopher? They need their father. The least
you could do is stay until they're grown."

"Aren't you listening, Mom?" Laura was mad—
Hailey could tell by the way she was breathing. "I
just told you he had someone in my bed, that he's
had other women from the very beginning. What
kind of example is that for the kids? You figure I
should just shut up and put up with that?"

Jean waved a hand in the air. "That's how men
are. You can learn to ignore it. It's not worth breaking up a home over. I certainly didn't when your
father—"

It was probably the shock on her daughters' faces
that stopped her.

"Daddy?" Laura shook her head. "Are you saying Daddy had affairs and you *ignored* it?"

Jean's mouth narrowed. "Some men are just like
that."

Hailey couldn't breathe. Once again she had the
feeling the world was tumbling down around her,
and this time it was her father's image that broke
into shattered fragments.

"I had you kids to think about. I didn't have a job in those days. How would I have supported you if I left him?" Jean was defiant. "And there would have been talk. You know, Laura, they always say it's the woman's fault when a man strays, that she lets herself go, or she doesn't fulfill her duties as a wife—"

"Are you insinuating that I'm no good in bed?" Laura made a rude noise. "That's crap. I'd like to see Frank try and tell that to Michael."

"Michael? Who's Michael?" Jean's eyes widened and her mouth fell open. "Oh, Laura," she wailed, "you aren't having an affair, are you?"

Hailey heard her sister gulp, and she felt sorry for her. Reaching over, she took Laura's hand. The palm was damp, and she was trembling.

Courage, sister. She was going to need it.

"Yeah, I am." Laura's voice quavered, but to her credit, she came out with the truth. "And I'm also pregnant, Mom. It's Michael's baby. And I'm not marrying him, or living with him, either, so don't go there."

Jean's skin had been flushed, but now it went so pale Hailey wondered if she was about to faint. Her mouth trembled and she whispered, "But…but what are you going to do? How are you going to live? Does Frank know?"

"Not yet."

"Well, then, just go back and he'll never even—"

"No." Hailey hadn't said anything until now, but this was going too far. "She can't do that, Mom. For heaven's sake, how can you even suggest it?"

"You stay out of this, Hailey." Jean's temper flared. "You don't know the first thing about what goes on in a marriage."

"Well, if it's what I've been hearing, I don't want to know."

Jean wasn't listening. "All I ever wanted for you girls was security. I never had that. Your father could have taken out a sizable life-insurance policy, but he didn't, so after he died it was a struggle to make ends meet. You have everything now, Laura, everything I ever wanted. How can you just throw it away?"

Laura thought it over. "It just takes too much out of me to pretend all the time that things are wonderful when they're not."

But Jean wasn't interested in emotion. "What about this Michael? Does he have any money?"

Laura sighed and shook her head. "He's a phys ed teacher. He earns a living, but he's not well-off. And anyway, I'm not relying on him to support *me*. He'll support his baby, of course. I've seen a lawyer, and she says she'll be able to get me support right away from Frank, for the kids and for myself."

Their mother snorted. "You have no idea what it's like to raise a family by yourself. You've led a sheltered life, Laura."

Hailey had had enough. "Lots of women do it, Mom. You did. Laura will do just fine. She has us to help her out, and she has a man who cares about her."

Jean scowled at her. "Of course Frank cares."

"I wasn't talking about Frank. I meant Michael."

The fight seemed to whoosh out of Jean and she burst into tears. "A teacher doesn't earn what a successful lawyer like Frank does. I wish you'd reconsider, Laura." She sniffled. "You'll never find as good a provider as Frank. You'll be sorry."

"If I am, at least it'll be because I made a decision on my own." Hailey could see her sister struggling for the right words. "All my life I've done what you wanted me to do, Mom, but I can't anymore. I need to find out what it is I really want."

Jean's tears had dried up and she was angry again. "Mark my words, by the time you do, you won't be able to afford it."

As the conversation went round and round the same issues, Hailey felt exhausted. Something was nagging at her, and she finally came out with it.

"If you figure marriage is the way to go, Mom, how come you never married again yourself? You must have had offers."

"The two men I might have considered weren't well-off," Jean replied defensively. "If I had married them, I would have lost your father's pension, and it was my security. No matter what happened, I knew I had that to fall back on."

The look on Laura's face mirrored Hailey's own amazement. Jean had valued money above everything else, even love, and she'd ended up alone. But she had the pension. It made Hailey want to bawl.

CHAPTER NINETEEN

ROY DIALED Hailey's cell number. When she answered, he could hear restaurant sounds in the background.

"Roy, hi, you got my message."

He hadn't, but before he could say so, she was talking again.

"Laura and I are just finishing dinner. Could you meet me someplace in half an hour? Because I really need to talk something over with you."

That made two of them. By the upbeat sound of her voice, he figured her news had to be a lot better than his.

He suggested a park, and he was waiting when she drove up.

His stomach was knotted as he hurried over to the truck, and an awful sense of foreboding clutched at his gut. She opened the door and slid down into his arms, and he held her close and never wanted to let her go.

"Hey, my obscene phone friend." She laughed and hugged him. Then she took his hand, linking her fingers through his, swinging their arms as they made their way to a bench underneath a willow tree.

"I wanted to talk to you about some stuff Margaret said. It kind of scared me."

"I know about it." He wished with all his heart that he didn't have to tell her the rest. There was no easy way to do it, so he opted for brutal honesty. "I've just come from an emergency court hearing, Hailey. Shannon Riggs and her lawyer and Tonya Cabral, Shannon's sponsor, were there. Margaret Cross sent a deposition."

Hailey rolled her eyes. "She's such a busybody, that woman. I suppose she said I wasn't fit to be David's foster mother because you and I were having an affair?"

"She probably said that, but it didn't have any bearing on what happened. She did support Shannon Riggs in her application for custody and offered her any personal assistance she could provide."

"She told me she was going to do that. She really hates me, and she doesn't want me to have David. But it doesn't make any difference, does it?"

He didn't answer.

"Roy?" She was frowning at him now. "You're scaring me. Tell me what happened."

There was no way around it. "The judge asked me what I thought was the best situation for David, and I said that I believed he should be returned to Shannon under close supervision." He was looking into her face as he said it, and her eyes widened as if he'd struck her. "That was the ruling the judge made. They nearly always rule what the social worker suggests."

She shook her head as if she didn't understand. "He's…he's going home with *her?*"

Roy took her hand, but she pulled it away. "Yeah. I suspect he's gone already. The order was immediate." He felt awful. "I'm so sorry, Hailey."

"Oh, God." She pressed her hands, one over the other, against her heart as if the pain there was unbearable. Her eyes were wild, her voice out of control. "Why, Roy? *Why* did you do this to me? I could understand if the judge ruled that way on his own, but why would you recommend that she have him when you know what she's like? And you know more than anybody how much I love him?"

All he had was the truth. "Because I've seen how he is with Shannon, Hailey. I heard him screaming for her. I saw him camped out by that bloody door on the ward. I saw how sick he got when she left." Roy had to make her understand so she wouldn't look like that, as if he'd struck her. "For David's sake, I couldn't recommend they be separated. I just couldn't do it. I know in my heart that this is one instance where the ministry is right, that whenever possible, it's best to leave kids with their natural parent." He took a breath and tried again. "But right or not, I feel like a shit about this. More than anything in the world, I wanted you to have David. I know how much you love him."

"No, you don't." Hailey glared at him. "If you did, you'd never have done this to me."

She swallowed hard, and the agony on her face made his chest hurt.

Her voice wobbled. "How…how could you, Roy?

How could you just change your mind? How could you even suggest he's better off with her than with me?'' She'd gone pale, and her freckles stood out like golden dots across her cheekbones.

"Hailey, please, listen to me. I thought of David, and only David. He's my priority here, no matter what else is going on, no matter what I personally might want. I thought about what he'd choose if he had the chance.'' Roy felt as miserable as he'd ever felt in his life. "And I knew he'd choose to be with her. He loves her.'' *And I love you.* But this wasn't the time to say it.

"He's a baby. He doesn't understand what's best for him.'' Her voice was thick with emotion. "I never dreamed you'd decide in her favor, Roy. She deserted him—you saw him when he first came in.'' She looked at Roy, and he could see the disillusionment in her lovely eyes, the way her mouth turned down, the way her jaw was set against him.

He scrambled for something, anything that would make her see reason. "This isn't personal, Hailey. This is my job. I warned you how this could go. I told you in the beginning there were no guarantees, that fostering could break your heart.''

"Yeah, you did. I was just a fool for thinking that you were on my side and that…that you actually cared what happened to David. She'll do the same thing again, you know. If she did it once, she'll do it again.''

A cold shudder ran down his spine. He'd given that a lot of thought. "I truly hope not.''

"Yeah, well, me, too.''

At that moment he would have done anything to ease her pain, but he couldn't think of what it might be. Worst of all, he still believed he'd made the only choice possible, given the circumstances. He'd never felt more helpless in his life.

"Hailey, don't let this come between us." He reached for her hand, but again she pulled it away. "I care about you. We've got something good here."

"No, we don't." The words were clipped, her tone harsh. "I trusted you, and you betrayed me. I can't do anything right now but feel. And it hurts...my heart hurts so much I can hardly stand it." She got to her feet, and he followed.

"I'm going home now." Her voice was flat. It scared him.

"Don't go while you're feeling this way. Come for a walk. Let me take you somewhere, anywhere. We can talk this out." He wanted to be with her when she cried. "Please, Hailey, I know you're mad, but c'mere. Let me hold you." He realized it wasn't for her sake. It was for his.

Not looking at him, she shook her head, and her voice was sad. "I just don't want to be with you right now, Roy."

Her words hurt more than he'd thought possible.

She got up and walked away from him, and he followed her, but she turned and waved him away.

At last he lost his temper. "Hailey, wait a god-damn minute here." He ran after her, took hold of her arm, turned her to face him. "For God's sake—"

"Let me go." Her eyes shot sparks, and there was fury in her tone. "Don't you think you've done enough already?"

He dropped his arms and she got into her truck and drove off.

That was that, then. He swore. He went home, put on his runners and ran until his entire body was soaked with sweat, his chest was on fire, and his calves were cramped. But it didn't help. Nothing did.

The phone rang, and he snatched it up, hoping it was Hailey.

"Hey, brother, how's it going? I haven't heard from you in a while."

It was Nicole. "I've had better days."

"Wanna tell me about it?"

"It's Hailey. And David." He started at the beginning and ended with the scene in the park. "I did what I knew was right, but in the process I lost her, Nick. I let her down, big time. And dammit, I really cared about her."

"Why the past tense? She's just angry and hurt. She'll come to her senses. Give her time to cool off and then tell her how you feel. And this time, try not to sabotage it, okay?"

"What do you mean, sabotage it?"

"I've watched you. It's easy to see what someone else is doing wrong, it's just our own stuff we're blind to. With you, the minute it starts looking serious, you find a reason to end it."

"The hell I do." Anger flared. "Why would I do a thing like that?"

"Who knows? Could be you have a little image

thing going, some issue with self-esteem. I dunno. All I'm saying is don't use this as your reason for giving up on Hailey. If you care about her, go after her. Persevere. Don't take no for an answer.''

After he hung up, Roy thought about it. Nicole didn't know what she was talking about. She'd been reading too many women's magazines. There'd always been good, valid reasons for ending his relationships, hadn't there? He thought about it as he showered and changed, then drove out to visit his parents at the retirement home.

He pulled into a parking space. As usual, his father was outside, pretending to weed the miniscule garden in front of the Zedycks' unit, but Roy knew Martin was waiting for him. The old man's weathered face creased into a smile, and although he wasn't a demonstrative man, he rested a hand on his son's shoulder.

"Hey, Pop, those zucchinis are something." It was tough to sound lighthearted when he felt miserable, but he gave it his best shot.

"I picked some for you to take. These little tomatoes, too—they're sweet. This time of year, harvest time, I miss the farm."

Martin said the same thing every month of the year, and every time he said it, Roy felt a pang of guilt. The old man had wanted to die on his own land, with his son taking over where he'd left off. It was the Old Country way.

"Mom feeling okay? Flu's all gone?"

"She coughs a little, but the doctor says she's

fine. She made you blackberry pie. Wouldn't let me near it till you got here."

Roy sat at the small table with his parents, dutifully eating pie that for the first time in living memory he really didn't want. He listened to his father's complaints about the way the place was run, caught his mother's faded blue eyes on him and the doting expression there.

He knew what was coming. His mother asked the same question every week, and this time he really dreaded it. She waited until her husband ran down and then leaned toward Roy, her ample bosom resting on the tabletop. "So, you meet some nice girl yet, *boyco?* You're not getting younger, you know, and me, neither."

She wanted grandbabies. He'd made the mistake of bringing a couple of women here to meet his parents. He hadn't brought anyone in a long time.

"I did meet someone, Ma. But it didn't work out."

"So what's to work out?" Frustration made her voice shrill. "That's what you always say. You young people, you want a guarantee. In my day we took our chances. We got married and we worked it out after."

"Leave the boy, Momma," Martin said now. "When it's time, he'll know."

"How *do* you know, Pop?" He'd never asked anything like that before, and both his parents gave him surprised looks when the words burst out of him. "How did you know, with Momma?"

Martin put a chunk of pie in his mouth and savored it before he answered. "It was the war—there wasn't time to think too much," he finally said. "I saw Rose, she was working in a bakery, and I just knew. It's like farming. You get a feeling when it's right to cut the hay or plant."

That wasn't a whole hell of a lot of help. "Did you date other people or just each other?"

"Ach, there were girls—there are always girls when you are a soldier," Martin said, winking at Roy. "They like the uniform."

Rose slapped his arm.

"But once I saw Rose, that was that. I had to fight for her, though. The owner of the bakery wanted her—they were engaged already. I just never gave up, and when I kissed her, she knew I was the one."

"Martin, you shouldn't tell the boy such things." Rose dropped her eyes and her lined face grew pink, and for an instant Roy saw her the way she must have been, with her soft hair and blue eyes and sweet smile.

"So you fell in love, the two of you?"

Martin had had enough. He scowled and waved a hand. "Love, all this talk of love nowadays. We just knew it was right," he said with finality, and Rose nodded her head in agreement.

"When it's right, you just know, *boyco,*" she said.

On the drive back into the city, Roy thought about it.

When he'd broken up with women before, it had been final. He'd accepted that it was over. Since he'd usually been the one to make the decision, there'd been a sense of relief when it ended. He didn't feel like that now.

He thought about what Nicole had suggested, that maybe he'd sabotaged things.

Reluctantly he admitted that in some aspects of his life, it was true. He hadn't been able to be the farmer that Martin wanted him to be. He sure as hell wasn't the lawyer or doctor that his birth parents might have expected. Did that sense that he disappointed people affect his relationships with women?

Hailey's face came to mind.

When it's right, you just know.

He did know. The problem was, how to convince her?

"HOW COULD HE BETRAY me this way?" Hailey's face was swollen and sopping wet from the washcloth Laura kept dipping in ice water.

"All along, he encouraged me. He made me believe that I was right for David. And then he does this. I didn't even see it coming. And besides that, I *slept* with him."

"So you slept with him just to get David?"

"Are you nuts, Laura?" Hailey was appalled. "Do you really think I'd do a thing like that?"

"Of course not. I just don't want *you* to get the two things mixed up." Laura dumped more ice into the basin of water. "One is about a little kid, and the other's about you falling for Roy and hating yourself for being human."

Hailey stopped crying and glared at her sister. "What's that supposed to mean?"

"Well, if you never let yourself care, you never get hurt."

"Well, I *did* let myself, and look where it's landed me."

"You're still on the list to adopt, you're approved to foster, and you'll get a baby soon. Your feelings for Roy shouldn't have anything to do with David."

"But they do. The two things are interconnected. I'm withdrawing my applications to foster *and* to adopt."

"Hailey, don't do that. You'll feel different once you get over this. There'll be other kids you'll love just as much as you love David."

That was hard to believe at the moment, hard even to imagine. She did love David, and the pain she felt at losing him was devastating. And worst of all was her love for Roy. She'd trusted him and he'd deliberately hurt her.

"If you want my honest opinion," Laura said— Hailey didn't particularly—"I think Roy is great, considering that he's a guy. He did what he believed to be best for David, even knowing you'd hate him for it. That takes a special kind of integrity."

"That takes a real mean streak. And I don't hate him." Hailey's tears started again. "I...I love him. That's why it hurts so much."

Laura sighed, wrung out the cloth and put it over Hailey's eyes. "This happy-ever-after stuff is such a crock. I'm never going to read *Cinderella* to Samantha again. I bought a gallon of chocolate-maple-nut ice cream. You want some?''

It didn't cure anything, but it helped.

ROY PHONED at seven-thirty the next morning, waking her up.

''Meet me for breakfast? There're things we need to discuss.''

''We don't have anything to say to each other, Roy. It all got said yesterday.''

''That's not so.''

She heard him take a deep breath and then expel it.

''I love you, Hailey. I didn't say that before, and I should have.''

It would have meant everything to her the day before yesterday. Now she had a wall around her heart, a barricade that kept her from letting anything else in. The silence stretched.

''I won't give up,'' he said quietly. ''I'll keep calling, and I'll keep telling you how I feel. And I'll be keeping a very close eye on David. I'll let you know how he's doing.''

The rat. He knew she needed to know that David was safe. He knew she'd take his calls, just because of that.

She couldn't stay home. She got in the truck and drove to Sam and Ingrid's. Gran was up, swathed in a black-and-silver Oriental housecoat. She took a look at Hailey's swollen face and poured her a mug of coffee.

''Sam had an early call. They're shooting that movie downtown and he's a stand-in for one of the actors. You want an omelet?''

"I'm not hungry, Gran. I need to tell you what's happened. David's gone back to live with his mother, and it's Roy's fault." The story poured out, and this time Hailey made it through without crying.

"I'm so sorry, honey." Ingrid put her arms around her. "I know how much you were counting on having David." She patted Hailey's shoulder, and it felt soothing and comfortable. "But I don't agree that it's Roy's fault."

Hailey reared back, shocked. "Of course it is. He made the recommendation. He told me the judge goes by what the social worker says."

Ingrid shook her head. "You told me how that little boy cried for his mother. Replacing a person isn't easy, and it's not always the answer. I think I would have done the same if I were Roy. The way to support kids is to support their mother."

Hailey had never gotten really angry at Ingrid, but she did now.

"How can you say that, Gran? You, of all people. Mom was alone after Dad died, and all you ever did was fight with her. You were good to Laura and me, but you sure didn't support Mom."

"I know I didn't." Ingrid looked stricken. "All of us have things we're sorry for, and that's a big one with me. I should have tried harder with Jean. I got my back up about certain things she said to me about your father, things I just couldn't countenance. Ed was my only son, and I never forgave her for it."

"I suppose she told you that Daddy had affairs with other women."

Ingrid nodded, and her eyes sparked with fresh anger. "She shouldn't have told you that. He was your daddy and you were close to him. There was no need for you to think badly of him after he was gone.''

"The first I heard of it was yesterday." Hailey told Ingrid what was going on with Laura. "Mom sort of blurted it out. I don't think she meant to."

"Well. See, again I jump to conclusions. I should have settled this with Jean a long time ago. I think it's time now. I'll do my best to make peace with her." Ingrid hesitated, then added, "But I want you to think carefully about Roy, Hailey. From what I've seen of him, he's a good man, and he seems right for you. I've made lots of mistakes, and I know how they haunt a person. I want to keep you from making one here."

Why does everyone keep taking his side?

"I don't trust him anymore. Trust is a big thing between two people."

"Ah, my Haileybop. Don't cut off your nose to spite your face."

When she got home, Hailey turned off her cell phone and ignored the numerous messages from Roy. It was hard to get ready for work, although she was relieved she was on evening shift, because Margaret would already have gone home by the time she got to St. Joe's. She wasn't sure if she could stop herself from physically attacking the older nurse if she saw her.

She made sure she arrived right at shift change, so there wouldn't be a lot of time for questions about David, but everyone wanted to know what had happened. They knew he'd been discharged, and that

Shannon and a social services worker had picked him up.

Hailey told the story again, weary to death of going over it.

The other nurses were sympathetic and outraged at Margaret's role in what had happened.

"She's handed in her notice—she's taking early retirement," one of her co-workers said. "I heard it from someone in the personnel office. She'll be gone at the end of September. Nobody's gonna miss her, that's for sure."

That night, for the first time she could ever remember, Hailey counted off the hours she had to work, longing to go home. When the new shift arrived and hers was finally over, she made her way out of St. Joe's, weary to the bone, squinting in the harsh sunlight as she headed for the parking area where she'd left the truck.

Her heart gave a thump and her mouth went dry because Roy was there, wearing shorts and a rumpled green golf shirt. He was leaning against her truck, and he straightened his long body and smiled at her. His eyes were bloodshot, as if he hadn't slept a whole lot.

"Can I interest you in some breakfast, Nurse Bergstrom?"

For an instant, passion leaped across the barrier she'd created. She wanted to throw herself into his arms, because only there would she be at peace. But David's round little face swam between them, and the pain cut into her heart. The peace would be shortlived—only the length of time it took for the passion to ebb and resentment to take its place.

"I can't." She looked at him, shook her head and told him the bald truth. "You hurt me, and I'm scared you'll do it again."

"You'd end what there is between us just because you're scared?" There was temper and challenge in his tone. "I thought you were braver than that."

"Well, you thought wrong." She dragged her keys out of her bag and walked around him to open the truck door. "Don't call me, please. Don't wait like this again. It's over."

"Don't do this, Hailey."

She was too tired to argue with him. She started the truck and backed out. As she drove away, she wasn't even crying.

CHAPTER TWENTY

SEVEN DAYS passed.

Laura helped dismantle the crib in the room that was to have been David's, and that same day Nicole got the court order, just as she'd said she would, and Laura and the kids moved back into their house. Frank had packed up his belongings and taken most of Laura's jewelry, as well as any paintings he considered valuable. He was still making threats, but Laura was no longer affected by them. Nicole had done a fine job of making her aware of her rights,

Hailey thought she'd be happy at having her privacy again, but the night her sister left, she wept. The house was empty and echoing without Laura and her niece and nephew.

In the two weeks that followed, Hailey volunteered for extra shifts. She and Margaret avoided each other as much as possible, and the older nurse no longer nagged about the way Hailey did her job. Maybe she sensed that Hailey would explode if she confronted her.

Roy called at least every other day, and Hailey was polite and distant. But inside, her emotions were like a volcano about to erupt. She resented Roy and she loved him. She couldn't stop herself from missing him, wanting him, or blaming him for the gaping hole David had left in her heart.

She asked Harry Larue about David one morning.

"Saw him just the other day," the pediatrician said. "He's doing great, eating well, healthy and happy. Want me to tell his mother you were asking about him?"

"Definitely not."

"Sorry." Harry avoided her eyes and hurried off. Of course he knew the whole story. Everyone knew. The nurses no longer asked about the baby she planned to adopt, and no one talked about David.

On her break, Hailey stayed at Laura's and deliberately turned off her cell phone. It wore her down, Roy's calling all the time. She helped the kids with homework and watched videos with them while Laura had a sleepover with Michael. On Sunday she and Laura cooked a roast and invited Jean for dinner.

Hailey watched her mother taking stock of Laura's house. When Frank had lived there, he'd demanded that it be kept in perfect order. Now it looked lived in, with shoes in a heap at the door and video games spread across the carpet.

Samantha and Christopher talked nonstop during the meal, telling their grandmother all about the puppy Laura had promised they'd get the following week.

"Daddy never let us have a dog," Samantha said. "He told us dogs make lots of mess, but we're gonna clean up the mess, right, Chris?"

"Right. And Daddy's not coming back to live here, so we get to keep the puppy, right, Mom?"

"Right."

The kids clapped, and Hailey saw the scandalized look Jean gave Laura. When the kids were excused, Jean said, "That's disgraceful, Laura. It sounds as if the children are choosing a dog over their father. Frank called me. The poor man's beside himself. I keep hoping you'll come to your senses."

Hailey was proud of her sister for smiling at their mother and saying, "I already have. That's why we're getting a puppy."

HAILEY WAS ON day shift the next morning, and as she was stowing her things in her locker, Karen breezed in.

"Hailey, hey, did you hear about Margaret?"

"What about her?"

"She had a heart attack last night—she's in intensive care."

A feeling of relief momentarily swept through Hailey, followed by a fierce pang of guilt. What kind of horrible person was she, feeling relieved because someone was ill?

"Is she going to be all right?"

"They're not sure—it was fairly major. She was alone when it happened, but somehow she managed to call 911. And guess what?" Karen couldn't hide her excitement. "There's a message for you at the desk. You're to call Melissa Clayton-Burke. I'll bet you anything she asks you to take over for Margaret."

KAREN WAS RIGHT. Melissa asked if Hailey would become acting head nurse on the pediatrics ward.

Hailey hesitated. She'd turned down opportunities in the past to be head nurse, mostly because the job she loved was direct patient care. As head, she'd spend less time with patients and more on administration. She'd be responsible for all the patients in peds, instead of the ones assigned to her. But if she said no, someone would be assigned who didn't know the department or the kids. Reluctantly she agreed.

When she arrived to start her shift, the others all knew, and a cheer went up. It was gratifying to have the support of her co-workers.

Her heart sank, however, when Mary said, "Brittany's bad—she had a really difficult night. I called her doctor and he ordered more meds, but she's still pretty miserable. Her temperature's up, and she's struggling to breathe. We called her mom about an hour ago, and she's taking the early-morning ferry over."

They were all quiet for a moment. Each of them knew that Brittany's disease had spread to her lungs and this relapse meant it wasn't likely she would survive much longer.

"She's fought so hard for so long." Hailey could feel sorrow like a hard, tight lump, right under her heart. "Maybe it's time for all of us to let go."

The others nodded agreement. Hard as it was, they knew that the time always came when some children needed permission from those around them, from those who loved them, to leave. Sometimes the child's parents intuitively did exactly that, but more often it became the nurses' job to gently explain that it was necessary.

"I'll speak to her mother when she gets here." Hailey knew Susan Whitcomb really well; they'd become friendly during Brittany's many admissions.

Hailey hurried to Brittany's room, relieved to find the little girl deeply asleep.

The first couple of hours convinced Hailey that administration wasn't where she wanted to spend the rest of her career. In the midst of playing a game with one of the kids, someone paged her because she was wanted on the phone. She was responsible for scheduling tests. Any problems with food trays were hers to sort out, and the constant interruptions began to wear on her.

When she had time, she checked Brittany again and found the little girl awake.

"Hey, chickadee, how's it going?"

Hailey hid her shock at Brittany's appearance. Even with oxygen, the fragile girl was laboring for breath. One glance told Hailey that she was nearing the end of her short life. Children often had a clarity about their eyes when the end was near, an otherworldly radiance. Brittany's gray eyes had it now.

"Your mom's coming soon," Hailey said as she gently did all she could to make the child more comfortable. "Let's straighten this sheet. It's all crumpled up under you. Want me to read to you?"

Brittany gave her head a slight shake. She looked so small and alone in the hospital bed.

"Want me to hold you?"

Brittany's nod and attempt at a smile were heart-breaking.

Hailey slipped off her shoes and got on the bed, praying there wouldn't be any interruptions. She gathered Brittany into her arms and rocked her gently.

"Don't be scared, honey." Her voice was thick with grief, but she held the tears back. "When it's time, the angels will come and get you, and nothing will hurt anymore."

"How...will...I know?" It seemed such an effort for her to speak.

"You'll hear the music." For Hailey, the effort was just as overwhelming. She wanted to cry, but she couldn't let herself do that. Not yet, not while Brittany needed her to be strong.

Brittany whispered, "Mama?"

"Your mama understands. She knows it's getting hard for you now. She'll be okay. She's a really strong lady."

The little girl nodded, and it seemed to Hailey that her breathing eased just a trifle. Time passed, and as long as she could, Hailey ignored the hands on her watch, the tasks that needed completing. At this moment nothing was more important than being here. At last Brittany fell asleep, and Hailey gently, carefully, slid the child out of her aching arms and climbed off the bed.

The rest of the morning was frantic, and it was past lunchtime when Brittany's mother, Susan Whitcomb, hurried up to the nurses' station.

"She's sleeping—she's slept most of the morning,'' Hailey told her, hugging Susan and drawing her into the nurses' lounge, thankful that it was deserted.

"Brittany's bad, isn't she?" Susan's eyes were wide and fearful, and her hands were trembling around the coffee mug Hailey handed her. She looked drawn and terribly strained.

In answer to her question, Hailey nodded. "Yeah, she is."

Susan's eyes welled up with tears and her voice wobbled. "Is it…is it time?"

"Almost."

Susan moaned in agony, and Hailey got up and took the other woman in her arms.

"I think she's holding on for you," Hailey explained. "I think it's time to let her know that it's okay to go when she's ready."

"God, Hailey," Susan sobbed. "I'm not sure I can do it. It tears me apart, I…I love her so much." When the tears slowed, Susan blew her nose hard. "You know, I was only fourteen when she was born."

Hailey tried not to reveal her shock. Susan looked much older than twenty-six.

"I was a wild kid. My boyfriend was an older guy, all of seventeen." Susan attempted a smile, but tears leaked steadily from her tired eyes. "He ran away when he found out, and everyone said I should give her up for adoption, that I was too young to raise her. I was going to, but then when she was born, I held her, and she looked up at me as if she knew me, and I just couldn't do it, you know?"

Hailey felt hot and then icy cold. She thought of David, of Shannon. She really didn't want to hear this, but she couldn't walk out on Susan. Besides, Susan's situation was totally different from Shannon's, wasn't it? Susan was a conscientious mother. She'd never have deserted her baby.

"It was so hard, learning how to take care of her," Susan was saying through her tears. "She had colic. I couldn't have done it without my mother and grandmother—they were both there for me. I remember a couple of times when I ran out the door and left them with Brittany when she was screaming." She blew her nose again and stood up. "I'll go down to her room now and see if she's awake. And—" her voice faltered "—I'll tell her it's okay."

"You've got my cell number," Hailey said, holding back her own tears. "You call me if you need me, Susan, anytime, day or night."

Susan nodded. "Thanks. Tom's coming tonight. His mother's staying with the boys. He'll be here with me."

Hailey worked an extra hour that afternoon, doing her best to finish everything her new position demanded. By the time she was ready to leave, she was both exhausted and frustrated.

She stopped by Brittany's room. Susan was sitting on the bed, cradling her daughter. Hailey gave them each a kiss and wearily made her way down to the parking garage.

She was near her truck when it hit her full force. She'd just advised Susan to let her daughter go, because it was best for Brittany. But what had Hailey done for David, for Shannon? She'd allowed her own overwhelming need to obscure the truth—that David really did need to be with his mother. The truth was bitter and agonizing, and she bent double with the pain. But even pain didn't last, and after long moments it ebbed into a kind of weary acceptance. Her hands trembled as she searched for her keys.

As she unlocked her truck, she gave in to the nagging little voice in her head. Cursing her conscience, she locked the vehicle again and went back into St. Joe's. She took the elevator up to intensive care, wondering just what the heck she was doing and why.

"She's improved somewhat since this morning—she's conscious and aware," the nurse at the station told Hailey when she asked about Margaret. "You can go in for a few minutes. She doesn't have any other visitors."

Hailey had only intended to find out how she was. Something made her ask, "Has anybody else been in to see her?"

"Melissa Clayton-Burke. Hers was the only emergency number Ms. Cross had listed. There was one next of kin, but it turned out to be an elderly woman with Alzheimer's in a rest home in Victoria. We didn't know who else to call. Is there anyone you know of?"

Hailey shook her head. How terribly lonely it must be not to have anyone to call in an emergency except the hospital administrator. Damn, she hated feeling sorry for Margaret, but she just couldn't help it.

As she made her way past the line of beds, she hoped the former head nurse would be asleep, but she wasn't. Margaret turned her head and looked up at her. Strange, Hailey thought, to see the woman without her cap. Her hair was matted down, there were oxygen plugs in her nose and IVs in her arm. She looked old and sad and very sick. Again, Hailey felt a pang of sympathy.

"Hi, Margaret." Hailey managed a smile. "I just wanted to say hello. Everyone on peds says hi. We're all hoping you'll be better soon."

It wasn't strictly true. Hailey had heard the other nurses talking, and there wasn't much affection for Margaret in what they said.

"Is there anything I can bring you? Anything you need or want?"

"No. Thank you." The words were breathy and faint.

"Okay." Damn, this was awkward. "Well, then, you just concentrate on getting better, okay?" She turned to go.

"Wait."

Hailey longed to pretend she hadn't heard, but she just couldn't do it.

"I'm...sorry." Margaret's speech was labored. "Wasn't right...of me. But the boy...needed his...mother."

Hailey could only nod. Why did every single person feel it necessary to tell her the same damn thing?

Maybe because she'd needed to hear it a number of times before she could accept it.

"You're…a good nurse, Hailey."

For a moment, Hailey thought she was hearing things. She gaped at Margaret. Why was she telling her this *now?*

"I'm having a tough time being a good nurse these days," she finally said. "I miss David something awful." Roy, too, but she couldn't say that.

"You'd make…a good mother." Margaret closed and opened her eyes. "But…I couldn't stand…that boy crying for her…like he did."

"Yeah." Hailey's sigh was deep and sad and healing. "I know. I guess I couldn't stand it either." She'd finally admitted what she'd known all along, what everyone had been trying to tell her. Roy had done the right thing, the only thing. She didn't blame him any longer. She had to tell him so.

"I'll come by and see you in the morning before I go on shift, Margaret. But right now, I gotta make a phone call."

WHEN HE WALKED into the apartment that evening, Roy's phone was ringing. He wasn't about to answer; he wanted to go for a run. He'd been running more than he had since he was on the high-school track team. It wasn't making him feel any better, but at least it tired him enough so that he slept at night.

The ringing stopped, and his machine clicked on. A woman's tense, high voice said, "I need to talk to Roy Zedyck right away. It's Tonya Cabral. It's about David."

CHAPTER TWENTY-ONE

ROY SNATCHED UP the receiver, and his stomach knotted as he listened to what Tonya had to say.

"I was out," she told him, "and the message was on my machine when I got home. It was Shannon asking me to keep David. She was on something when she called—I could tell by her voice. I went over to her place, but she's not there. Neither is David."

He called the police. Then he raced out to his car. It took him twenty-five horrible minutes to get to the apartment hotel where Shannon had been living. A police car was at the curb when he arrived. Inside, the door to Shannon's apartment was open.

The young constable there shook his head at Roy, confirming what Tonya had said. "No sign of the kid here."

"Was there an address book, a number scribbled anywhere beside the phone, any indication of where she might have taken the baby?" Roy found it an effort to keep his voice even.

"Nothing. There's food in the fridge, milk, bread. I talked to the neighbors. Nobody has any idea how long she's been gone."

"She's being supervised twice daily—someone

from Social Services would have come by mid-
morning.'' He dialed Marty on his cell phone to get
the number of the social worker. When Roy reached
her, he could tell by her voice that she was ill. She
said she had the flu, that she'd asked someone else
to go by and check on Shannon. Roy punched in the
relief number she gave him, but no one answered.

He called Tonya Cabral and got a meager list of
other people Shannon might have asked to baby-sit.
With the constable's help, Roy found their ad-
dresses. By the time he'd located all of them, it was
long past midnight, and the effort had been fruitless.
They all said they hadn't spoken to Shannon for
days.

Roy couldn't think of anything else to do but wait.
Please, God, don't let it be too late for David.
The prayer was a desperate litany. There was one
more call he had to make. Feeling sick and scared
and responsible, and knowing she had every right to
say I told you so, he called Hailey.

SHE'D JUST FALLEN ASLEEP when the phone rang.

''Mmm?'' She couldn't wake up.

''Hailey?'' It was Susan Whitcomb, and her voice
was thick with tears. ''Hailey, please, could you
come? I'm at St. Joe's, and Brittany—I know she's
going now and, oh, God, I…I don't know what to
do. I can't stand this.'' The words ended in a desperate wail.

''I'll be right there.''

The moment Hailey hung up, the phone rang

again, and she snatched the receiver, thinking it was Susan calling back.

"Hailey, it's Roy."

The tense and somber tone of his voice sent fear shooting through her.

"Shannon's disappeared, and we can't locate David. She called Tonya, wanting her to baby-sit. Tonya was out, the machine took the message. Shannon was high when she called. I've notified the police. I've tried to locate people who know her, but I can't find him. I'm calling you because you love him, because you have a right to know."

Fear, stark and terrible, washed through her like icy water, and she knew he was expecting her to say I told you so.

It took all she had to reassure him while her insides wound into knots.

"Roy, you'll find him, and he'll be fine. She loves him. She'll have left him somewhere safe. Look, I have to go to St. Joe's right now—one of my patients is dying. Can you meet me there in about an hour in the coffee shop?"

"I'll wait for you."

The drive through Vancouver's deserted streets was eerie. The long hot spell had finally broken and it was sheeting down rain. Hailey stared out at it as she drove, thinking of David, of Brittany, of Roy. Would he forgive her for being so single-minded, so selfish, so blind to everything he was?

And David. Where was he? *Let him be safe. Please let him be safe.*

She raced up to the pediatric floor and made her

way straight down the quiet hallway to Brittany's room. The nurse on shift was just coming out of the room, and she shook her head at Hailey, tears brimming in her eyes. Hailey could hear Susan's keening cries as she opened the door, and she knew that Brittany was gone.

Susan was cradling her daughter's frail form against her breast, rocking back and forth, her face ravaged with tears, tendons in neck and arms standing out. Her husband, Tom, stood beside the bed, his face twisted with grief.

"She won't let go," he said. "She won't put her down."

Hailey went to Susan, slipping her arms around her and Brittany. She held them both silently until the storm of awful grief quieted and the frantic grip Susan had on the child finally eased.

"Look how beautiful she is," Hailey said, gently taking the girl from Susan's arms and laying her on the bed. "She's at peace, Susan. She's not in pain anymore."

For the next half hour Hailey quietly related all the memories she had of Brittany, her wide smile, her love for Stephen King novels, her sense of humor, her bravery, and at last Susan calmed. She allowed Hailey to lead her from the room to the nurses' lounge. Tom followed and Hailey made them both a cup of hot, sweet tea. At last, Susan turned to her husband for comfort, and Hailey watched as the two of them embraced. Susan had told her of the goodness of this gentle man, how hard he worked to support their family, how much he loved Brittany.

When they went, arm in arm, to say a final goodbye, Hailey went into the washroom. She closed the door to a cubicle and sobbed out her own grief for the girl she'd loved and nursed for so long. When the storm of tears was over, she washed her face and then made her way down to the coffee shop.

Roy wasn't there. The man behind the counter knew Hailey, and he beckoned her over.

"Mr. Zedyck say, please go to emergency, Miss Hailey."

They must have found David. Heart hammering with a mixture of hope and dread, Hailey tore down the corridor and burst through the doors into the ER.

She saw Roy standing outside a treatment room, and she hurried over to him. His green eyes, filled with weariness and remorse, met hers, and at the last moment, she kept on moving, flying straight into his arms.

"Hailey, thank God you're here." He gathered her close, and she could feel the tension in his body.

"I love you, Roy. I'm so sorry for being selfish." It needed to be said before anything else.

When she looked up at him, his face was ravaged with emotion. There was moisture in his eyes. He let her go reluctantly, and when she could breathe again, she said, "Is David okay?"

"I hope so. The police are picking him up right now. He should be here in a few minutes."

It took her a moment to digest that. "Then

who…'' She gestured at the treatment room. *''Shannon?''*

Roy nodded. ''I came in through emergency because I wanted to make certain David wasn't here, and I happened to see medics bringing someone in with an overdose. Her face was covered with a breathing mask, but I saw the tattoos on her arms and knew who it was.''

''Is she…?''

''They've given her Narcan.''

Hailey knew the powerful drug blocked the narcotic receptors. People on the edge of death from overdose made what seemed a miraculous recovery when injected with Narcan.

''She's conscious,'' Roy said. ''She told me where she left David.''

''Not…not alone?'' The words were a prayer.

Roy shook his head. ''With someone named Janet Riley, a woman she met at the library.'' He glanced toward the street doors. ''Here they are now.''

Hailey ran toward the police officer carrying David. The toddler was wrapped in a gray blanket and wearing blue flannel pajamas several sizes too big, and his eyes were confused and heavy with sleep. He spotted Hailey.

''Lee-lee, I got Bonzo.'' From the depths of the blanket he drew out the battered dog and held it out for her to see.

''Good for you. Bonzo looks healthy. And so do you, punkin.'' She smiled at him and took him into her arms. She cuddled him close, burying her face in his curls and the sweetness of his neck, fighting tears of relief. David put up with it for a moment, but then he looked around and his lip quivered.

"Where my mommy? I want my mommy."

One of the ER doctors came out of the cubicle just then. "Miss Riggs is conscious and she wants to talk to you, Mr. Zedyck."

Hailey nodded to Roy. "David and I'll go to the cafeteria and get some juice."

"Where Mama?" The little boy wasn't letting up, and Hailey was afraid that in a moment he'd start screaming, so she decided in favor of the truth.

"Mommy's sick. She's right in there with the doctor. We can go see her soon, okay? Let's go find some juice first."

David scowled, but he didn't make a fuss. He was thirsty and he drank the apple juice she bought him in one long swallow, and then pointed at the corridor. "Go Mama now."

"Okay, Mr. One-Track Mind." Hailey stuffed Bonzo in her coat pocket, and with David heavy on her hip, made her way back to emergency.

"Shannon wants to talk to you alone," Roy told her, meeting her outside the treatment cubicle. "They said it's okay for you to go in."

Hailey hesitated. She didn't want David to see his mother if she was sick. She tried to hand him to Roy, but the child clung to her and shook his head, his lower lip sticking out mutinously, his arms locked around Hailey's neck.

"Mama," he insisted.

She gave up and stepped inside, and David let out a squeal when he saw Shannon. She was sitting on the edge of the treatment table, an IV in one arm, but otherwise she looked quite normal.

"Mama." David scrambled from Hailey's arms into Shannon's. He patted her face with his hands and touched the IV with a finger. "Mama sore?" He pressed his lips to her cheek.

The girl was weak, and it was obvious it was all she could do to hold on to him. Hailey stayed close, supporting David's back in case he slipped from Shannon's grasp.

"Davie, hey, my big boy." Shannon closed her eyes and her face contorted in agony as he wrapped his arms around her neck. After a moment she looked at Hailey and her mouth trembled. Her face was ashen, and the bones stood out in skeletal relief.

"You were right," she whispered. "I'm not a good mother to him. Maybe I can't ever be. I know…" Her voice broke, and it took time for her to be able to go on.

Hailey waited, not daring to hope. Her heart was pumping, and her arms ached from supporting the boy in Shannon's thin arms.

"I know you love him a lot, and…and Roy told me you're a good person." She seemed to gather every ounce of strength, and her voice was suddenly loud and strong in the small room. "I want you to take him. I'll…I'll sign the papers so you can adopt him. He deserves better than me." She held David convulsively close, and then she loosened her hold on him, looking into his face, trying desperately to smile through the tears raining down her cheeks.

"Mama has to go into the hospital, Davie.

Mama's sick. Remember when you were in the hospital? Mama can't take care of you, so you go home with Hailey, okay?''

"No." David's chin wobbled.

"Yes." Shannon's voice was firm.

For one endless moment Hailey considered accepting. But Susan's story about being a teenage mom was fresh in her mind, and Bonzo weighed heavily in her pocket, the battered symbol of a little boy's love for and need of his mother.

She cleared her throat and looked directly into Shannon's ravaged face, sending a silent prayer of thanks to Brittany's mother, who had taught her so much about love and what it really meant.

"I'll take him now and care for him, if Roy says it's okay, but only till you get your life straightened out." It took everything Hailey had to say these words. "People can't be easily replaced, Shannon, and he loves you. He's a powerful reason for you to take control of your life. He's such a special little boy."

Shannon's tears turned to wrenching sobs. David patted her head and started to cry, too. Exhausted, Shannon lifted David into Hailey's arms and collapsed on the bed.

Hailey hauled Bonzo out of her pocket and offered him to David, thinking to comfort him, but David took the dog and stretched toward his mother. With Hailey holding him, he tucked it into the crook of Shannon's arm. He didn't struggle as Hailey carried him out of the room, but he did cry, deep, heart-breaking sobs that Hailey felt in every pore of her body.

Outside, Roy was waiting. He draped an arm around both of them.

"I think you'd better get this boy home and into bed," he said.

Her heart leaped. "Will you come with us?"

"Nothing in this world could stop me."

ROY DROVE the truck, and David cried himself to sleep in the car seat they'd borrowed from the hospital. The next days and weeks would be agonizingly hard for him, and for Hailey, because the fact was, he wanted and needed Shannon.

"Shannon said…" Hailey began, but he shook his head.

"We'll figure all that out later. Right now there's something more important to discuss." He pulled the truck into a bus zone and put the gearshift in park. The wipers went on struggling with the downpour. A streetlight provided just enough illumination for Hailey to see his face, his eyes, as he turned toward her then reached across and covered her hand with his, where it cradled David's shoulder.

"Hailey, I love you. I want to be with you always. Will you marry me?"

A city bus pulled up behind them and the driver honked his horn.

Roy didn't budge. His eyes were on her face, and everything she'd ever dreamed of was here, in the cab of an old pickup at three o'clock on a rainy morning.

"Okay," she said. What was it with her vocabulary? She cleared her throat. "Yes. Yes, of course I will. Marry you."

The bus driver honked again as Roy leaned across the gearshift and the sad, sleeping boy and kissed her, but Hailey didn't think it was an angry or impatient honk.

She chose to believe it was a benediction.

EPILOGUE

HE WAS TALL for five, taller than most of the kids starting kindergarten that warm September morning. He'd used gel on his hair, brushing his unruly dark curls nearly flat, and the green backpack he'd chosen looked too big for his shoulders.

He clung to his beloved daddy's hand until they reached the door where the teacher waited. She was a slender young woman in jeans and a Batman sweatshirt, and Hailey smiled at her. Her name was Amy, and they'd met the previous week at a welcome-to-kindergarten evening. Hailey felt she could trust someone who wore a Batman shirt the first day of school.

"Hello, David." Amy crouched down so she was at his level. Hailey noticed that he'd already let go of Roy's hand.

"Welcome to kindergarten. Want to come in and meet the other kids?"

David nodded. Amy stood up and smiled at the three adults.

"He'll be just fine," she assured them, her hand on David's shoulder. She bent to him again. "Maybe you oughtta say goodbye to your little sister?"

David turned and grinned at Emily Ann, enthroned in her stroller. The grin revealed the gap where his two front teeth hadn't yet grown in. His blue eyes danced with excitement, and his husky voice was confident.

"Bye, Em. Bye, Mom. Bye, Lee. See you after school, Daddy."

Without a single backward glance, he turned and went inside.

Emily let out an imperious howl and banged her heels against the footrest. "Me, me, me go David!" she demanded, struggling to get out and follow her brother. Her red curls stood out like a flag, and her imperious personality was evident in her voice.

Hailey wheeled the stroller quickly away, pulling a toy car out to distract her howling daughter. Emily Ann threw it on the sidewalk.

Shannon picked it up. Her eyes were wet, and she swiped at them with her sleeve as she stuck the toy into the carrier. "Well, I guess Davie's a big boy now. Our baby's grown up." Her voice was wobbly. "I'll probably see you guys tomorrow. Right now I've got to get to work." She gave Hailey a quick, hard hug and then loped toward the bus stop. At twenty, she still resembled a skinny kid, tight black pants hugging nonexistent hips, hair dyed a shocking pink and cropped within an inch of her scalp.

The familiar, comforting weight of Roy's arm came around Hailey's shoulder, and she blinked away the suspicious dampness in her eyes as she turned and smiled up at him.

"He'll be okay," she said. It was really a question.

"He'll have made friends with half the class by now," Roy assured her.

She knew it would be like that. David had a winning personality, a kind, caring and generous nature that attracted adults and children alike. In many ways, he was old beyond his years. He'd had to be. He was still helping to raise his mother to adulthood.

"If only your daughter was half as agreeable as our son," Hailey teased. Emily Ann was this minute taking off her sandals to pitch at her mother in protest at not being allowed to go with her adored big brother.

Roy recovered one and stuck it in his jacket pocket. "We ought to let Ingrid raise her—they're so much alike." The words were tough, but the tone betrayed that Em had her daddy wrapped around her tiny finger. She also had her paternal grandparents completely charmed, as well as Ingrid and Sam. Even Jean was beguiled, although these days Jean was preoccupied with the retired doctor she was seeing.

As for Em's godmother, Nicole—well, thanks to her, Emily Ann had a wardrobe to rival any royal princess, and she already knew a weed from a flower. She couldn't quite climb into the tree house Nicole had built, but the scrapes on her arms and legs attested to Em's strength of mind—nothing was going to deter her for long. Nicole, either. She'd finally given the legal firm her resignation, effective the end of the year, and she'd had cards made up that read, "Need a cultivated gardener? Call the Ace of Spades."

"Shannon seems to like this new job." Hailey said to Roy; David's mother was selling aromatherapy products. Hailey couldn't count the number of jobs Shannon had held and then sabotaged in the past three years. She'd been in drug rehab twice more since the first time, but it had been fourteen months now since the last episode. Maybe it was safe to hope that this time she'd make it.

"I've been asked to give a talk on open adoption at the upcoming convention," Roy said. "Any chance you'd come along and tell them your side of things?"

"I'd have to be honest about how tough it is," Hailey warned. Shannon had been as much a part of their lives as David had, and the challenges she'd presented had been far greater than any they'd faced with him. There'd been times when Hailey wished she'd accepted the offer Shannon had made that long-ago night in St. Joe's ER. She and Roy had started their marriage with a two-year-old crying for his mother and a troubled teen to nurture, and it hadn't been easy.

Gratifying, though. It had been gratifying.

"Maybe it's not always as challenging as it's been for us." Roy leaned over and kissed her windblown curls. "But then, we're the type who thrive on challenge."

It was a common bond, one of the many they shared. Roy's job was difficult and draining. He'd turned down two offers of promotion because a move into upper management meant he'd no longer be directly involved with people like David and

Shannon, and he understood that they symbolized the work he was born to do.

Hailey worked two or three days a week at St. Joe's, doing her best to comfort the kids in the pediatric ward and make them laugh. She'd worked as head nurse for a full year after Margaret's death, but it hadn't suited her.

She was lucky that day care had never been a problem. Laura had taken care of David from the first, and after her own sweet Matthew was born, Laura had started an exclusive and very successful day care center, remaining defiantly single while staying very much in love with Michael.

"I think this contrary girl of ours needs a nap." Roy now had Em's other shoe poked into his jacket pocket, along with her pink socks. He was carrying her fluffy sweater. Their little daughter was red-faced and screaming, struggling to remove her shirt. Her major form of protest for the past few weeks had been stripping off all her clothes.

"She's a nudist by nature, like her daddy." The memory of that long-ago dinner always made Hailey grin.

"I don't have to be at work until after lunch," Roy said, giving her a lecherous look. "Got any left-over lasagna?"

"I keep a supply frozen, just for romantic moments like these." She laughed with him, loving him, wanting him more than ever, as he did her, and her heart swelled with gratitude and joy.

He leaned toward her and whispered something wicked and erotic and enticing in her ear, and around them, the September morning seemed to shimmer.

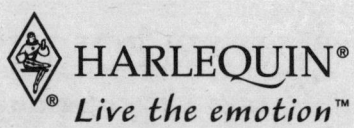

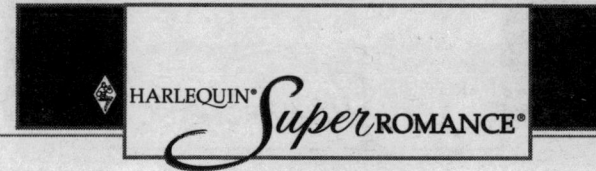

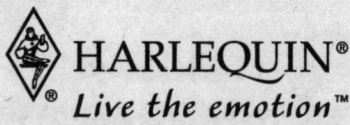

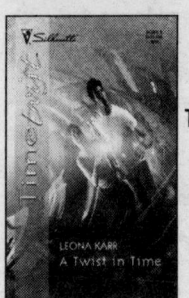

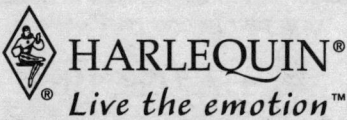

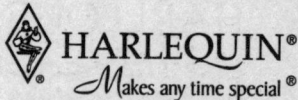

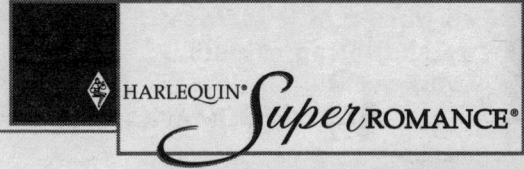

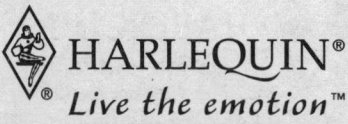

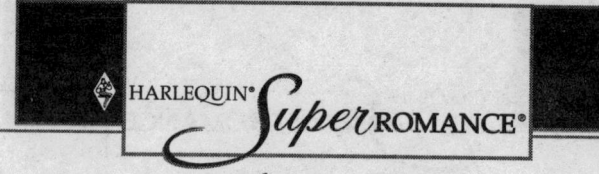

The Target

The action-packed new story by

Kay David

Part of

The GUARDIANS

To some, the members of the bomb squad are more than a little left of normal. After all, they head toward explosives when everyone else is running away. In this line of work, precision, knowledge and nerves of steel are requirements—especially when a serial bomber makes the team The Target.

This time the good guys wear black.

Harlequin Superromance #1131 (May 2003)

Coming soon to your favorite retail outlet.

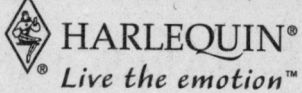

HARLEQUIN®
Live the emotion™

Visit us at www.eHarlequin.com

HSRTGKDM